PRAISE FOR KENT HARUF

'Haruf's fiction, though emotionally rich, is delivered in surprisingly naked language; it is delicate and meticulous, but unembellished. The author fades out of view, becoming not the reporter speaking to the camera, but the invisible operator behind the lens. We are left alone in the world of Holt, watching and listening to the small warm hum of daily life, unable to tear ourselves away until the hidden cameraman stops the film and we step out, blinking, into the cold light of day'   *Waterstone's Books Quarterly*

'Two taciturn bachelor brothers, a dim-bulb couple living in a trailer, a quiet preteen boy living with his grandfather, a social worker, and a young mother abandoned by her husband . . . The plain truth is you can't stop reading or caring about them'   *Boston Globe*

'Haruf makes us care about these plain-spoken, small-town folks without ever resorting to sentimentality or clichés. Instead, he uses their language to capture the mood and mores of the town . . . His story possesses the haunting appeal of music, the folksy rhythms of an American ballad and the lovely, measured grace of an old hymn'   *New York Times*

'Highly charged and compassionate . . . Every action in Holt casts a long shadow, and the gist of Haruf's story is what happens when those shadows touch. The results are equal parts grace and calamity . . . slow, deliberate, highly charged'   *New Yorker*

'A kind book in a cruel world . . . Honest impulses, real people and the occasional workings of grace'   *Washington Post*

'Melancholy truths set to gorgeous melody . . . Haruf sings the second verse of his moving hymn to life on America's great plains'   *Kirkus*, starred review

Eventide

KENT HARUF is the author of *Plainsong* and lives with
his wife, Cathy, in the mountains of Colorado.

KENT HARUF

Eventide

A novel

PICADOR

First published 2004 by Alfred A. Knopf,
a division of Random House, Inc., New York, and simultaneously
in Canada by Random House of Canada Limited, Toronto

First published in Great Britain 2005 by Picador
First published in paperback 2005 by Picador

This edition first published 2006 by Picador
an imprint of Pan Macmillan Ltd
Pan Macmillan, 20 New Wharf Road, London N1 9RR
Basingstoke and Oxford
Associated companies throughout the world
www.panmacmillan.com

ISBN-10: 0-330-43372-5

1 3 5 7 9 8 6 4 2

A CIP catalogue record for this book is available from
the British Library.

Printed and bound in Great Britain by
Mackays of Chatham plc, Chatham, Kent

Abide with me: fast falls the eventide;
The darkness deepens; Lord, with me abide.
When other helpers fail, and comforts flee,
Help of the helpless, O abide with me.

—Henry F. Lyte

Eventide—the time of evening; evening

Eventide

Part One

1

THEY CAME UP FROM THE HORSE BARN IN THE SLANTED
light of early morning. The McPheron brothers, Harold and Raymond. Old men approaching an old house at the end of summer. They came on across the gravel drive past the pickup and the car parked at the hogwire fencing and came one after the other through the wire gate. At the porch they scraped their boots on the saw blade sunken in the dirt, the ground packed and shiny around it from long use and mixed with barnlot manure, and walked up the plank steps onto the screened porch and entered the kitchen where the nineteen-year-old girl Victoria Roubideaux sat at the pinewood table feeding oatmeal to her little daughter.

In the kitchen they removed their hats and hung them on pegs set into a board next to the door and began at once to wash up at the sink. Their faces were red and weather-blasted below their white foreheads, the coarse hair on their round heads grown iron-gray and as stiff as the roached mane of a horse. When they finished at the sink they each in turn used the kitchen towel to dry off, but when they began to dish up their plates at the stove the girl made them sit down.

There's no use in you waiting on us, Raymond said.

I want to, she said. I'll be gone tomorrow.

She rose with the child on her hip and brought two coffee cups and two bowls of oatmeal and a plate of buttered toast to the table and then sat down again.

Harold sat eyeing the oatmeal. You think she might of at least give us steak and eggs this once, he said. On account of the occasion. But no sir, it's still only warm mush. Which tastes about like the back page of a wet newspaper. Delivered yesterday.

You can eat what you want after I'm gone. I know you will anyway.

Yes ma'am, probably so. Then he looked at her. But I'm not in any rush for you to leave here. I'm just trying to joke you a little.

I know you are. She smiled at him. Her teeth were very white in her brown face, and her black hair was thick and shiny and cut off neat below her shoulders. I'm almost ready, she said. First I want to feed Katie and get her dressed, then we can start.

Let me have her, Raymond said. Is she done eating?

No, she isn't, the girl said. She might eat something for you though. She just turns her head away for me.

Raymond stood and walked around the table and took up the little girl and returned to his seat and sat her on his lap and sprinkled sugar on the oatmeal in his bowl and poured out milk from the jar on the table and began to eat, the black-haired round-cheeked girl watching him as if she were fascinated by what he was doing. He held her easily, comfortably, his arm about her, and spooned up a small portion and blew over it and offered it to her. She took it. He ate more himself. Then he blew over another spoonful and gave that to her. Harold poured milk into a glass and she leaned forward over the table and drank a long time, using both hands, until she had to stop for breath.

What am I going to do in Fort Collins when she won't eat? Victoria said.

You can call on us, Harold said. We'll come see about this little girl in about two minutes. Won't we, Katie.

The child looked across the table at him, unblinking. Her eyes were as black as her mother's, like buttons or currants. She said nothing but took up Raymond's calloused hand and moved it toward the cereal bowl. When he held out the spoon she pushed his hand toward his mouth. Oh, he said. All right. He blew over it elaborately, puffing his cheeks, moving his red face back and forth, and now she would eat again.

When they were finished Victoria carried her daughter into the bathroom off the dining room to wash her face and then took her back to their bedroom and changed her clothes. The McPheron brothers went upstairs to their rooms and got into town clothes, dark trousers and pale shirts with pearl snaps and their good white hand-shaped Bailey hats. Back downstairs they carried Victoria's suitcases out to the car and set them in the trunk. The backseat was already loaded with boxes of the little girl's clothes and blankets and bed-sheets and toys, and a child's padded car seat. Behind the car was the pickup and in its bed, together with the spare tire and the jack and a half dozen empty oil cans and dry wisps of brome hay and a piece of rusted barbed wire, were the little girl's high chair and her daybed, its mattress wrapped in a new tarp, all of it lashed down with orange binder twine.

They returned to the house and came out with Victoria and the little girl. On the porch Victoria paused for a moment, her dark eyes welling with sudden tears.

What's the matter here? Harold said. Is something wrong?

She shook her head.

You know you can always come back. We're expecting you to. We're counting on it. Maybe it'll help to keep that in mind.

It isn't that, she said.

Is it because you're kind of scared? Raymond said.

It's just that I'm going to miss you, she said. I haven't been gone before, not like this. That other time with Dwayne I can't even remember and I don't want to. She shifted the little girl from one arm to the other and wiped at her eyes. I'm just going to miss you, that's all it is.

You can call if you need something, Harold said. We'll still be here at the other end.

But I'm still going to miss you.

Yes, Raymond said. He looked out from the porch toward the

barnlot and the brown pastures beyond. The blue sandhills in the far distance low on the low horizon, the sky so clear and empty, the air so dry. We're going to miss you too, he said. We'll be about like old played-out workhorses once you're gone. Standing around lonesome, always looking over the fence. He turned to study her face. A face familiar and dear to him now, the three of them and the baby living in the same open country, in the same old weathered house. But you think you can come on? he said. We probably ought to get this thing started if we're going to.

RAYMOND DROVE HER CAR WITH VICTORIA SITTING BESIDE him so she could reach into the back and tend to Katie in her padded chair. Harold followed them in the pickup, out the lane onto the gravel county road, headed west to the two-lane blacktop, then north toward Holt. The country both sides of the highway was flat and treeless, the ground sandy, the wheat stubble in the flat fields still bright and shiny since its cutting in July. Beyond the barrow ditches the irrigated corn stood up eight feet tall, darkly green and heavy. The grain elevators in the distance showed tall and white in town beside the railroad tracks. It was a bright warm day with the wind coming hot out of the south.

In Holt they turned onto US 34 and stopped at the Gas and Go where Main Street intersected the highway. The McPherons got out and stood at the pumps, gassing up both vehicles as Victoria went in to buy them cups of coffee and a Coke for herself and a bottle of juice for the little girl. Ahead of her in line at the cash register a heavy black-haired man and his wife were standing with a young girl and a small boy. She had seen them walking at all hours along the streets of Holt and she had heard the stories. She thought that if it weren't for the McPheron brothers she might be like them herself. She watched as the girl moved to the front of the store and took a magazine from the rack at the plateglass windows and flipped through it with her back turned away as if she were not related in any manner to the people at the counter. But after the man had paid for a box of cheese crackers and four cans of pop with food stamps, she put the magazine back and followed the rest of her family out the door.

When Victoria came out, the man and the woman were standing in the tarred parking lot deciding something between themselves. She couldn't see the girl or her brother, then turned and saw they were standing together at the corner under the traffic light, looking up Main Street toward the middle of town, and she went on to where Raymond and Harold were waiting for her at the car.

IT WAS SHORTLY AFTER NOON WHEN THEY DROVE DOWN the ramp off the interstate and into the outskirts of Fort Collins. To the west, the foothills rose up in a ragged blue line obscured by yellow smog blown up from the south, blown up from Denver. On one of the hills a white A was formed of whitewashed rocks, a carryover from when the university's teams were called the Aggies. They drove up Prospect Road and turned onto College Avenue, the campus was all on the left side with its brick buildings, the old gymnasium, the smooth green lawns, and passed along the street under the cottonwoods and tall blue spruce until they turned onto Mulberry and then turned again and then located the apartment building set back from the street where the girl and her daughter would now live.

They parked the car and the pickup in the lot behind the building, and Victoria went in with the little girl to find the apartment manager. The manager turned out to be a college girl not unlike herself, only older, a senior in sweatshirt and jeans with her blonde hair sprayed up terrifically on her head. She came out into the hallway to introduce herself and began at once to explain that she was majoring in elementary education and working as a student teacher this semester in a little town east of Fort Collins, talking without pause while she led Victoria to the second-floor apartment. She unlocked the door and handed over the key and another one for the outside door, then stopped abruptly and looked at Katie. Can I hold her?

I don't think so, Victoria said. She won't go to everybody.

The McPherons brought up the suitcases and the boxes from the car and set them in the small bedroom. They looked around and went back for the daybed and high chair.

Standing in the door, the manager looked over at Victoria. Are they your grandfathers or something?

No.

Who are they? Your uncles?

No.

What about her daddy then? Is he coming too?

Victoria looked at her. Do you always ask so many questions?

I'm just trying to make friends. I wouldn't pry or be rude.

We're not related that way, Victoria said. They saved me two years ago when I needed help so badly. That's why they're here.

They're preachers, you mean.

No. They're not preachers. But they did save me. I don't know what I would've done without them. And nobody better say a word against them.

I've been saved too, the girl said. I praise Jesus every day of my life.

That's not what I meant, Victoria said. I wasn't talking about that at all.

THE MCPHERON BROTHERS STAYED WITH VICTORIA Roubideaux and the little girl throughout the afternoon and helped arrange their belongings in the rooms, then in the evening took them out to supper. Afterward they came back to the rented apartment. When they were parked in the lot behind the building they stood out on the pavement in the cool night air to say good-bye. The girl was crying a little again now. She stood up on her toes and kissed each of the old men on his weathered cheek and hugged them and thanked them for all they had done for her and her daughter, and they each in turn put their arms around her and patted her awkwardly on the back. They kissed the little girl. Then they stood back uncomfortably and could not think how to look at her or the child any longer, nor how to do much else except leave.

You make sure to call us, Raymond said.

I'll call every week.

That'll be good, Harold said. We'll want to hear your news.

Then they drove home in the pickup. Heading east away from the mountains and the city, out onto the silent high plains spread out flat and dark under the bright myriad indifferent stars. It was late when they pulled into the drive and stopped in front of the house. They had scarcely spoken in two hours. The yardlight on the pole beside the garage had come on in their absence, casting dark purple shadows past the garage and the outbuildings and past the three stunted elm trees standing inside the hogfencing that surrounded the gray clapboard house.

In the kitchen Raymond poured milk into a pan on the stove and heated it and got down a box of crackers from the cupboard. They sat at the table under the overhead light and drank down the warm milk without a word. It was silent in the house. There was not even the sound of wind outside for them to hear.

I guess I might just as well go up to bed, Harold said. I'm not doing any good down here. He walked out of the kitchen and entered the bathroom and then came back. I guess you've decided to sit out here all night.

I'll be up after a while, Raymond said.

Well, Harold said. All right then. He looked around. At the kitchen walls and the old enameled stove and through the door into the dining room where the yardlight fell in through the curtainless windows onto the walnut table. It feels empty already, don't it.

Empty as hell, Raymond said.

I wonder what she's doing now. I wonder if she's all right.

I hope she's sleeping. I hope her and that little girl are both sleeping. That'd be the best thing.

Yes, it would. Harold bent and peered out the kitchen window into the darkness north of the house, then stood erect. Well, I'm going up, he said. I can't think what else I'm suppose to do.

I'll be up shortly. I want to sit here a while.

Don't fall asleep down here. You'll be sorry for it tomorrow.

I know. I won't. Go ahead on. I won't be long.

Harold started out of the room but stopped at the door and turned back once more. You reckon it's warm enough in that apartment of hers? I been trying to think. I can't recollect a thing about the temperature in them rooms she rented.

It seemed like it was warm enough to me. When we was in there it did. If it wasn't I guess we'd of noticed it.

You think it was too warm?

I don't guess so. I reckon we'd of noticed that too. If it was.

I'm going to bed. It's just goddamn quiet around here is all I got to say.

I'll be up after a bit, Raymond said.

2

THE BUS CAME FOR THEM ON THE EAST SIDE OF HOLT AT seven-thirty in the morning. The driver waited, was turned sideways in the seat staring at the front of the trailer house. She honked the horn. She honked a second time, then the door opened and a young girl in a blue dress stepped out into the untended yard of cheatgrass and redroot, walking toward the bus with her head down, and climbed the metal steps and moved to the middle where there were empty seats. The other students watched her pass in the narrow aisle until she sat down, then started talking again. Now her mother came out of the trailer holding her younger brother by the hand. He was a small boy dressed in blue jeans and a shirt that was too big for him buttoned up to his chin.

After he had climbed aboard the bus the driver said: I shouldn't have to wait for these kids like this. There's a schedule I got to follow, if you didn't know.

The mother looked away, peering through the row of windows until she saw the boy was seated beside his sister.

I'm not going to tell you again about this, the driver said. I've had it with you people. There's eighteen kids I got to pick up. She swung the door closed and released the brake and the bus jerked down Detroit Street.

The woman stared after her until the bus turned the corner onto Seventh and then looked all around as if someone along the street might come to her aid and tell her what to say in reply. But there was no one else outside at this time of morning and she went back to the trailer.

Old and dilapidated, it had once been bright turquoise but the color had faded to a dirty yellow in the hot sun and the blasting wind. Inside, clothes were piled in the corners and a trash bag of empty pop cans was leaning against the refrigerator. Her husband sat at the kitchen table drinking Pepsi from a large glass filled with ice. Before him on a plate were the leftovers of frozen waffles and fried eggs. He was a big heavy black-haired man in outsized sweatpants. His enormous stomach was exposed below his maroon tee-shirt and his huge arms dangled over the back of his chair. He was sitting back resting after breakfast. When his wife came inside he said: What'd she do? You got that look on your face.

Well, she makes me mad. She isn't suppose to do that.

What'd she say?

She said she got eighteen kids to pick up. She said she don't have to wait for Richie and Joy Rae like that.

I'll tell you what I'm going to do, I'm calling the principal. She isn't allowed to say nothing to us.

She isn't allowed to say nothing to me never, the woman said. I'm telling Rose Tyler on her.

IN THE WARM MID-MORNING THEY LEFT THE TRAILER AND walked downtown. They crossed Boston Street and followed the sidewalk to the back of the old square redbrick courthouse and entered a door with black lettering spread across the window: HOLT COUNTY SOCIAL SERVICES.

Inside on the right was the reception room. A wide window was set above the front counter, and hollowed into the wood under the glass was a security pocket through which people passed papers and information. Behind it two women sat at desks with files stacked on the floor beneath their chairs, with telephones and more files on the desktops. Pinned to the walls were large calendars and official bulletins issued by the state office.

The man and woman stood at the window, waiting as a teenaged girl ahead of them wrote on cheap yellow tablet paper. They leaned forward to see what she was writing and after a moment she stopped and gave them an annoyed look and turned away so they couldn't see what she was doing. When she was finished she bent and spoke into the gap beneath the window: You can give this note to Mrs. Stulson now.

One of the women looked up. Are you talking to me?

I'm finished with this.

The woman rose slowly from her desk and came to the counter as the girl slipped the paper under the glass. Here's your pen back, she said. She dropped it into the hollow.

Is there any message with this?

I put it all on that paper, the girl said.

I'll give it to her when she comes in. Thank you.

As soon as the girl was gone the woman unfolded the paper and read it thoroughly.

The couple stepped forward. We're suppose to see Rose Tyler now, the man said. She got an appointment with us.

The woman behind the window looked up. Mrs. Tyler is with another client at the moment.

She was suppose to see us at ten-thirty.

If you'd care to have a seat I'll tell her you're here.

He looked at the clock on the wall beyond the glass. The appointment was ten minutes ago, he said.

I understand that. I'll tell her you're waiting.

They looked at the woman as if expecting her to say something else and she looked steadily back at them.

Tell her Luther Wallace and Betty June Wallace is here, he said.

I know who you are, the woman said. Take a seat, please.

They moved away from the counter and sat down in chairs against the wall without speaking. Beside them were boxes of plastic toys and a little table with books and an open carton of crayon stubs and broken pencils. No one else was in the room. After a while

Luther Wallace removed a jackknife from his pocket and began to scrape at a wart on the back of his hand, wiping the knife blade on the sole of his shoe and breathing heavily, beginning to sweat in the overheated room. Beside him Betty sat looking at the far wall. She appeared to be thinking about something that made her sad, something she could never forget in this world, as if she were imprisoned by the thought of whatever that was. She held a shiny black purse on her lap. She was a large woman not yet forty, with a pockmarked face and limp brown hair, and every minute or two she drew the hem of her loose dress modestly over her knees.

An old man came out from a door behind them and limped across the room with his metal cane. He pushed the door open and went out into the hall. Then the caseworker, Rose Tyler, stepped into the waiting room. She was a short square dark-haired woman in a bright dress. Betty, she said. Luther. Do you want to come back?

We just been sitting here waiting, Luther said. That's all we been doing.

I know. I'm ready to talk to you now.

They stood up and followed her down the hall and entered one of the little windowless interview rooms and sat down at a square table. Betty arranged the skirt of her dress as Rose Tyler closed the door and seated herself across from them. She set a file on the table and opened it and turned through the pages, reading each one rapidly, and at last looked up. So, she said. How have you been this month? Is everything going the way you want it to?

Oh, we been doing pretty good, Luther said. I guess we don't have to complain. Do we, dear.

I still got this pain in my stomach. Betty laid a hand gently over her dress as if something was very tender there. I don't hardly sleep at night, she said.

Did you see the doctor like we talked about? We made an appointment for you to see him.

I went to him. But he didn't do me no good.

He give her a bottle of pills, Luther said. She been taking them.

Betty looked at him. But they don't do me no good. I still hurt all the time.

What are they? Rose said.

I give the doctor's slip to the man at the counter and he filled it out. I got them at home on the shelf.

And you don't remember what they are?

She looked around the bare room. I don't remember right now, she said.

Well, they come in a little brown bottle, Luther said. I tell her she got to take one every day.

You do need to take them regularly. They won't help you unless you do.

I been, she said.

Yes. Well, let's see how you feel when you come in next month.

They better start doing something pretty soon, Betty said. I can't take much more of this.

I hope they will, Rose said. Sometimes it takes a while, doesn't it. She took up the file once more and looked at it briefly. Is there anything else you want to talk to me about today?

No, Luther said. Like I say, I guess we been doing all right.

What about that bus driver? Betty said. I guess you're forgetting about her.

Oh? Rose said. What's the trouble with the bus driver?

Well, she makes me mad. She said something to me she isn't suppose to say.

Yeah, Luther said. He sat forward and put his thick hands on the table. She told Betty she don't have to wait on Richie and Joy Rae. She said she got fifteen kids to pick up.

Eighteen, Betty said.

It ain't right for her to talk to my wife that way. I got a mind to call the principal about it.

Just a minute, Rose said. Slow down and tell me what happened. Did you have Richie and Joy Rae out at the curb on time? We've talked about that before.

They was out there. They was dressed and ready.

You need to do that, you know. The bus driver's doing the best she can.

They come right out after she honked.

What's the bus driver's name? Do you know?

Luther looked at his wife. Do we know her name, honey?

Betty shook her head.

We never did hear her name. The one with the yellow hair is all we know.

Yes, well. Would you like me to call and find out what's going on? Call that principal too. Tell him what she been doing to us.

I'll make a phone call for you. But you have to do your part too.

We already been doing our part.

I know, but you need to try to get along with her, don't you. What would you do if your children couldn't ride the bus?

They looked at Rose and then across the room at the poster taped on the wall. LEAP—Low-Energy Assistance Program, all in red letters.

Let's see then, Rose said. I've got your food stamps here. She produced the stamps from the file on the table, booklets of one, five, ten, and twenty-dollar denominations, each in a different color. She slid the packets across the table and Luther gave them to Betty to put in her purse.

And you received your disability checks on time this month? Rose said.

Oh yeah. They come in the mail yesterday.

And you're cashing the checks like we talked about and putting the money in separate envelopes for your various expenses.

Betty's got them. Show her, dear.

Betty removed four envelopes from her purse. RENT, GROCERIES, UTILITIES, EXTRAS. Each envelope with Rose Tyler's careful printing in block letters.

That's fine. Now is there anything else today?

Luther glanced at Betty, then turned toward Rose. Well, my wife keeps on talking about Donna. Seems like she always got Donna on her mind.

I just been thinking about her, Betty said. I don't see why I can't call her on the phone. She's my daughter, isn't she.

Of course, Rose said. But the court order stipulated that you have no contact with her. You know that.

I just want to talk to her. I wouldn't have no kind of contact. I just want to know how she's been doing.

Calling her would be considered contact, though, Rose said.

Betty's eyes filled with tears and she sat slumped in her chair with her hands open on the table, her hair fallen about her face, a few strands stuck to her wet cheeks. Rose extended a Kleenex box across the table, and Betty took one and began to wipe at her face. I wouldn't bother her, she said. I just want to talk to her.

It makes you feel bad, doesn't it.

Wouldn't you feel bad? If it was you.

Yes. I'm sure I would.

You just got to try and make the best of it, dear, Luther said. That's all you can do. He patted her shoulder.

She isn't your daughter.

I know that, he said. I'm just saying you got to get on the best way you know how. What else you going to do? He looked at Rose.

What about Joy Rae and Richie? Rose said. How are they doing?

Well, Richie, he's been fighting at school, Luther said. Come home the other day with his nose all bloody.

That's cause them other kids been picking fights with him, Betty said.

I'm going to teach him how to fight them back one of these days.

What's causing this, do you think? Rose said.

I don't know, Betty said. They just always been picking on him.

Does he say anything?

Richie don't say nothing to them.

That's because I been teaching him: Turn the other cheek, Luther said. When they smite thee on one cheek, turn him the other one. It's out of the Bible.

He only has two cheeks, Betty said. How many cheeks is he suppose to turn?

Yes, Rose said, there are limits, aren't there.

We come to the limits, Betty said. I don't know what we're going to do.

No, Luther said, otherwise I guess we don't got too much to complain about. He sat upright in his chair, apparently ready to leave, to move on to whatever came next. I guess we been doing pretty good for ourselves. You get what you get and don't have a fit, what I always tell people. Somebody told that to me one time.

3

HE WAS A SMALL BOY, UNDERWEIGHT FOR HIS AGE, WITH thin arms and thin legs and brown hair that hung over his forehead. He was active and responsible, and too serious for a boy of eleven. Before he was born his mother decided not to marry the man who was his father, and when he was five she died in a car wreck in Brush Colorado on a Saturday night after she'd been out dancing with a redheaded man in a highway tavern. She had never said who his father was. Since her death he had lived alone with his mother's father on the north side of Holt, in a dark little house with vacant lots on both sides and a gravel alley out back that had mulberry trees grown up beside it. At school he was in the fifth grade and he was a good student but spoke only when called on; he never volunteered anything in the classroom, and when he was let out of school each day he went home by himself or wandered around town or occasionally did yardwork for the woman who lived up the street.

His grandfather, Walter Kephart, was a white-haired man of seventy-five. For thirty years he'd been a gandy dancer on the railroad in southern Wyoming and northeastern Colorado. When he was almost seventy he got pensioned off. He was a silent old man; he would talk a good deal if he'd been drinking, but he was not a drunk and generally would take a drink at home only if he were sick. Each month when his pension check came he'd cash the check and spend an evening drinking at the Holt Tavern on the corner of Third and Main, where he would sit and visit with other old men in town and tell stories that were not exaggerated so much as they were simply enlarged a little, and then he'd remember for an hour or two what he had been able to do in the long-ago oldtime when he was still young.

The boy's name was DJ Kephart. He took care of the old man, walking him home along the dark streets in the night when his grandfather was finished talking at the tavern, and at home he did most of the cooking and cleaning, and once a week washed their dirty clothes at the Laundromat on Ash Street.

One day in September he came home from school in the afternoon and the old man said the neighbor woman had been over, asking for him. You better go see what she wants.

When did she come?

This morning.

The boy poured out a cup of cold coffee from the pot on the stove and drank it and started toward the woman's house. It was still hot outside, though the sun had begun to lean to the west, and the first intimations of fall were in the air—that smell of dust and dry leaves, that annual lonesomeness that comes of summer closing down. He walked past the vacant lot with its dirt path leading to a row of mulberry trees at the alley and then the two widows' houses, both set back from the quiet street behind a dusty stand of lilac, and came to her house.

Mary Wells was a woman just past thirty with two young girls. Her husband worked in Alaska and returned home infrequently. Slim and healthy, a pretty woman with soft brown hair and blue eyes, she could have done all the yardwork herself but she liked helping the boy in this small way and always paid him something when he worked for her.

He knocked on the door of her house and waited. He thought he should not knock a second time, that it would be impolite and disrespectful. After a little while she came to the door wiping her hands on a dish towel. Behind her were the two girls.

Grandpa said you came over this morning.

Yes, she said. Will you come in?

No, I guess I better get started.

Don't you want to come in first and have some cookies? We've been baking. They're just fresh.

I drank some coffee before I left home, he said.

Maybe later then, Mary Wells said. Anyway I wondered if you had time to work in the backyard. If you don't have something else you need to be doing right now.

I don't have anything else right now.

Then I can use you. She smiled at him. Let me show you what I have in mind.

She came down the steps, followed by the two girls, and they went around the corner of the house to a sun-scorched garden beside the alley. She pointed out the weeds that had come up since he'd last been there and the rows of beans and cucumbers she wanted him to pick. Do you mind doing that? she said.

No, ma'am.

But don't let yourself get too hot out here. Come sit in the shade when you need to.

It's not too hot for me, he said.

I'll send the girls out with some water.

They went back inside and he began to weed in the rows between the green plants, kneeling in the dirt and working steadily, sweating and brushing away the flies and mosquitoes. He was accustomed to working by himself and used to being uncomfortable. He piled the weeds at the edge of the alley and then began to pick the bushbeans and cucumbers. An hour later the girls came out of the house with three cookies on a plate and a glass of ice water.

Mama said for you to have these, said Dena, the older girl.

He wiped his hands on his pants and took the glass of water and drank half of it, then he ate one of the big cookies, eating it in two bites. They watched him closely, standing in the grass at the edge of the garden.

Mama said you looked hungry, Dena said.

We just baked these cookies this afternoon, Emma said.

We helped, you mean. We didn't bake them ourselves.

We helped Mama bake them.

He drank the rest of the water and handed them the glass. There were muddy prints and streaks on the outside.

Don't you want these other cookies?

You eat them.

Mama sent them for you.

You can have them. I've had enough.

Don't you like them?

Yes.

Then why won't you eat these?

He shrugged and looked away.

I'll eat one, Emma said.

You better not. Mama sent them out for him.

He doesn't want them.

I don't care. They're his.

You can have them, he said.

No, Dena said. She took the two cookies from the plate and put them down in the grass. You can eat them later. Mama said they're yours.

The bugs'll get them first.

Then you better eat them.

He looked at her and then went back to work, picking green beans into a white-enameled bowl.

The two girls watched him work, he was on his knees again crawling, his back to them, the soles of his shoes turned up toward them like the narrow faces of some strange being, his hair dark with sweat at the back of his neck. When he reached the end of the row the girls left the cookies in the grass and went back inside.

AFTER HE WAS FINISHED HE TOOK THE BEANS AND THE cucumbers to the back door and knocked and stood waiting. Mary Wells came to the door with the two girls.

My, look at all you found, she said. I didn't think there were that many. You keep some of them yourself. Now, let me get you some money.

She turned back into the house and he stepped away from the open doorway and looked out across the backyard toward the neighbors' yard. There were patches of shade under the trees. Where he stood on the porch the sun shone full on his brown head and on his sweaty face, on the back of his dirty tee-shirt and the corner of the house. The girls were watching him. The older one wanted to say something but couldn't think what it should be.

Mary Wells came back and handed him four dollars folded in half. He didn't look at the money but put the bills in his pants pocket. Thank you, he said.

You're welcome, DJ. And take some of these vegetables with you. She handed him a plastic bag.

I better go then. Grandpa'll be getting hungry.

But you take care of yourself too, she said. You hear me?

He turned and went around to the front yard and started up the empty street in the late afternoon. He had the money in his pocket and the bag of green beans and two of the cucumbers.

When he was gone the girls walked out to the edge of the garden to see if he'd eaten the cookies, but they were still in the grass. There were red ants crawling on them now and a line of ants moving away in the grass. Dena picked up the cookies and shook them hard, then threw them out into the alley.

AT HOME HE FRIED HAMBURGER IN AN IRON SKILLET AND boiled some red potatoes and the green beans Mary Wells had given him and set out bread and butter on the table together with the sliced cucumbers on a plate. He made a new pot of coffee and when the potatoes and beans were ready he called his grandfather to the table and they began to eat.

What'd she have you doing over there? the old man said.

Pulling weeds. And picking vegetables.

Did she pay you?

Yes.

What'd she give you?

He drew the folded bills from his pocket and counted them out on the table. Four dollars, he said.

That's a lot.

Is it?

It's too much.

I don't think it is.

Well, you better hang on to it. You might want to buy something someday.

After supper he cleared the table and washed the dishes and set them to dry on a towel on the counter while his grandfather went into the living room and turned on the lamp beside the rocker and read the *Holt Mercury* newspaper. The boy did his schoolwork at the kitchen table under the overhead light and when he looked in an hour later the old man was sitting with his eyes shut, their paper-thin lids cross-hatched by tiny blue veins and his dark mouth lapsed open, breathing harshly, and the newspaper spread across the lap of his overalls.

Grandpa. He touched his arm. You better go to bed.

His grandfather woke and peered at him.

It's time for bed.

The old man studied him for a moment as if trying to think who he was, then folded the paper together and set it on the floor beside the chair and, pushing against the arms of the rocker, rose slowly and walked into the bathroom, and afterward went back to his bedroom.

The boy drank another cup of coffee at the kitchen sink and dumped the dregs in the drain. He rinsed out the pot and turned off the lights and went back to bed in the little room next to his grandfather's, where he read for two hours. Through the wall he could hear the old man snoring and coughing and muttering. At ten-thirty he cut the light out and fell asleep and the next morning he got up early to make their breakfast and afterward went to school across the tracks to the new building on the south side of Holt, and at school he did willingly and skillfully all that was required of him but didn't say much of anything to anybody throughout the day.

4

THEY HAULED THE BLACKBALDY YEARLING STEERS TO
town in the gooseneck trailer and jumped them out into the alley at
the load-in dock behind the sale barn and the yard crew sorted them
into a pen. The veterinarian inspected them and found none of the
respiratory diseases he looked for in yearlings, nor the cancer eyes
nor Bang's nor the occasional malformed jaw he might expect in
older cattle, and the brand inspector cleared them without question.
Afterward they were handed the chit saying the steers were theirs
and how many of them there were, and then they drove home again
and ate in the kitchen in the quiet and went up to bed, and the next
morning in the stilldark they rose from bed and chored out.

Now at noon they were seated at a square table in the little dirty
sale barn diner ordering lunch. The waitress came with a pad and
stood over them, sweating and red-faced. What are you two going to
have today?

You look about like you was flat wore out, Harold said.

I've been at this since six this morning. Why wouldn't I be?

Well, you might just bust something. You better take it easy.

When would I do that?

I don't know, Harold said. That's the question. You got any
specials going on?

Everything's special. What have you got in mind?

Well, he said, I've been considering the noble pig. I've seen about enough of these blackbaldy steers the last couple days to put me off beef for a week.

We have ham steak and there's bacon if you want that. We could make you up a ham sandwich.

Bring me a ham steak. And mashed potatoes and brown gravy and whatever else comes with it. And black coffee. And some punkin pie if you would.

She wrote rapidly in her pad and looked up. Raymond, what about you?

That sounds about right, he said. Just bring me the same as Harold. Only what other brand of pie you got?

I have apple blueberry butterscotch lemon. She glanced over at the counter. I think I got one piece of chocolate meringue.

Blueberry, Raymond said. But take your time. There isn't any rush about this.

I just wish he'd hire another girl, she said. That's all it'd take. You think Ward's ever going to do that?

I can't see it happening.

Not in my lifetime, she said, and walked toward the kitchen and said something to two men at another table as she passed by.

She returned balancing two cups of coffee and a bowl of lettuce salad for each of them and a plate of white bread with little pats of butter and set it all down and went away again. The McPheron brothers took up their forks and began to eat. While they were eating, Bob Schramm came over. Anybody sitting here? he said.

You, Harold said. Set down.

Schramm pulled out a chair and sat and took off his black hat and placed it crownside down on the vacant chair and put a finger to each ear and turned up the plastic dials in his hearing aids, then smoothed the hair on the top of his head. He looked around the crowded room. Well, I just heard old John Torres died.

When was this? Harold said.

Last night. Over to the hospital. Cancer, I guess. You knew him, didn't you.

Yeah.

He was something, old John was. Schramm looked at them, watching them eat. Here he was, what, about eighty-five, he said, and the last time I seen him he's bent over so bad his chin about catches on his belt buckle and I says how you doing, John, and he says oh, pretty good for a old fucker. That's good, I say, at least you're still fuckin, and he says yeah, but I been having trouble splitting this cottonwood, it's soft in the middle, kind of spongy and you can't get it to split right. You shove the wedge in and it's like sticking a fork in a pan of this caliche mud. Well, you can see where I'm going with this, Schramm said. Here's old John still trying to split firewood at his age of life.

Sounds about like him. Harold reached for a piece of bread and buttered and folded it and bit a large half moon out of the middle.

Well, he smoked two packs of Lucky Strikes every day, Bob Schramm said, and he never mistreated a human being in this world. I always set down with him and when I poured my coffee I poured him one too. This one time he come in and he says how you doing, and I says oh not too good, I got something on my mind, some people upsetting me. And he says who is it, you want me to take care of them, and I says oh no, that's all right, I'll take care of things, because I knew what he'd do or have somebody else do for him. They'd wake up with their throats cut, is what I'm talking about. Well, he come out of San Luis Valley. You didn't want to fool with him. Even if he never hurt nobody before, it don't mean he couldn't arrange for it to happen this time, even if he wasn't going to be the one doing it himself.

The waitress arrived at the table carrying two big platters of ham steak and mashed potatoes and gravy and green beans and apple sauce. She placed them in front of the McPherons and turned to Schramm. What about you, what are you going to have?

I haven't even give it any thought yet.

I'll have to come back, she said.

Schramm watched her leave and looked around, gazing over at the next table. Don't they give you menus here no more?

It's above the counter, Raymond said. On the wall there.

I thought they used to give you menus.

It's up there now.

Is menus that expensive?

I don't know how expensive menus are, Raymond said. You mind if we go ahead and eat?

No. Hell. Don't wait on me. He studied the menu printed on pasteboard above the counter while the McPheron brothers leaned forward over their plates and began to eat. He reached in the hip pocket of his pants and withdrew a blue handkerchief and blew his nose, shutting his eyes all the while, then folded the handkerchief and put it away.

The waitress came back and refilled the coffee cups. Schramm said: Oh, just bring me a hamburger and fries and some coffee, why don't you.

If you want any dessert you better say so now.

I don't guess so.

She walked off to another table and poured coffee there and went on.

When's the funeral going to be? Harold said.

I don't know. I don't even know if they was able to locate his kinfolk yet, Schramm said, to tell them he died. But there'll be a lot that wants to attend.

People liked him, Raymond said.

Yeah, they did. But here you go. I wonder if you ever heard this one. There was this time old John was carrying on with Lloyd Bailey's wife. I seen them myself once, they was in her new Buick hid out down in the bar ditch alongside the tracks out at the Diamond T crossing, the car lights all shut off, that Buick bouncing on its springs a little and the radio turned down low playing something Mexican out of Denver. Well, mister, they was having theirselves a good time. Well, so that fall old John and Lloyd's missus jumped up and run off to Kremmling across the mountains there and holed up in a motel room. Shacked up, living like man and wife. But it wasn't nothing to do there unless you was a hunter and wanted to take a potshot at a deer or a bull elk. It's just a little place, you know, along the river, and ruttin in a kingsize motel bed can get tiresome after a while, even if you can lay the room off on somebody else's credit card. So after a while they come back home and she went back to Lloyd and says to him you going to let me come back or do you want to divorce me? Lloyd, he slapped her so hard it spun her head around, and he says all right then, I guess you can come back. Then Lloyd and her went off on a running drunk. They got about as far as Steamboat Springs, I guess, and turned around. When they come back they was still together. I believe they still are. Lloyd, he said it took him all of a two-week drunk to wash old John Torres out of his system.

How long did it take to wash him out of the wife's system? Harold said.

That I don't know. He never said. But that's one thing about him for sure. Old John could get to you.

I don't guess he's getting to nobody now, is he.

No sir. I reckon his day is over.

Still, I guess he had his fun, Raymond said. He had himself a good run.

Oh, he did that, Schramm said. None much better. I always thought a lot of old John Torres.

Everybody did, Raymond said.

I don't know, Harold said. I don't imagine Lloyd Bailey thought that much of him. Harold put his fork down and looked around the crowded diner. I wonder what become of that punkin pie she was going to bring me.

WHEN THEY HAD FINISHED LUNCH AND LEFT MONEY ON the table for the waitress the McPherons moved next door into the sale barn for the one o'clock start. They climbed up the concrete steps into the middle of the half circle of stadium seats and sat down and looked around. The pipe-iron corral of the sale ring lay below, with its sand floor and the big steel doors on either side, the auctioneer already in place behind his microphone sitting next to the sale barn clerk in the auctioneer's block above the ring, both of them facing the ranks of seats across the ring, and all the animals sorted in pens out back.

The seats began to fill with men in their hats or caps and a few women in jeans and western shirts, and at one o'clock the auctioneer cried: Ladies and gentlemen! Well all right now! Let's get to going!

The ringmen brought in four sheep, all young rams, one with a horn that had splintered in the waiting pen and the blood was trickling from its head. The sheep milled around. Nobody much wanted them and they finally sold the four rams for fifteen dollars each.

Next they brought in three horses one after the other. A big seven-year-old roan gelding came first that had white splashes on its underbelly and more white running down the front of its hind legs. Boys, the older of the ringmen hollered, he's a well-broke horse. Anybody can ride him but not everybody can stay on him. Boys, he'll get out there and move. And he understands cattle. Seven hundred dollars!

The auctioneer took it up, chanting, tapping the counter with the handle end of his gavel, keeping time. A man in the front row allowed that he would give three hundred.

The ringman looked at him. You'll give five hundred.

The auctioneer took that up, and the roan horse sold finally for six hundred twenty-five, bought back by its owner.

They sold an Appaloosa next. Boys, she's a young mare. Not in foal. Then they sold a black mare. She's a young thing now, boys. About two years old, not broke. So we're just going to sell her that way. Three hundred fifty dollars!

After the horses were done the cattle sale began, and it was this that most people had come for. It went on for the rest of the afternoon. They sold the old stuff first, then the cow-calf pairs and the butcher bulls and finally the lots of calves and yearlings. They pushed the cattle in from one side, held them in the ring for the bidding, and moved them about to show them to best advantage, the two ringmen stepping out or tapping them with the white prodsticks, then pushed them through the other metal door into the outback for the pen-back crew to sort out. Each pen was numbered with white paint to keep the animals separate, and all of them had yellow tags on their hips saying which lot they belonged to. On the wall above the metal doors electronic boards blinked TOTAL LB. and HEAD CT. and AVERAGE WT. There were advertisements on the walls for Purina and Nutrena feeds and Carhartt equipment. And below the auctioneer's booth this sign: NOTICE ALL GUARANTEES ARE STRICTLY BETWEEN BUYER & SELLER.

The McPheron brothers sat high up in their seats and watched. They had to wait until late in the afternoon for the sale of their year-lings. Around three in the afternoon Raymond went down into the diner and brought back two paper cups of coffee, and sometime later Oscar Strelow sat down in front of them and turned sideways in his chair to talk, remarking on a pen of his cattle that one time sold so poorly he'd driven out and got drunk afterward and when he got home in that sorry state his wife was so mad she wouldn't talk to him but went straight into town the next morning and bought a brand-new Maytag washing machine, writing out a check for the entire amount right there, and Oscar said he didn't think it was a good idea to offer any comment about it to his wife just then and he still never had.

They kept running the cattle through. The younger of the ring-men was the one watching the bidders and they looked at him pur-posefully, making a nod or raising a hand, and he'd holler Yup! looking back and forth from one bidder to the other, Yup! and when the last bidder gave up and looked away the auctioneer up in the block cried: I sold them out at one hundred sixteen dollars to number eighty-eight! and the young ringman released the cattle out of the ring. Then the older ringman in a blue shirt with a big hard belly hanging down above his belt buckle let the next lot in through the steel door on the left and began to holler.

Boys, they're a nice pair of steers. I'm going to let you all in for ninety-five dollars!

Boys, she's a long-haul calf. She looks a little like a milk cow. Seventy-four dollars!

The only thing wrong with this one is she's got a short tail and that's stupid!

Boys, she's got a little knot on her jaw. Dry it, it won't amount to nothing.

A heifer girl and a good one!

All right. Seventy-seven dollars! Let's not play games.

The cattle sale went on. And one time there was a big lot, eighty head of them, that the ringmen ran through fifteen and twenty at a time until they came to the last bunch and these they kept back in the ring as representative of the whole lot, and all the while the older ringman was hollering: Boys, they're a good outfit. Take a good look at them, you're not going to see them again. They're a good feeding outfit, boys. Eighty cows. Eighty dollars. Come on!

And there was one other time in the afternoon when Harold, sitting up in his seat above the sale ring, began to bid on a pen of butcher cows. After he bid a second time Raymond turned to look at him. Was that you? He thought that was you trying to bid on them.

It was.

Well what the hell are you doing?

Nothing. Having a little fun.

We don't need no more cattle. We're trying to sell some here today.

I ain't going to buy any. I'm just having some fun raising the price for somebody else.

What if you get stuck with them?

I won't.

Yeah. But what if you do.

Then I reckon you'll just have to get your pocketbook out and pay for them.

Raymond turned away. You know something, he said. You're starting to get a little mushy in the head in your advanced years, did you know that?

Well, we got to have some fun, don't we? Victoria's not here no more.

But we don't need no more cattle.

You already said that.

I'm saying it so you'll hear me.

I hear you. But I still say we got to have some kind of enjoyment in life.

I know we do. I ain't arguing with you about that.

AT LAST THE AUCTIONEER CAME TO THE BLACKBALDY yearlings the McPherons had hauled in. The steers came into the sale ring in a swirling mass, their heads down, all moving, trying to turn back into themselves to hide.

The ringman hollered: Boys, they come right off the grass. They'll do everything you want them to do. Good stretchy steers. These are yearling kind of cattle, boys. And good ones they are!

Ninety dollars!

The auctioneer started his chant. Well all right now. You got to like them. Fifteen steers weighing a average of eight-oh-eight. They'll hang a good carcass for you, boys. Here we go now. Hey I got a bid now, ninety-dollar bid now, ninety-na-quarter now, now a half, now a half, got seventy-five, now ninety-one, now one-na-quarter now, now half, bid's one-na-half, now one-na-half the bid now, now seventy-five.

The McPherons watched the fifteen steers milling about in the ring below, frightened and uncertain in this great commotion and noise, their eyes rolled back, one bawling into the dust-filled air and another taking it up, the men and women in the stadium seats all looking on through the pipe-iron bars of the ring, the brothers watching from above, viewing their own cattle with a strange emotion, having brought them in to sell but knowing too well what effort they'd put into them and what trouble there'd been over the past year and with which one or two there'd been the trouble and even knowing for four or five of them which mother cow they'd come out of. But watching the two brothers, you could not have told anything by what showed on their faces. They looked on impassively at the sale of the fifteen steers as if they were attending an event of no more significance than the rise and fall of a dry little wind.

We all in now? the auctioneer cried. We all done here? Ninety-one seventy-five, ninety-two? ninety-two? ninety-two? He flipped the gavel around, taking it by the handle, banged it sharply on the wood block on the counter and sang into the microphone: I sold them out at ninety-one seventy-five to—he looked at the bidder across the ring in the fifth row, a fat man in a straw hat, a cattle buyer for a feedlot, who flashed four fingers twice—to number forty-four!

Sitting beside the auctioneer the sale clerk wrote it down in her ledger, and the ringmen released them and ran in the next lot.

Well, Harold said, looking straight ahead. That'll do.

It'll serve, Raymond said, looking as though he too were talking to no one, talking about not even yesterday's news, but about last week's, last month's.

They stayed on in their stadium seats to watch the present lot of cattle being sold, and the next lot, then they rose and moved stiffly down the steps and out of the sale barn. The yard crew and the penback crew had done their work and they received the cashier's check—less the selling commission and the charges for the brand inspection, the feed, the health inspection, the insurance, and the fee that went to the meat board. The woman in the office handed the check to Raymond and congratulated them both. Raymond looked at the check briefly and folded it once, put it in his old leather purse and snapped it shut, poking the purse away in the inner pocket of his canvas chore jacket. Then he said: Well, it wasn't too bad, I guess. At least we never lost no money.

Not this time, Harold said.

Then they shook the woman's hand and went home.

AT HOME UNDER THE FADING SKY THEY WALKED DOWN TO the horse barn and cow lots and out to the loafing shed to check on things, and the cattle and horses looked all right. So they came back up across the gravel drive to the house. But the day's excitement was gone now. They were tired and bleary now. They heated up canned soup on the stove and ate at the kitchen table and afterward set the dishes to soak and then removed themselves to the parlor to read the paper. At ten o'clock they turned on the old console television to catch whatever news there might be showing from somewhere else in the world before they climbed up the stairs and lay down tired in their beds, each in his own room across the hall from the other, consoled or not, discouraged or not, by his own familiar time-worn memories and thoughts.

5

THEY CAME DOWN THE PLANK STEPS OUT OF THE TRAILER
into the bright sun in the middle of morning and rounded the corner
in the packed dirt and arrived at the rusted shopping cart that waited
like something patient and abiding among the dry cheatgrass and
pigweed. They shoved it rattling away from the trailer out into
Detroit, walking the cart ahead of them, headed downtown, Luther
pushing, panting steadily, Betty coming along quiet beside. They
walked paired up under the trees, with one of the front wheels of the
cart flapping loose whenever it hit a crack in the concrete or a stone of
any size, and passed through the intersection in front of a car delayed
behind a stop sign and came one block more and crossed against traffic and entered at last the store at the corner of Second and Main.

The grocery was a long narrow brick-faced building running
back to the alley with wood floors formed of old-fashioned tongue-
and-groove oak boards that were oiled and darkened, a place fragrant
and dusty and a little dim, with narrow aisles between shelves and
tiers of foodstuffs.

Luther pushed the cart past the bins of apples and oranges, the
cabbage heads and leaf lettuce next to the wall, his wife following
behind in her loose dress. In the next aisle, beyond the fresh-
butchered meat in the cooled trays, the frozen foods were displayed
behind the tall glass doors. He stopped now and began to hand the

cold boxes to Betty, who stacked them in the cart, and they moved forward and he took down more. Frozen spaghetti, cold pizza, boxes of burritos and meat pies and waffles and berry pies and chocolate pies and lasagna. Salisbury steak dinners. Meals of macaroni and cheese. All frozen in their bright hard vivid boxes.

He pushed on and she followed him up the next aisle, where they stopped to study the canned pop. He turned to her. You going to want something else this time? Or you going to stay with that same old strawberry?

I can't make up my mind.

How bout some of this black cherry?

You're getting me confused.

Maybe you want some of both of them.

Yes, she said, whyn't you do that.

He lifted two cases of the pop from the shelf and stooped over to slide the cases onto the undershelf of the cart, his great hindquarters exposed above his gray sweatpants, and stood panting, red-faced, and yanked his shirt down.

You all right, dear?

Yeah. But them's heavy when you got to bend over like that.

You better not have no cardiac arrest on me.

No ma'am. Not here. Not today.

They pushed on. Around the corner among the paperware and detergent, a plump woman was blocking the aisle, making up her mind about dish soap. Oh I'm sorry, she said, then looked up and saw who it was. She said no more but shoved her cart only a little out of the way.

That's fine, missus, Luther said. I can make it okay. He squeezed his cart through, and Betty turned sideways, shuffling by. The woman stared after them until they had disappeared around the end and then stood fanning the air in front of her face.

In the next aisle they looked for some time among the various cereals. One of the store employees came by, a boy in a green apron, and Luther stopped him. Bud, what happened to that cereal with raisins in it? All them raisins in it.

Isn't it here?

We been looking all over.

The boy searched among the shelves, bending over and looking up high. We might have some in back, he said finally.

We'll wait for you, Luther said. Go ahead.

The boy glanced at him and pushed through the swinging doors into the back of the store. Then the plump woman rolled her cart up behind them.

Luther moved their cart to the side. He's went out back to look for that cereal, he said.

What? she said. Did you say something to me?

He's went out in back there to get our cereal. We're just waiting on him.

She stared at him, she turned to look at Betty, then she walked rapidly away.

Cause they ain't none of it on the shelf here, Luther called after her.

The boy came back and told them he couldn't find any of the cereal they wanted.

Did you look everywhere pretty good? Luther said.

Yeah, I looked. If we have any it'll be out here on the shelves.

But they ain't none of it out here. We know that already. You got to have some of it in the back.

No. I looked. We must of sold it all.

Luther turned to Betty. He says they don't have none, dear. Says they're out of it.

I heard him.

What you want to do about it?

I was counting on a box of cereal to carry home.

I know. Only he says they must of sold it all.

The boy was watching them talk, his head going back and forth. You could buy a box of this other cereal, he said, and buy a box of raisins and put that in it. It'd be about the same thing.

Put raisins in the box, Luther said.

Put raisins in one of these other cereals, the boy said.

Right here, you mean?

No. When you get home. After you buy them and take them home.

Huh. Luther looked around. You want to do that, honey?

You decide, Betty said.

Well, the cereal's here, the boy said. The raisins are over in aisle two in the middle on the right. If that's what you want to do. It doesn't make any difference to me. He turned and walked toward the checkout.

They studied the boxes of cereal. In the old rusted cart their cartons had begun to defrost, water condensing on the cardboard in the warm air.

I can't see how that'd be any good, Luther said. Can you?

I don't want none of that, Betty said.

No ma'am.

It wouldn't taste the same.

It wouldn't taste the same in a hundert years, Luther said.

They went on and picked up a plastic jug of milk and two dozen eggs in the next aisle and came to the bakery and took three loaves of the cheap white bread, and at last came to the front of the store and lined up behind the register, waiting for their turn. Luther pulled a magazine from the rack in front of them and looked at pictures of half-naked women in the glossy pages.

Who you looking at? Betty said. You better keep your eyes saved for me. She took the magazine out of his hands and put it back. I'm your wife.

They's too skinny anyhow, he said. Not enough meat on them for what I like. He pinched Betty's hip.

You better stop that too, she said, and smiled at him and looked away.

The checkout lane cleared and they began to set their groceries on the belt and Luther bent over and lifted up the cases of pop with a grunt.

The woman at the register was working briskly. How're you folks doing today? she said.

We're doing pretty good, Luther said. You?

I'm still above ground, the woman said. Every day above ground is a good day, isn't it.

Yes ma'am. I believe you got that right.

We're doing pretty good, Betty said, except for that cereal we couldn't find.

Didn't we have any?

No ma'am, said Luther. You're all out.

Well. I'm sorry.

When their charges were totaled Betty took the booklets of food stamps from her purse and handed them to Luther and Luther presented them to the woman. Behind them a man with cans of beans and stew and a carton of cigarettes in his cart stood watching them. The clerk tore out the stamps and rang up and slipped the stamps under the tray in the register and made the last dollar's change in actual coins. The boy in the green apron sacked their groceries and loaded them back in the cart.

You have a good day, Luther said, and they pushed out through the electric door onto the sidewalk.

The man behind them shook his head at the checkout woman. Would you look at that. They're eating better than you and me and they're on food stamps.

Oh, let them be, the woman said. Are they hurting you?

They're eating a steak dinner and I'm eating beans. That's hurting me.

But would you want to be them?

I'm not saying that.

What are you saying?

I'm not saying that.

On the sidewalk Luther and Betty started back toward the east side of Holt with their grocery cart. It was hotter now, the sun risen higher in the blue sky. They kept to the shade under the trees and once or twice in every block they stopped to rest, and then shoved on, homeward.

6

THEY WERE COLLECTED IN A CIRCLE ON THE PLAYGROUND
when he came out at noon recess. Even from a distance he could see
they were from his own grade, with a few of the younger ones from
the lower grades there too, gathered inside the chain-link fence
beyond the end of the school building. Now and then one of them
hollered something brief and excited, and he went down to see what
it was about.

Two little boys from the first grade were facing each other across
five feet of red gravel, and the older boys were trying to make them
fight, saying things, goading them. One boy they taunted more than
the other, the one whose lank brown hair appeared as if it had been
cut by someone barbering with his eyes shut. He knew who it was—
his classmate Joy Rae's little brother—and inside the ring he looked
ragged and scared. His outsized shirt was buttoned to his chin and
had holes at the elbows, and his jeans had a purple tint as though
someone had washed them together with something red. He seemed
ready to cry.

One of the boys next to DJ was yelling at him: Go ahead. Why
won't you fight?

He's a chickenshit, a boy across the ring hollered. That's why. He
flapped his arms and crowed and hopped up and down. The kids next
to him hooted.

The other boy in the ring was somewhat bigger, a blond boy in jeans and red shirt.

Go on. Hit him, Lonnie.

They don't want to fight, DJ said. Let them go.

Stay out of this. The boy next to him stepped out and shoved the blond boy forward, and he swung and hit Joy Rae's brother on the side of the face and then stepped back to see what he'd done and her brother put his hand up to his cheek.

Don't, Joy Rae's brother said. He spoke very softly.

Hit him again. You better hit him.

He doesn't want to fight, DJ said. He's had enough.

No he hasn't. Shut up.

The boy shoved the blond boy again, and he hit her brother and grabbed him around the neck and they went down in the gravel. The blond boy rolled over on top of him, their faces close to each other, and hit him in the face and throat, and her brother tried to cover his face with his hands. His eyes looked frightened and his nose was bleeding. He began to wail.

Then the circle was broken by a girl rushing into the ring, Joy Rae, in a blue dress too short for her. You're hurting him, she cried. Stop it. She ran over and pulled the blond boy off her brother, but the first big boy, the loudmouthed one, shoved her and she tripped over the little boys and fell on her hands and knees in the gravel. One knee was cut but she jumped up and pulled at the blond boy crying: Let go, you little son of a bitch.

The big loudmouthed boy grabbed her and this time hurled her backward into the ring of onlookers, and two boys grabbed her by the arms.

She twisted and kicked at them. Let go of me, she screamed.

DJ stepped into the ring and pulled the blond boy off and stood her brother on his feet. He was crying hard now and his face was smeared with blood. The ringleader grabbed DJ by the arm. What do you think you're doing, asshole?

He's had enough.

I'm not done with him yet.

Then a boy cried: Oh shit. Here comes Mrs. Harris.

The sixth-grade teacher came striding into the circle. What's this? she said. What's going on here?

The boys and girls began to walk off fast with their heads down.

Every one of you come back here, she called. Come back here.

But they all went on, some of them running now. The two boys holding Joy Rae let her go and sprinted off as Joy Rae hurried over to her brother.

What's this about? the teacher said. She put her arm around the little boy and lifted his chin to see in his face. Are you all right? Talk to me. She wiped at the blood with a handkerchief. His eyes were red and there were bruises starting on his cheeks and forehead and the front of his shirt was ripped open. What's this about? She turned to DJ. Do you know?

No, he said.

Who started it?

I don't know.

You don't know, or you're not telling me?

He shrugged.

Well, you're not helping anybody by not telling.

I know who it was, Joy Rae said, and named the big boy who'd been out in the ring.

He's in very serious trouble then, the teacher said.

She led Joy Rae and her brother into the school building, but DJ lingered on the playground until the bell rang.

AFTER SCHOOL HE WAS WALKING HOME THROUGH THE park next to the railroad tracks when two boys appeared from behind the rusted WWII tank that served as a monument. They rushed up at him across the newly mown grass. How come you told old lady Harris on me? the big loudmouthed boy said.

I didn't.

You told her I made those little kids fight.

I never told her anything.

Then how come I caught hell from her and Mr. Bradbury? Now I have to bring my mom to school tomorrow. Because of you.

DJ looked at him, then at the other boy. They were both watching him.

I'm going to kick your ass, the first boy said.

Yeah, how'd you like to get your ass kicked, the other one said. He gave a signal with his hand and a third boy came out from behind the tank, and they took turns shoving him until one of them grabbed him around the neck while the other two hit him in the head and sides, then they threw him down and held his face in the grass.

The first boy kicked him in the ribs. You lying sack of green shit. You better learn to keep your mouth shut.

Living with a old man.

Yeah. They probably fuck each other. The boy kicked him again. You been warned, he said, then they walked off toward downtown.

He lay in the grass looking at the spaced and orderly trees in the park and the clear sky through the trees. Blackbirds and starlings were pecking in the grass around him.

After a while he got up and went home. In the little dark house his grandfather was sitting in his rocking chair in the living room.

Is that you? he called.

Yes.

I thought I heard somebody out there.

It's only me.

Come in here.

In a minute, he said.

What are you doing?

I'm not doing anything.

7

WHEN THE PHONE RANG IT WAS HALF-PAST SIX IN THE
evening on a Saturday and Raymond got up from the kitchen table
where he and Harold had been eating a supper of beef steak and pan-
fried potatoes and took up the phone in the dining room where it
hung on the wall on a long cord, and on the other end it was Victoria
Roubideaux.

Well now, is that you? he said.

Yes. It's me.

We just was finishing supper.

I hope I didn't interrupt you. I could call later if you want.

You didn't interrupt a thing. I'm just glad to hear from you.

How's the weather there? she said.

Oh, you know. About like always this time of year. Starting to
turn off cold at night but it's still nice in the daytime. Most days it is.

He asked her how the weather was for her, there in Fort Collins
next to the mountains, and she said it was dry and cold at night there
too but that the days were still warm, and he said that was good, he
was glad she was still getting some warm days. Then there was
silence until she thought to say: What else is going on at home?

Well. Raymond looked out through the curtainless windows
toward the barnlots and pens. We took those yearling steers into the
sale barn last week.

The ones from over south?

That's right.

Did you get your price?

Yes ma'am. Ninety-one seventy-five a hundredweight.

Isn't that good. I'm glad.

It wasn't too bad, he said. Well anyway, now how about you, honey? What's going on up there?

She told him about her classes and professors and about an exam coming up. She told him one professor said albeit so often in his lectures that the students all counted the times.

Albeit? Raymond said. I don't even know what that means.

Oh, it means something like although. Or even so. It doesn't really mean anything. He's just talking.

Huh, Raymond said. Well, I never heard of it. So have you been making any friends up there?

Not too many. I talk with this one girl some. And the apartment manager, she's always around.

No young boys?

I'm too busy. I'm not interested anyway.

And how about my little girl. How's Katie?

She's fine. I put her in the university day care while I'm in class. I think she's starting to get used to it. At least she doesn't complain anymore.

Is she eating?

Not like at home.

Well. She needs to eat.

She misses you, Victoria said.

Well.

I miss you too, she said.

Do you, honey?

Every day. You and Harold both.

It isn't the same around here, I can tell you. Far from it.

Are you all right? she said.

Oh yeah. We're doing okay. But here, now I better put Harold on. I know he wants to say hello. And you take care of yourself now, honey. Will you do that?

You too, she said.

Harold came out from the kitchen and took up the phone while Raymond went back to start the dishes. Harold and Victoria talked about the weather and her classes again, and he asked why she wasn't out having fun since it was Saturday night, she should be doing something to enjoy herself on a Saturday night, and she said she didn't feel like going out, maybe she would some other weekend, and he said weren't there any good-looking boys at that college, and she said maybe there were but she didn't care, and he said well, she better keep her eyes open, she might see one she liked, and she said well, she doubted that, and then she said: But I hear you did all right at the sale barn last week.

Not too bad, Harold said.

I hear you got almost ninety-two. That's really good, isn't it.

I'm not going to complain. No ma'am.

I know how much it means to you.

Well, he said. Now what else about you? You need any money yet?

No. That's not what I was calling for.

I know. But you be sure to say so. I got a feeling you wouldn't tell nobody even if you did.

I'm all right for money, she said. It's just good to hear your voice. I guess I was feeling a little homesick.

Oh, he said. Well. And since Raymond was making enough noise doing dishes that he couldn't hear what Harold was saying on the phone, he told Victoria how much his brother missed her and how he talked about her every day, speculating on what she was doing there in Fort Collins and making suggestions as to how the little girl was faring, and as he went on in this vein it was clear to the girl that he was talking as much about himself as he was his brother and she felt so moved by this knowledge she was afraid she was going to cry.

After they hung up Harold went back to the kitchen where Raymond was just emptying the dishpan, pouring the water out into the sink. The clean dishes were drying in the rack on the counter. How'd she sound to you? Raymond said.

She sounded to me, Harold said, like she was kind of lonesome.

I thought so. She didn't sound quite right to me.

No sir, she didn't sound quite like herself, Harold said. I reckon we better send her some money.

Did she say something about that?

No. But she wouldn't, would she.

That wouldn't be like her, Raymond said. She never would say anything about what she wanted even when she was here.

Except for the baby sometimes. She might of said something about her once in a while.

Except for Katie. But it wasn't just money, was it.

It wasn't even about money, Harold said.

The way she sounded. The way her voice was.

No, it wasn't money that made her voice sound that way. It was the rest of it too.

Well, I reckon she's kind of lonesome, Raymond said. I'm going to say she kind of misses being here.

I guess maybe she does, said Harold.

Then for the next half hour they stood in the kitchen, leaning against the wooden counters drinking coffee and talking about how Victoria Roubideaux was doing a hundred and twenty-five miles away from home, where she was taking care of her daughter by herself and going to classes every day, while here they themselves were living as usual in the country in Holt County seventeen miles out south of town, with so much less to account for now that she was gone, and a wind rising up and starting to whine outside the house.

8

WHEN ROSE TYLER CAME OUT FROM THE KITCHEN TO THE front door of her house on a weekday night in the fall, the sky above the trees was heavily clouded and there was the smell in the air of rain coming, and on the doorstep under the yellow porch light stood Betty Wallace with the two children and out in the yard in the dry grass in the shadow of a tree was Luther Wallace looking big and hulking and dark.

Betty, Rose said. Is something the matter?

I didn't want to bother you this time of night, Betty said. But I got an emergency. Could you drive me and my kids over to my aunt's house? She looked out at Luther in the front yard. He's being mean to me.

Do you want to come inside?

Yes. But he don't have to. I'm mad at him.

Perhaps he better come too so we can all talk this over.

Well, he better behave hisself.

Rose called to Luther and he came up on the porch. He looked sad and disturbed. Even in the cool night air he was sweating, his great wide face as red as flannel. I never done nothing to her, he said.

You ain't at home now, Betty said. You better behave yourself at Rose's house.

Well, you better be quiet and shut your mouth and not tell no lies to people.

I ain't telling no lies. What I tell is the truth.

There's things I can tell too.

You don't have no reason to tell something on me.

Yes sir, I do.

Here now, Rose said. We're going to be civil. Or you can both go on back home.

You hear? Betty said. You better mind Rose.

Well, she ain't just talking to me.

Hush, Rose said.

They entered the house through the front hall and went into the living room, and Joy Rae and her brother Richie looked at everything with a kind of awe and surprise, as if they were seeing a set display of furniture and paintings arranged for view in a city museum. They sat down with their mother on the flowered couch and were very quiet and still—only their eyes moved, looking at everything. Luther had started to sit in a wood rocker but it was too small and Rose brought him a chair from the kitchen. He sat down carefully, testing with his hand for the seat of the chair.

Betty, why don't you start, Rose said. You said you wanted to go to your aunt's house. What was that about?

That was about he's being mean to me, Betty said. He just slapped me for no reason. I never did nothing to him.

I never either slapped her, Luther said.

Oh, he's the one lying now.

I just pushed her a little. Because she did something to me. Well, she said I was eating too much.

When was this? Rose said.

Bout a hour ago, Betty said. Joy Rae wasn't eating her dinner and he tells her you better—

I said you better eat if you want to keep your strength up.

No. He says you better eat or I'm going to eat it for you. Joy Rae, she said she didn't want it. Said she was sick of this same old food all the time. So then he took her macaroni-cheese dinner off her plate and ate it looking right at her. I guess you'll eat it next time, he says. I don't care, she says. You going to learn to care, he says, and that's when I come between them and he says watch out, and I says no, you watch out.

Then what happened? Rose said.

Then nothing happened, Luther said.

Then he slapped me, Betty said.

That's a lie. I only just pushed her a little.

You slapped me in the face. I can still feel it. I feel it right now. Betty lifted her hand and caressed her cheek and Luther looked at her from across the room with slit eyes.

The children sat on the couch and appeared to be uninterested in what was being said, as if they were not involved in these matters or couldn't affect their outcome even if they were. Studying the furniture and the pictures on the walls, they sat next to each other without so much as glancing at the three adults.

Rose stood and went to the kitchen and came back with a plate of chocolate fudge and held the plate in front of the children before offering it to Betty and Luther. She sat again. I think we all need to cool down, she said.

I just want to go to my aunt's house, Betty said. I can cool down over there.

Does she want you to come?

We been there before.

But does she want you now?

I think she does.

Didn't you call her?

No. Our phone ain't working.

What's wrong with it?

It don't have no dial tone.

Rose looked at her. Betty sat slumped beside the children, her lank hair fallen about her pocked face, her eyes reddened. Rose turned to Luther. What do you think about this, Luther?

I think she ought to come home like she's suppose to.

But she says she doesn't want to be in that house right now.

I'm her husband. The Bible says man is lord of his own castle. He builds up his house on a rock. She's suppose to mind what I say.

I don't have to mind him, do I, Rose.

No. I think Luther's wrong about that.

I want to go to my aunt's house, Betty said.

WHEN THEY BACKED OUT FROM THE DRIVEWAY LUTHER was standing forlornly in the headlights, the beams sweeping across him while he looked back at them with his hands in his pockets. Overhead, above Holt, the rain seemed nearer. Betty sat in the front seat with Rose, the children in back, staring out the window at all the houses and the intersecting streets and the tall trees. The houses all had lights burning beyond the window shades, and there were bushes and narrow little sidewalks leading around back to the dark alleys. The streetlamps glowed blue at the corners and the trees were evenly spaced along the sidewalks. Rose drove them through the quiet streets and at the highway she turned east.

As they approached the Highway 34 Grocery Store Betty said: Oh, I forgot my napkins.

What do you mean? Rose said.

It's my time of month come round again. I don't have my napkins. I'll have to change sometime.

Do you want to stop and buy some?

If you please. I better.

They pulled in and parked among the cars near the front doors. Beyond the plateglass windows the store was brightly lit and there were women standing at the checkout. Go ahead, Rose said.

Betty looked toward the store but didn't get out.

What is it now?

I don't have no money. I didn't bring my pocketbook. Could you loan me some? I'll pay you back first of the month.

Rose gave her some bills and Betty went inside. When she disappeared into the aisles, Rose turned in the seat to look at the children. Are you two all right back there?

She's not going to want us, Joy Rae said.

Who isn't?

Mama's aunt.

Why do you say that?

Last time she said not to come back again. I don't see why we have to go out there.

Maybe you won't have to stay very long. Just until your parents can calm down a little.

When's that going to be?

Soon, I hope.

I don't want to go out there either, Richie said.

Oh? Rose said.

I don't like it out there.

Cause you wet the bed the last time and she got mad, Joy Rae said. He wets the bed.

So do you.

Not no more.

Betty came back with a paper bag and Rose drove east from town on the highway out into the flat open treeless country, then turned north a mile to a little dark house. A light came on above the front door as the car stopped. Okay, Rose said. Here we are.

Betty looked at the house and got out and climbed the steps to the door and knocked. After some time a woman in a red kimono opened the door. Her hair was flat on one side, as if she'd been in bed already. She was smoking a cigarette and she looked past Betty at the car. Well, she said. What do you want now?

Can me and my kids stay here tonight?

Oh lord, what happened this time?

Luther slapped me. He's being mean to me again.

I told you the last time I wasn't going to do this again. Didn't I.

Yes.

I don't know why you two even stay together.

He's my husband, Betty said.

That doesn't mean you have to stay with him. Does it.

I don't know.

Well I do. I got to get up in the morning and go to work. I can't be running you all over town.

But he's being mean. I don't want to stay with him tonight. Betty looked back toward the car. Rose had turned the engine off.

Then suddenly the rain started. It came down slanted brightly under the yardlight next to the garage and glinting and splashing under the yellow porch light. Betty began to get wet.

Oh, all right, the aunt said. But you know you'll just go back to him. You always do. But you listen to me now, it's just for tonight. This ain't going to be anything permanent.

We won't make no trouble, Betty said.

You already have.

Betty looked away and put her hand up over her face, shielding her face from the rain.

Well, tell them to come in, the aunt said. I'm not standing out here all night.

Betty waved toward the car for the children to come.

I think you better go on, Rose told them. I think it'll be all right.

Joy Rae took the bag from the front seat and she and her brother got out and hurried through the rain up onto the porch, then followed their mother inside. The aunt looked again at the car. She flipped her cigarette out into the wet gravel and shut the door behind her.

THE WIND WAS BLOWING THE RAIN SIDEWAYS IN GUSTS when Rose pulled into the driveway at her house, and when she stopped she got a sudden fright. Luther was leaning against the garage door. She turned off the ignition and the headlights and got out, watching all the time to see what he might do. She walked around to the side door and he followed a few steps behind. Rose, he said, can I ask you something?

What do you want to ask?

Could you borrow me a quarter?

I think so. Why?

I want to call Betty and say I didn't mean her no kind of hurt. I want to tell her to come back home.

You could call from here.

No, I better go downtown. I been rained on already.

She took a quarter from her purse and handed it to him, and he thanked her and told her how he'd pay her back, then walked off toward Main Street. She watched as he passed under the streetlamp at the corner, a great dark figure splashing through the shining puddles in the wet night; his black hair was plastered over his head and he went on in the rain, bound for a public phone booth on a corner.

9

ON A SATURDAY AFTER BREAKFAST, AFTER HE HAD DONE up the dishes, he came outside and without specific intention or any direction in mind started up the street in the bright cool morning and passed the vacant lot and the houses where the old widows lived in individual silence and isolation. Dena and Emma were out in front of their mother's house, and they had a new bicycle that they'd bought with the money their father in Alaska had sent. Dena knew how to ride already but Emma was only learning. Dena was on the bicycle now, riding on the sidewalk, and she stopped in front of DJ and stepped down, straddling the bike. Her little sister ran up beside them. You want to ride? she asked him.

No.

Why not? Don't you know how?

No.

You could learn, Dena said. Look at me, I'm already riding.

I don't know anything about it.

Haven't you ever tried before?

I don't have a bike, he said.

Why don't you? Emma said.

I never bought one.

Don't you have any money?

Be quiet, Emma.

But he said —

Never mind, Dena said. You want to ride this one?

It's a girl's bike. I ought to learn on a boy's bike.

You want to or not? She got off and held the handlebar out to him and he looked at her and took hold of the rubber grip and stepped over the low crossbar. When he tried pushing the bike forward the pedal came around and hit him in the back of the leg.

How do you? he said.

Get this one pedal to come up. Now step down on it.

The bike went forward and wavered and stopped.

Do it again.

He went ahead a little farther.

Get your other foot up at the same time on the other pedal.

He went forward once more and wobbled and put both feet down.

You have to keep pedaling. You don't stop.

He pedaled down the block on the sidewalk and the two girls trotted beside until he veered off into a bush and tipped over. He got up and pulled the bike upright. How do you stop it?

Dena put her foot up. Like that, she said.

Don't you have hand brakes?

No. Just the pedals.

He started again and rode down the driveway into the street and rode along pedaling steadily as they ran beside him. The bike stammered and wobbled and he almost hit them once. They screamed in delight, their faces pink as flowers, and he pedaled away. Dena called: Try and stop, try and stop. He stood up on the pedals and braked suddenly, then put his feet down to catch himself. They ran up beside him.

It's easy, Dena said. Isn't it?

I know.

He rode up and back in the street and turned and rode toward them and lifted one hand from the handlebar to wave and put his hand back quickly and rode past and came back once more, but he was too fast this time and drove the bike into the two sisters in the middle of the street and hit the older girl hard and they crashed over, sprawling out in the pavement, the bike over them. He had torn the skin from his elbow and knee and the girl was hurt in the hip and chest. She was crying a little, holding her hip. He felt sick to his stomach. Blood trickled down his arm and the knee of his pants was ripped. He got up feeling sick and lifted the bike off her, then took her hand and helped her to her feet. I'm sorry, he said. Are you all right? I'm sorry.

She looked at him and crossed her arms over her chest where she felt bruised. Why didn't you put the brakes on? Didn't you remember that?

No.

You can't forget that.

I better go home, he said. He was inspecting his elbow. I need to wash this off.

Mama will fix it for you. Come in the house.

You're dripping on your shoes, Emma said.

He looked down. I know, he said. There were bloody spots on the toes and laces.

Let Mama fix it for you, Dena said.

They walked the bicycle out of the street onto the grass and let it flop down. Before they got up to the house Mary Wells came out and stood in the front door. She had seen them from the window coming toward the house and for some reason her eyes were red. She took them into the house.

Inside, he cupped his hand under his elbow so he wouldn't drip on the carpet and she led him back to the bathroom. The two girls followed and watched while he held his arm over the sink and their mother rinsed his arm, the blood thinning and dripping into the basin while she washed tenderly, touching the cut place with the tips of her fingers, brushing the grit away. When his elbow was clear, the blood seeped out like little red berries. She told him to hold a washcloth to it, then had him put his foot up on the toilet seat and she lifted his pants and his knee was bleeding too. The blood had run into his sock. She cleaned off his knee with another washcloth. The two girls peered over her shoulder, their faces serious and absorbed, wondering. And while their mother was tending him, her eyes suddenly filled with tears and the tears ran down her cheeks onto her chin. DJ and the two girls looked at her in astonishment, and they felt a kind of fear at seeing a grown-up cry.

It's all right, DJ said. It's not that bad.

It's not that, she said. I was thinking of something else.

Mama? Dena said.

She went on cleaning his knee, squeezing antiseptic ointment from a tube and taping a bandage over it, and then did the same to his elbow. All the time she kept wiping at her eyes with the back of her hand.

Mama. What's wrong?

Don't bother me, she said.

But will you look at me too?

Why? Are you hurt?

Yes.

Where?

Here. And here.

Her mother turned to DJ and Emma. You two go on out. Now, she said to Dena, let me see.

DJ and the younger sister went out to the front room and stood beside the piano where the light came in from the front window. The little girl looked up at his face as if she expected him to do something.

What's wrong with her? he said. What's making her cry like that?

Daddy.

What do you mean?

He called last night and she's been crying. He said he's not coming home.

Why not?

I don't know why not.

Didn't he say?

I don't know.

Mary Wells came out with Dena from the bathroom. You kids go outside now, she said.

I don't want to, the little girl said.

Why don't you?

I want to stay with you.

All right. But you two go out. I'm not feeling very well, she said. She had begun to cry again. They watched her out of the corners of their eyes. Go on, she said. Please.

I want to stay too, Dena said.

No. One's enough in here. Go on now. You and DJ do something outside.

OUTSIDE, THEY PUSHED THE BIKE AROUND THE CORNER of the house to the backyard and stood by the garden looking at the alley. Let's go someplace else, Dena said.

I don't want to go downtown. I don't feel like seeing anybody right now.

We don't have to see anybody, she said.

They walked out into the alley in the tire tracks running on either side of the weeds that grew down the center of the gravel like a low hedge and passed the backyards of the old widow women and the vacant lot next door and then his grandfather's house and the vacant lot beyond. At the street they crossed over and entered the alley in the next block. On the left was an old blue wooden house, its backyard overgrown with lilac bushes and mulberry trees. Nobody had lived in the house for years. The porch screen was hanging loose and there were scraps of metal scattered under the bushes. An old black Desoto had been shoved under a mulberry and its pale-green windows had been starred and shot through by boys with pellet guns. All the tires were flat. At the alley was a small unpainted shed.

They peered in through the little window, the panes old and wavy, coated with dirt and brown cobwebs. They could only make out a push mower and a garden tiller. The door creaked open when they lifted the metal latch and they went in through long strings of cobwebs. The shed was dark and shadowy inside, with a dirt floor black with oil. There was a shelf along the back wall. Beneath it a whitewall tire. There were woven baskets with wire handles stacked one inside the other, and a rusted hand saw, and a carpenter's hammer, both its claws broken off. Below the window was a dead house sparrow, dry as dust on the dirt floor, weighing nothing. They looked at everything, lifting the tools and setting them back in their outlines of dust.

We could make something of this, Dena said.

He looked at her.

This place here.

It's just dirty in here. It's dark.

We could clean it out, she said.

He looked at her and she seemed dim and shadowy in the thin light coming through the window. He couldn't see her eyes. She had lowered her face. She was holding something in her hands, but he couldn't see for sure what it was. We could bring things here, she said.

Like what?

I don't know, she said. You don't have to if you don't want to.

She was looking down at whatever it was she had in her hands.

Maybe I do, he said.

It was an old red coffee can. He could see that now and she was poking around to see what was inside. In the dim light he studied her soft unknowable face, a girl's face. Didn't you hear me? he said.

What.

I said maybe I do.

I heard you, she said.

Part Two

Part Two

10

SHE HAD THE AUNT WHO LIVED OUT IN THE COUNTRY
east of Holt and she had the uncle who lived in town, who was Hoyt
Raines, on her mother's side.

On a windy afternoon at the beginning of October he was waiting on the front porch of their trailer when they came home from
Duckwall's. He was wearing a black baseball cap with purple trim-
ming and his face was hidden beneath the bill.

He was a tall thin man with the same dark lank hair that Betty
had and he had her own pale blue eyes. He worked in town and out
in the country on construction outfits and for tree-trimming opera-
tions, and in the summer months he joined harvesting crews that
began cutting wheat in Texas and finished in Canada. He almost
never worked at any one job longer than a single season. He'd work a
while and get laid off for one reason or another, or he'd get disgusted
and quit on his own. When he was out of work he'd lounge about in
his rented rooms on the south side of Holt, living on his last paycheck until the money ran out. The past five or six months he'd been
milking cows for a dairy north of Holt, and for him this was almost
heroic, the way he kept on. Even so—and this was more like him—
every three weeks or so he'd come into the milking parlor at six or
seven in the morning, arriving in his own good time, arriving late
and still drunk and still wooden-eyed, smelling of the cheap bar

whiskey he'd drunk the night before, and in this stupefied state he'd begin milking the expensive Holstein cows, cleaning the milk-dripping udders with a wet rag and attaching the milker-cups in clumsy haste, and the last time this had happened, it was two weeks ago, he had milked one of the sick cows into the fresh tank and the manager had had to empty the entire tank or risk being discovered and fined. Fourteen hundred gallons of fresh milk had had to be run out into the floor drain. The manager fired him on the spot—told Hoyt to go home, said he was never to come back, he didn't want ever to see his miserable face again. Well goddamn it, Hoyt said, what about my paycheck? You still owe me for this week's pay.

It'll be in the mail, you sorry son of a bitch, the manager said. Now get the hell out of here.

That day he went back to town still smelling faintly of whiskey, with also the reek of the milking parlor, that peculiar intense distinct odor which hung on in his clothes and hair and which even soap and water couldn't remove, and made his first stop at the Holt Tavern on Main Street though it was still only the middle of morning. There he began to drink and to explain to anyone who would listen—three old men and a couple of sad-eyed old women were already there—what had happened.

Now he was sitting on the porch step in the sun, smoking a cigarette, when his niece and Luther walked up across the weedy yard.

Looky who's here, Luther said.

I wondered when you two would decide to come home, Hoyt said.

We been downtown buying a new phone.

What do you want a phone for? Who's going to call?

We got to have a phone. I'm starting a business.

What kind of business?

A mail-order one. Home-based.

Hoyt looked at him. Well, he said, if you want to believe that. He stood up and turned to Betty. Aren't you going to give your uncle a hug?

She stepped toward him and he hugged her hard, then let her go and slapped her sharply on the rear.

Don't, she said. My husband don't like people messing with me.

You think Luther cares?

You better mind your manners.

That's right, Luther said. You ought to mind your manners around here.

What's crawled up your ass? I come over to see you two. I got something I want to propose. And here you're already giving me a raft of shit.

Well, Luther said. You shouldn't say that.

What you want to propose? Betty said.

Let's get out of this wind, Hoyt said. I can't talk out here.

THEY MOVED INSIDE THE TRAILER AND SAT AT THE kitchen table after Betty cleared a place for her uncle. He took off his cap and set it on the table and ran his fingers through his hair as he looked around. You need to clean this place up, he said. Good Christ, look at it. I don't see how a person can live like this.

Well, I ain't feeling very good, Betty said. My stomach keeps hurting me. I can't hardly sleep at night.

She been taking pills for it, Luther said. But it don't seem like it makes no difference. Does it, honey.

It ain't yet.

That don't mean you have to live like this, Hoyt said. You could do some of it yourself, Luther.

Luther didn't respond. He and Betty stared across the room as if there were something hanging on the wall they had failed to notice.

Hoyt was still smoking his cigarette. Betty, he said, get your uncle a ashtray. I wouldn't want to dirty your nice floor.

We don't have any. Nobody ever smokes in here.

They don't? He stared at her, then stood up and ran water from the faucet onto his cigarette and dropped it in the sink among the dirty dishes. He sat down again and sighed, rubbing his eyes elaborately. Well, I guess you heard, he said.

About what? Luther said. We didn't hear anything.

You didn't hear I lost my job? That son of a bitch out to the dairy laid me off two weeks ago. And that cow wasn't even marked good. There's suppose to be orange crayon smeared on her bag. How was I expected to remember she was sick? So I milked her into the tank like you're suppose to, and the son of a bitch fired me. Then this morning that other son of a bitch over to the apartment house kicked me out.

What happened with him? Luther said.

Nothing. Maybe I was a day or two behind on the rent, but I was about sick of his shit anyway. And he knows what he can do with that goddamn apartment of his. Hoyt looked at them. They were turned toward him, watching him like oversized children. So what do you think about all that? he said.

I think it's too bad, Betty said. They shouldn't of treated you that way.

No sir, Luther said. That ain't right for people to treat you like that.

Hoyt waved his hand. I know all that, he said. I'm not talking about that. I'll take care of his fat ass one of these days. And he knows it. That much is understood. What I'm talking about is this here. I want to make you a proposition. I'll come over here and move in with you two, and I'll pay you some rent while I get on my feet. It'll be good for all of us. That's what I'm talking about.

Luther and Betty glanced at each other over their lunchtime dishes. Outside, the wind was shaking the trailer each time it gusted up.

Go ahead, Hoyt said. Feel free to say something. It's not that difficult.

I don't know, Betty said. We only got three bedrooms. Joy Rae and Richie sleeps in their own rooms.

They got to have their own rooms, Luther said. And we got ours. We ain't got no other space.

Just a minute now, Hoyt said. Think about what you're saying. Why can't one of them move in with the other one? What's wrong with that idea? They're just little kids.

I don't know, Betty said. She looked about the room as though she'd misplaced something.

What would your mom say? Hoyt said. You not wanting to take

in her own brother, not inviting him to come in out of the cold when he needed some help. What do you think she'd say to that?

It ain't very cold out right now, Betty said.

Are you trying to be smart? That's not what I'm talking about. I'm talking about you letting me move in here.

Well, we want to help you, she said. It's just— She gestured vaguely with her hands.

I'll tell you what, Hoyt said. At least let me take a look. Let's see what we're talking about here. There's no harm in looking, is there?

Abruptly he stood up. They traded glances and followed him down the hallway past the bathroom. Hoyt looked into the bedrooms as he passed, first Luther and Betty's bedroom, then Richie's, before coming to a closed door at the end of the hall; he pushed the door open with his foot and walked into Joy Rae's room. In all the house it alone was neat and clean. The single narrow bed against the wall. A wooden dresser draped with a thin pink scarf. A meager box of jewelry and a brush and comb displayed over the scarf. The faded oval rug on the floor next to the bed.

This here'll do, he said. At least it's cleaned up. She can move in with her brother and I'll stay in here.

Oh, I don't know about that, Betty said, standing behind him in the doorway.

It's just for a little while. Till I get going again. Where's your charity? Don't you have no heart?

I got my kids to think about too.

How is me moving in here going to hurt your kids?

Joy Rae fixed it up all by herself.

All right, he said. I'm your uncle, but if you don't want me moving in all you got to do is say get out. I'm not stupid.

I don't know what to say, she said. Luther, you say something.

Luther looked up the hallway. Well honey, Uncle Hoyt says it's just for a little while. He lost his own apartment. He ain't got no other place to go. Seems like we could help him out a little bit.

There, Hoyt said. That's somebody that cares.

I know one thing, Betty said. Joy Rae isn't going to like it.

· · ·

THEY TOLD HER OF THESE NEW ARRANGEMENTS WHEN SHE got home from school that day, and she went immediately to her room and shut the door and lay on the bed and cried bitterly. But that night, as ordered, she moved her things into Richie's room and hung up her few dresses in the little closet and set out the box of cheap jewelry on the half of the dresser she'd claimed for herself, then picked up his shoes and toys and clothes and put them away.

When she got into bed that night it was too narrow for two of them, even as small and as thin as they were, and in the night after they'd gone to sleep Richie began to dream violently, thrashing in bed, and she was forced to wake him.

Quit your kicking. Quit it, Richie. It's just a dream, so be quiet.

Then she looked up from the bed and saw her mother's uncle standing in the doorway staring at them, only his face visible in the shadow. He was leaning against the door frame. She pretended to be asleep and watched him through the darkness, and she could smell him. He'd been out drinking. She had been sitting at the table after supper when he'd asked her father for five dollars. He couldn't be expected to stay home at night, he'd said, he was still a young man and nobody was about to tie him down. Her father had looked suddenly afraid, and he'd glanced ceilingward for help but none had come, so he'd handed over five dollar bills out of his wallet. Now she kept watching him across the dark, and after a while he left the doorway and went down the hall to her room.

But even after he'd gone Joy Rae couldn't fall asleep for an hour or more. Then she woke in the morning to discover she was sleeping in a wet bed. Her brother had wet himself in the night and her gown was soaked with it, her legs cold and damp. It made her want to cry. She got up and wiped at her hips and legs with a dirty tee-shirt and began dressing for school. She woke her brother. He whimpered and complained, standing beside the bed.

Hush up, she said.

She helped him skin off his wet underpants. He was shivering and there were goose bumps running down his legs.

We got to get ready for school. The bus is coming. Hush up that crying, you little baby. I'm the one ought to be crying.

11

FIRST THEY SET TO CLEANING IT, AS PEOPLE DO WHEN they move into a new house. They wanted it clean before they did anything else to it. They brought water from his grandfather's house, carrying the bucket between them, their hands together on the wire bail, the water sloshing cold against their pants, and in the dark shed beside the alley they washed the dust off the single window and swept out the dirt and the trash with a short stub of a straw broom. Together they hauled out the pieces of scrap iron that were covered with dust and rolled out the whitewalled tire and pushed the old mower and the garden tiller under the mulberry bushes next to the Desoto. Then they swept the dark oily dirt floor a second time and sprinkled water in the corners and scrubbed down the walls of rough-sawn lumber. When they were finished the shed smelled clean, of damp earth and wet wood.

Then they began their search. In the afternoons after school and on succeeding Saturdays they collected things, foraging out into the alleys of Holt. At first they searched only the alleys of their own neighborhood, but after a few days they began to move into the alleys four and five blocks away.

They found a discarded kitchen chair and a wooden table with a splintered leg, then two old china dinner plates together with three silver forks and a serving spoon and a single steel-bladed knife. The next day they discovered a cast-off framed picture of the baby Jesus, with fat legs and fat feet, and a halo shimmering above his brown curls, altogether naked save for a white cloth draped about his hips. There was a sweet look of entreaty on his face, and they carried the picture back and hung it on a nail.

And five blocks away they discovered a rose-patterned carpet beside a trash can in the alley behind a brick house. The carpet was stained the color of coffee at one of its corners. They hauled it out into the alley, studied it, walked on it, then rolled it up and began lugging it home. But it turned out to be too heavy and down the alley they dropped it. I'll go get something, he said. He went back to his grandfather's house and returned with the wagon he had received as a present at Christmas when he was a first-grader and they balanced the carpet on the wagon and started back, both ends dragging in the weeds and gravel.

In the next block an old lady was standing at the back of her house in a black scarf and a man's long black overcoat. When they approached she stepped out into the alley. What are you kids doing? What's that you have?

It's just a rug.

You stole it, didn't you.

They looked at her. One of her eyes was blue and clouded and her nose dripped.

Let's go, DJ said. They started on around her.

Stop where you are, she said. She began to trot after them, wobbling in the red gravel. Thieves! she cried. Stop now!

Now they ran, the wagon bouncing behind them, the carpet leaping and scraping in the gravel until it finally tipped off. Panting, they looked back. She stood in the middle of the alley far behind. She was calling to them but they couldn't tell what it was. Just then she removed the black scarf from her head and waved it at them like a flag or warning, and without the scarf they could see her head was as bald as a brass ball.

You better watch out for her, Dena said.

She'll find you, he said. She'll come to your house.

They laughed, then lifted the carpet onto the wagon and carried on at a calm pace. At the shed they spread the carpet over the dirt floor, the stained end turned under, and swept it clean. Then they set the table on the carpet and placed the chair beside the table in the exact center of the room where the afternoon sun shone in through the window and the dust motes danced in the air like tiny creatures in dim water.

ON THE DAYS THAT FOLLOWED THEY WENT OUT AGAIN. One Saturday morning they found a second chair. Another day they turned up five red candles in a cardboard box and a glass candle holder that was only chipped at one corner. Back in the shed they lit one of the candles and sat down and looked at each other. It was late afternoon, almost evening, and suddenly they heard a car coming up the alley, the tires crunching in the gravel. They sat without breathing, each staring into the eyes of the other, and then the car went by without stopping and they began to talk softly in the flickering candlelight while, outside, the air grew dark around them.

I've got to go. Grandpa will be wanting supper.

You don't have to go yet, she said.

I'll have to go pretty soon.

12

THEY WERE LATE GETTING IT DONE. IT WAS ALREADY the middle of fall. They had been delayed by helping Victoria Roubideaux get settled in Fort Collins, and afterward by the unaccustomed listlessness that came with her absence, then they had busied themselves selling the yearling steers at the sale barn. So it was the middle of fall, already October, before they got around to moving the range bulls out of the pasture where the cows were.

That would have had something to do with it. Except that afterward, lying in his white bed in the Holt County Memorial Hospital staring out the window at the leafless trees, Raymond couldn't say for certain if even this much were true—this despite the fact that he and his brother had dealt with cattle all their lives.

There were six of them in the corral, all black Angus bulls. Black cattle were preferred now. Forty years ago it had been whiteface Herefords. Now it was black cattle because they graded out higher at the slaughterhouses. Convention and caprice were about all it was.

They had moved the bulls into the plank corral next to the barn on the morning of this cold crisp day. The sky was overcast and high, not like it wanted to rain or snow, just high and completely covered and cold.

They had been checking each of the bulls, deciding if they wanted to get rid of any, and there was the one bull that was acting up, turning snorty like he was on the fight. He had always been all right before, a little high as black Angus bulls can be, but nothing out of the ordinary. He was five now; they'd bought him three years ago at the sale barn, paying twenty-five hundred dollars for him. They had checked the records beforehand, reading who his sire was, how much milk his dam gave, what his birth, weaning, and yearling weights were, what his fertility check showed. And they'd looked him over thoroughly in the numbered pen before the auction ever started, and they both had approved of his confirmation. He was already thick and heavy as a two-year-old, with thick muscling and a thick neck and a great wide hornless blunt head, and clear black eyes that looked at them from under black eyelashes that were almost like a girl's, but with something else there too in his eyes as if he knew too well what he was capable of. He was upstanding, long in the body, with a good straight back, and his legs were set under him. He looked as if he could get around and cover the country. His sheath was satisfactory too, high enough that it wouldn't snag on sagebrush or soapweed and get so lacerated and cut up that the scar tissue would prevent him from being able to cover the cows he was set to.

So they had bid on him when he'd come into the ring and afterward Raymond had written out the check to the woman in the office, then they'd hauled him home in the stock trailer. And in due time his calves had been good ones, all healthy and vigorous, fast gainers, like he was. Yet from the beginning he'd tended to be a little snorty.

Now he was the last of the six bulls they were looking at on this cold and overcast morning in October. The other bulls were already sorted into the next corral. The McPheron brothers were inside the corral with him, studying him, walking around him, the corral dirt under their feet soft and loose, dusty with the wisps of dried manure. They were dressed for the weather and looked almost like twins in their canvas chore jackets and their jeans and boots and leather gloves, their old white dirty hats pulled low over their eyes on their round heads. Their faces were chafed red, their eyes bleary with the dust, and their noses had begun to run a little in the cold.

Well, Raymond said, he looks all right.

He'll do for another year, Harold said. He's taken a little gaunt in the flank there. But he's all right.

While they were talking about him the bull eyed them steadily. He turned to face them head-on as they walked around him.

He don't look like he wants to quit.

Not today, Raymond said. He looks like he could go on for another five years. He'll probably outlast the both of us.

All right then, Harold said.

He walked past the bull over to the heavy pipe-iron gate to throw it open so the bull could pass in with the others. Nervous from being kept back by himself, the bull moved up snorting and pawing to go through, but the gate was open only a little when he rushed the narrow opening, and all his weight was carried forward, slamming into the end-post of the gate as he hit it with his shoulder, and he was knocked backward, his feet slid in the dirt, and he went down as the gate clanged shut. He rose up massively and lunged forward, bellowing and snorting, his great head swinging back and forth, his eyes fixing on Harold. He dropped his head and smashed Harold in the chest, knocking him off his feet against the closed gate. You son of a bitch! Harold hollered. He slapped at him, tried to kick at him. But the bull smashed him again, lifting him, burying his head in Harold's chest and stomach, splaying him out flat against the iron gate. Harold tried to holler but nothing came out. The bull stepped back and Harold slid down in the dirt, and then the bull began to ram at him with his head.

Raymond saw it all and came running up from behind, whipping the bull in the hip with his gloved fist and grabbing his tail to distract him, to turn him away. Goddamn you! he hollered. Hey! Hey! The bull spun around, swinging heavily, all his power and weight, and flung Raymond across the corral, sprawling him out on the ground, and then came after him, his head down, swinging and plunging, and slammed him in the back. Raymond rolled onto his face in the dirt and managed to scramble up. Hey! he hollered. Hey! The bull knocked him down again, smashed him in the leg, Raymond all the time was trying to kick at him, and then he scrambled up once more and limped backward, moving away. The bull stood looking at him.

Then the bull turned again toward Harold, who lay on his face across the corral. The bull trotted across to him and began bumping

at him with his thick head. Tumbling in the dirt, kicking and twist-
ing, Harold finally rolled under a short plank panel they'd nailed into
the corner of the corral to prevent cattle from climbing into the
stock tank. Inside the little enclosure he was out of reach. His face
was filthy now, there was blood smeared across his nose and cheeks.
He turned his head and vomited into the dirt and tried to breathe.
The bull sniffed at him through the fence panel.

Seeing his brother safe for the moment, Raymond hurried limping into the barn and grabbed a hay fork leaning against the wall and
stumbled back out in a kind of one-legged hopping motion, and went
out and around the fence and climbed into the corral on the far side
to shove the gate open again. The bull stepped forward, sniffing at
the gate, then plunged through, and seeing Raymond on the other
side of the plank fence, the bull snorted and swung around, pawing
dirt up over his back. You son of a bitch, Raymond said. Try something now. He hollered and waved his arms, and as the bull turned
away he jabbed him in the hip with the hay fork. Bright blood
spurted out and the bull bellowed, he spun back to face Raymond
again, his head lowered, tossing back and forth, but the old man
stood him off, brandishing the long-handled hay fork as if he and the
bull had been flung together in some ancient arena, and all the time
Raymond was speaking in a low hard mean voice. Come on, goddamn you. Come on. The bull snorted once more and at last moved
away.

Raymond fastened the gate and hobbled across the corral to the
corner where his brother lay in the dirt. Harold had removed his
gloves and he was touching at his chest very carefully.

How bad is it? Raymond said, kneeling over.

Bad, Harold said. He was only whispering, his voice raspy and
tight. I can't get my breath. I'm all busted inside.

I'm going to run up to the house and call somebody.

I ain't going nowhere.

I'll just go up and call.

No. Stay here, Harold said. I mean I ain't going nowhere ever.

I got to call the ambulance.

I won't last till you get back. They can't do nothing for me.

You don't know that.

Yeah, I do, Harold whispered.

He looked up at his brother kneeling beside him across the fence panel. Raymond's face looked scared and dirty. His own face was chalk white now under the dirt and blood.

Pull me out from under this fence. I don't want to die cramped up in here.

I don't dare to move you, Raymond said. I got to call somebody.

No. Start pulling. I can't wait for you to get somebody else.

Hold on then. Goddamn it anyway.

He took Harold's canvas jacket at the shoulder and gripped his belt and began dragging him slowly through the loose dirt. His brother grunted and gritted his teeth, tears started up in his eyes, and there was blood trickling from the corner of his clenched mouth. Raymond slid him out from under the fence and Harold lay on his back at the edge of the corral, breathing in shallow gasps, with his hands moving at his chest, squeezing and pushing at his ribs as if this might help him breathe more easily. He opened his eyes and reached a hand up and wiped at his mouth. I'm missing my hat, he said.

I'll get it. Raymond stood and limped out into the corral and picked up the hat and slapped it against his leg and then limped back and knelt again. When Harold raised his head he fit the hat onto his short iron-gray hair. His hair was filthy. The back of the hat was crumpled so Raymond smoothed it out.

All right, Harold said. Thanks. He shut his eyes and tried to breathe. It's getting cold, he whispered.

Raymond removed his canvas jacket and spread it over him.

After a while Harold opened his eyes. He shivered and peered around. Raymond?

Yes.

Are you here?

I'm right here, Raymond said. Right next to you.

Harold looked up into his brother's face and Raymond took hold of his thick calloused hand.

You got to take care of her by yourself now. His voice was just a thin raspy sound. That little girl too. I won't be here to see how they come out. I was looking forward to it.

You'll see them, Raymond said. You're going to come out of this.

No. I'm done here, Harold said. I'm about finished.

He closed his eyes and shivered again, his breaths coming slower and harder. Then he stopped breathing. After a while he breathed once more, a long single rattling suck of air. Then he seemed to settle into the dirt more comfortably. After that he didn't breathe again. Raymond watched him and his brother's eyelids fluttered once, that was all, then Raymond began to weep, the tears ran down his face in dirty runnels. He held on to his brother's hand and looked out through the corral toward the pastures and the blue sandhills beyond. The hills lay far away in the distance on the low horizon. The wind had started up again. He could feel it now. He looked again at his brother and pulled the canvas coat up over his blood-smeared face. He knelt for a long while beside him, not moving, an old man with his old brother scuttled down in the loose dirt of a plank corral under an overcast October sky.

13

IT WAS AN HOUR AND MORE BEFORE RAYMOND ROUSED himself. Then he pulled himself up and limped across the gravel drive to the house and made the call. When the ambulance from Holt drove up in front of the house he told them to go down and collect his brother. The two men in their shiny jackets drove to the corral and gathered Harold up and carried him to the ambulance on a transfer board with a blanket spread over him, and then they drove both McPheron brothers into town to the emergency ward at the hospital. The doctor pronounced Harold dead on arrival.

Raymond lay on the narrow emergency-room bed behind green privacy curtains as the doctor examined him. The nurses had already removed his chore coat and flannel shirt and jeans so he lay now in a thin white cotton gown. The doctor felt his chest, listened to his heart and his lungs and felt tentatively along his leg. Afterward he ordered complete X rays that revealed cracked ribs on the right side of his chest and a broken bone in his lower left leg. They wanted to move him into surgery at once.

Wait now, Raymond told the nurse. Before you run me in there I want to call somebody. I ain't going to be no good later.

Who do you want to call?

Tom Guthrie and Victoria Roubideaux.

Tom Guthrie, the high school teacher?

Yes.

But I don't believe school's let out yet for the day.

For God's sake, Raymond said.

All right, she said. Never mind. We'll call and see if we can get him on the phone.

Also I want you to call Fort Collins, Raymond said. Get Victoria Roubideaux for me.

Now who's she, Mr. McPheron?

A young girl away at college, with her baby. Her name will be amongst the new listings.

But who is she to you? Is she your daughter?

No.

But usually we only make these kind of long-distance calls to relatives.

Just call her on the phone, Raymond said. Can't you do that?

If she were a relative, a niece, or something like a daughter.

She is like a daughter to me. More than like a daughter. She's what I've got to think of right now.

Well. The nurse looked at him. He was watching her intently, his face washed clean now, the scratches on his cheeks and forehead showing vivid and inflamed. All right, she said. But it's not the usual procedure. How do you spell it?

Raymond turned away. Good Christ, he said.

Very well, she said. I'll figure it out. Which one do you want to talk to first?

The girl. She'll have to know about this.

But you're sure you feel like talking right now. You must be in a lot of pain.

Just get me the phone once you get connected to her, he said. She's going to hate this. I'm pretty sure she loved my brother. I sure God know he loved her.

The nurse went out and he lay in the bed with the green curtains drawn around him. They had started an IV already and had strapped a blood pressure cuff to his arm and propped up his leg with a pillow. He lay looking at the white tiled ceiling, then he shut his eyes and despite his best intentions to the otherwise he was weeping again. He reached up out of the bedsheet and wiped his face and waited for the nurse to bring him the phone. He was trying to think how he was ever going to tell Victoria Roubideaux about what had happened.

Then the nurse came in with the phone and he said: Is that her?

Yes. I finally located her. Here, take it.

He held the phone to his ear. Victoria?

What's wrong? she said. Her voice sounded small and thin. Is something wrong? Has something happened?

Honey, I got something I got to tell you.

Oh no, she said. Oh no. No.

I'm just afraid I do, he said. And then he told her.

14

In the late afternoon Tom Guthrie stood in the hospital room beside Raymond, who lay in the white bed under the sheet in his hospital gown. They had wheeled him into the room after the surgery and they had started to put him into the bed next to the door but he'd told them he wanted the bed near the window.

Along with Guthrie in the room was Maggie Jones, another teacher from the high school. They'd been together since Guthrie's wife had moved to Denver, though Maggie still lived in her own house on South Ash Street. Now she was sitting in a chair drawn up close to Raymond's bed. The doctor had set the bone in his leg and put a cast over the leg below the knee, and there were elastic bandages wrapped around his chest to hold his ribs securely and to ease his breathing. His broken leg was raised onto pillows. He breathed shallowly, with little sharp exhalations, and his face showed what he had suffered. His face was drawn and pale, sallow under the red weathering. He looked old. He looked old and worn-out and sad.

I couldn't stop him, Raymond said. They're too big. Too strong. I tried but I couldn't. I couldn't save my brother.

Nobody could have saved him, Guthrie said. You did what you could.

Maggie put her hand on the old man's arm and patted him softly. You did everything you could, she said. We know that.

It wasn't enough, Raymond said.

It was quiet in the room, the light coming in aslant through the window. Outside the hospital along the street the bare trees looked orange in the late afternoon sun. Down the hall they could hear people talking and then there was some laughter. Someone came walking past in the hallway and they looked up when he went by. It was one of the preachers in town, come to call on the sick and the lame.

Tom, can you look after things for a couple days? Raymond said. I can't think who else to ask.

Of course, Guthrie said. Don't even think about it.

You'll need to let the bulls out and check they got water. And then if you'd check the cows and calves to the south.

Of course.

I still got the calves in there with the cows, and every cow and heifer is suppose to be carrying a new calf. They ain't due till February but you can't ever tell what they'll do. He looked at Guthrie. Well, you know all that.

I'll go out there right away, Guthrie said. As soon as I leave here. What else do you need me to do?

I don't know. Well, there's the horses too. If you don't mind.

I'll check them.

And can I check on things in the house? Maggie Jones said.

Oh, Raymond said. He turned to look at her. No. I don't want you to bother. It'll be a mess in there.

I've seen plenty of messes before, she said.

Well. I don't know what to say.

Just try to rest. That's all you have to do.

I can't, Raymond said. I shut my eyes and every time I see Harold out there in the corral. Laying out there in the dirt and the bull hitting him again.

He was looking at Maggie's face as he talked, looking up at her as though he were pleading some case that was already lost but one that he couldn't let go of. There were tears in his eyes.

Yes, Maggie said. I know. You'll be able to rest pretty soon. She touched his shoulder and smoothed back the stiff iron-gray hair on his round head. He felt ashamed to have her touch him in this manner but he allowed it for a moment. Then he moved his head from under her hand and turned away. Maggie was crying now too. Beside her Guthrie stood watching the old man. He wanted to think of words that would make some difference but there were none in any language he knew that were sufficient to the moment or that would change a single thing. They stayed quiet for some time.

THERE WAS A COMMOTION OUT IN THE HALL AND THEN Victoria Roubideaux came into the room carrying Katie in her arms. She came directly to the bed and looked down at Raymond. He looked up at her and shook his head. Honey, he said.

Yes, she said. I'm here now. She tried to smile.

Let me have Katie, Maggie said. She stood and took the little girl and Victoria sat down in the chair beside the bed and leaned over and kissed Raymond on the forehead. I came as fast as I could.

I hope you didn't take any risk driving.

No. It was fine.

Thank you for coming. I didn't know what I was going to do without you.

I'm here now, she said again.

He lifted his hand out of the sheet and she took it. I just couldn't stop it from happening, he said.

I know you would've done everything you could.

He looked into her face. He wanted to tell her one thing more but for a moment he couldn't speak. He had told her most of what he had to say on the phone. Honey, he said, you know Harold he was talking about you at the end. You and Katie. The last thing he had on his mind was you and that little girl. I think he would of wanted you to know that.

Thank you for telling me, she whispered. The tears ran down her cheeks, and she ducked her head and her dark hair fell about her face. She held his hand and sobbed quietly.

Guthrie said softly: Raymond. Why don't Maggie and I go on now. We'll come back later tonight.

I'll still be here, Raymond said. I don't think I'll be going anywhere else for a while.

Maggie returned the little girl to her mother and she and Guthrie went out of the room into the hall.

Victoria settled the child on her lap. Raymond looked at the little black-haired girl in her red coat and long stockings and he reached up and took hold of her foot. She was frightened by him and drew back.

Oh, honey, Victoria said. He won't hurt you. You know who Raymond is. But the little girl turned and faced away, hiding her head in her mother's neck. Raymond put his hand back under the sheet.

It's just that she's scared to see you this way, Victoria said. She's never seen anyone in a hospital bed before. We're all frightened to see you this way.

I don't imagine I look like much, Raymond said. Nothing you'd care to study.

GUTHRIE AND MAGGIE LEFT THE HOSPITAL AND DROVE first to Guthrie's house across the tracks on the north side of Holt on Railroad Street. Inside the house he left a note on the kitchen table for his two boys, Ike and Bobby, telling them to do their chores at the barn and then to heat up some soup on the stove, that he'd be home later in the evening. He explained that Raymond McPheron was in the hospital and needed his help but that he'd call them later from the ranch or the hospital lobby. Then he and Maggie drove in Guthrie's old red pickup back through town and out south on the two-lane blacktop to the McPheron place. The sun was setting now and all the flat country around them was cast in gold, with long shadows fallen out from behind the ordered fence posts above the bar ditch.

They turned off the blacktop onto the gravel road and then south again down the lane going back to the house and stopped at the wire gate. Maggie got out and went up to the house and Guthrie drove on and parked by the barn and got out into the cold evening air. The six bulls stood waiting in the corral, their backs to the wind, and he walked around to the gate to the pasture, climbed over the fence, and shoved the gate open. The bulls looked at him, and first one and then the others began to move heavily out of the corral. He stood back and watched as they trotted through the gate. There was the one that came limping and even in the darkening light he could see the patch of dried blood caked on its hip. Moving into the pasture, the bulls slowed once more to their own heavy unhurried pace, and he shut the gate behind them and checked the water level in the stock tank, then went back to the barn and drove the pickup over to the south and threw open the barbed-wire gate and passed through, rattling and jarring out into the pasture as he looked at all the cows and calves and heifers. The cattle faced him in the headlights, their eyes shining like bright rubies. When he approached they shied away from the pickup, the calves galloping off with their tails up, and he saw nothing of concern. Two old blackbaldy cows followed him but soon they stopped and stood still, staring after the pickup as he came bouncing back across the rough ground, the headlights picking up the clumps of sagebrush and soapweed ahead, and he came through the gate and shut it behind him, and then walked the saddle horses into the barn and forked hay to them from the loft, and once more got into the pickup and drove up to the house.

The lights were all on inside the house now. Maggie Jones had already washed the dishes and had set them to dry on the counter, and she had scrubbed the enameled top of the old stove, tidied the kitchen table and set chairs in place around it and had swept the floor. She was in the downstairs bedroom when Guthrie came in and found her.

You about ready to go? he said.

I thought Raymond had better stay down here, she said. He won't want to climb the stairs with that cast on his leg.

I hadn't thought of that, Guthrie said. He watched her draw the sheet tight and tuck it in and spread a quilt over the bed. What about Victoria and Katie? I thought this was their room.

I'm going to move the crib out into the parlor. And make up a bed on the couch for Victoria.

You think she's going to stay a while.

She'll want to.

What about her classes?

I don't know. She'll want to be here to take care of him. I know that.

He isn't going to like it, Guthrie said. Raymond won't want her staying home and missing school on his account.

No. He won't. But I think he'll have to accept it. Will you help me take this crib apart so we can get it through the door?

I'll get my tools.

Guthrie went out to the pickup and found pliers and a couple of screwdrivers and a wrench in the toolbox behind the cab and came back inside. After taking the crib apart and wheeling it into the parlor, they put it back together and stood it against the wall, then made up a bed on the old couch with clean sheets and a pair of green wool blankets and a much-yellowed pillow that Maggie found in the closet. They stood back and looked at this new arrangement. The walls of the room were papered over with an ancient flower pattern that was a good deal faded and showed water stains at the ceiling, and the two plaid recliner chairs were set across from the old console television.

I think we can go now, Maggie said.

They shut the lights off and went out to the pickup. From the outside the paintless clapboard house appeared all the more desolate in the blue glow of the yardlight at the corner of the garage. So insubstantial and paltry that the wind might blow through and find no resistance at all.

WHEN THEY HAD COME OFF THE GRAVELED COUNTY ROAD and had turned north on the blacktop toward Holt, Maggie said: I can't help but worry about him. What do you think he's going to do now?

What can he do? Guthrie said. He'll do what he has to.

You'll help him, won't you.

Of course I will. I'll be out there tomorrow morning before

school. And I'll come out again after school lets out. I'll bring Ike and Bobby with me. But he's still going to be alone.

She'll want to stay with him.

Victoria, you mean.

Yes. And Katie.

But that can't last forever. You know that.

I know, Maggie said. It wouldn't be good if it did. Not for him or them either. But I'm still worried about him.

They drove on along the blacktop. The narrow highway looked empty and forlorn ahead in the lights of the pickup. The wind blew across the flat open sandy ground, across the wheat fields and corn stubble and across the native pastures where dark herds of cattle grazed in the night. On either side of the highway farmhouses were set off by faint blue yardlights, the houses all scattered and isolated in the dark country, and far ahead down the highway the streetlights of Holt were a mere shimmer on the low horizon.

Maggie sat next to Guthrie in the cab and stared ahead at the center stripe in the road. I think I'll ask Victoria if she wants to stay with me, she said. She won't want to be alone in that house tonight.

She's going to have to stay in it sometime.

Not tonight, Maggie said. She's had enough to get used to for one day.

She's not the only one, Guthrie said. That poor old son of a bitch. Think of him.

Yes, Maggie said. She looked at Guthrie and slid over nearer in the seat and sat close beside him. She put her hand on his thigh and left it there as they rode along in the dark. They passed the small square sign at the side of the road that announced they had entered the limits of Holt.

In town they turned left onto US 34 and turned again onto Main Street and parked in front of the hospital. They got out in the chill air and went inside and found that Victoria was still seated in the chair beside Raymond's bed. Since they had left two hours earlier she had not moved. It was as if she would not even consider the possibility of moving, as if she thought by sitting beside his bed, refusing to move, she might prevent anything else from happening to him, or to anyone else she loved in this world. She was still holding Katie on her lap, and Raymond and the little girl were both asleep.

Then, hearing Maggie and Guthrie come into the room, Raymond woke. He looked up and it was clear, by what showed in his face, that he had just remembered. Oh Lord, he said. Oh Lord.

15

Later, Guthrie and Maggie left the room and went out, and Victoria stayed in the hospital and tended to Raymond and told him she would go to Maggie's house after visiting hours were over.

The orderly brought Raymond a tray of supper but he didn't want it. It tasted like nothing he cared for and he wasn't hungry anyway. Victoria fed some of the applesauce to Katie and she took the spoon and ate it herself and afterward sat on the floor with pencils and crayons, drawing pictures until she grew tired, then Victoria put her in the empty bed next to the door and spread the light cotton blankets over her.

She's all wore out, Raymond said.

I thought she would sleep in the car driving up here but she didn't, Victoria said. She jabbered all the way.

Victoria was holding Raymond's hand. She was sitting next to him as before in the chair beside his bed, the door half closed against the noise of people going by and the low murmuring of people talking out in the hallway.

How's school going? he said. Still doing all right?

It's okay. It doesn't seem very important right now.

I know. But you'll have to keep on.

I'm going to stay home for a while.

You don't want to miss your school.

It won't hurt to miss some. This is more important. She straightened the bedsheet at his neck.

Raymond looked at her and then at the tiled ceiling, shifting a little in the bed. I can't quit thinking about him, he said. He stays at the front of my mind all the time.

Do you want to talk about it?

It happened so fast. You can't predict what an animal is going to do. You never can. I knew that bull was that way, but he'd never hurt nobody before.

You couldn't do anything, she said. You have to know that.

But it doesn't help, just knowing it. I keep going over all of it again in my head. There ought to of been something I could do.

Did he suffer? Victoria said.

Yes. He was awful bad at the end. I'm only glad now it didn't last too long. I didn't know how bad it was really. I thought he'd make it, I thought he'd come out of it. We been together all our lives.

You always got along together, didn't you.

Yes, honey, we did. We never did have much of a fight. We had our disputes sometimes but they never amounted to anything. They was always done the next day. We just agreed on most things. Even without having to talk about them.

Did you ever think of doing anything else?

Like what, honey?

I don't know. Like getting married, maybe. Or living apart.

Well. There was this one time Harold had him kind of a interest in a woman, but then she got interested in somebody else. That was a long time ago. She still lives here in town, with two grown-up kids. He always figured he was too slow, I guess. It might not of ever got anywhere anyway. Harold was pretty set in his ways.

They were good ways though, Victoria said. Weren't they.

I think they were, Raymond said. He was a awful good brother to me.

He was good to me too, Victoria said. I keep expecting him to come walking in that door any minute now, saying something funny, and wearing that old dirty hat of his, like he always did.

That was him, wasn't it, Raymond said. My brother always did have his own way of wearing a hat. You could tell Harold from a distance anywhere. You could tell him two blocks away. Oh hell, I miss him already.

I do too, she said.

I don't imagine I'll ever get over missing him, Raymond said. Some things you don't get over. I believe this'll be one of them.

16

WHEN HE GOT HOME FROM PLAYING IN THE SHED WITH
Dena, his grandfather had already gone to bed in his little room at
the back of the house, and when he switched on the light the old man
raised up on his elbows in his long underwear, with his white hair
disheveled and a wild look in his eyes.

Turn that off, he said.

What's wrong, Grandpa?

I don't feel very good.

Do you want supper?

I want you to turn that goddamn light off is what I want.

DJ cut off the light and went out to the kitchen. He made toast
and coffee and carried these on a dinner plate back to the bedroom
but now the old man was asleep.

In the night he heard him get out of bed. His grandfather stayed
in the bathroom a long while before shuffling back to his room.
Through the thin wall he could hear the bedsprings creaking under
his weight, and then he began to cough. After a while there was the
sound of his spitting.

In the morning when he went in to see him the old man was
awake. He looked small under the heavy quilt, his white hair sticking
out sideways, his thick red hands beyond the cuffs of his underwear
lying slack and empty over the blanket.

Are you going to get up, Grandpa?

No. I don't feel like it.

I made fresh coffee.

All right. Bring that.

He brought the coffee and the old man sat up and drank a little, then set the cup on a chair next to the bed and lay back again. He started coughing as soon as he was stretched out. He twisted around to reach under the pillow and pulled out a filthy handkerchief and spat into it and then used it to wipe his mouth.

You must be sick, Grandpa.

I don't know. You better get on to school.

I don't want to.

Go on. I'll be all right.

I should stay home with you.

No. It ain't nothing to worry about. I been sicker than this before and always come out of it. I took a fever of a hundred and six one time before you was ever born. Now go on like I told you.

He went unhappily to school and sat all morning at his desk at the rear of the room while his mind wandered back to the house. Through the tedious hours of the morning he paid little attention to his schoolwork. The teacher noticed his lack of attention and came to his desk and stood beside him. DJ, is something wrong? You've done nothing all morning. It's not like you.

He shrugged and stared ahead at the blackboard.

What's bothering you?

Nothing's bothering me.

Something must be.

He looked up at her. Then he lowered his head and took up the pencil on his desktop and started to work at the math problems she'd assigned them to do. The teacher watched for a moment and returned to her desk at the front of the room. When she looked at him again a few minutes later, he'd already stopped working.

At noon when they were released from school for the lunch hour he began immediately to run. He raced home through the town park and across the shining railroad tracks and didn't stop until he got to the house. He paused in the kitchen to catch his breath, then walked down the hall to his grandfather's room. The old man was still in bed, coughing steadily now and spitting into the dirty hand-kerchief. He hadn't drunk any more of the coffee. He looked up when DJ entered the room, his face very red and his eyes wet and glassy.

You look worse, Grandpa. You better go to the doctor.

The old man had lowered the window blind during the morning and the room was dark now. He looked like someone who had been put away in a dim back room and left there to his own devices.

I ain't seeing no doctor. You can just forget about that.

You have to.

No, you head on back to school and mind your own business.

I don't want to leave you.

I'm going to get out of this bed. Is that what you want?

DJ left the room and went out in front of the house, looking up and down the empty street. Then he ran across to Mary Wells's house and knocked on the door. After some time she opened the door wearing an old blue bathrobe, and the pretty grown-up woman's face he was used to seeing, always made up with pink rouge and red lipstick, was now plain and bare. She looked haggard, as though she hadn't slept in days.

What are you doing here? she said. Aren't you supposed to be in school?

Grandpa's sick. I just came home to check on him. Something's wrong with him.

What is it?

I don't know. Could you come over and look at him?

Yes, she said. Come in while I get dressed.

He waited for her near the door but didn't sit down. He was surprised to see the newspapers on the floor and the various magazines and pieces of mail scattered around. Two half-filled coffee cups were set on the side table next to the couch, and milky coffee from one of the cups had spilled out in a gray pool on the polished wood. In the dining room last night's dishes were still on the table. It was clear she had troubles of her own. Dena had said so when they were out in the shed, but she wouldn't talk more about it.

Mary Wells came out of the bedroom in jeans and a sweatshirt, and she had brushed her hair and had put on some lipstick, but that was all. She didn't say anything and they went outside. They started across to his grandfather's house.

How long has he been sick? she said.

I don't know if he is sick for sure. But he seems like it.

How long has he seemed sick?

Since yesterday. He keeps coughing and he won't get out of bed.

They crossed the vacant lot and went into the little house. She had never been beyond the front door, and he felt embarrassed for her to see the inside, to see how they lived. She looked around. Where is he?

Back here.

He led her through the hall to the dark bedroom that smelled of sweat and stale coffee and his grandfather's sour bedding. He could smell it now in her presence. The old man lay in the bed, his hands outside the blanket. He heard them come in the room and opened his eyes.

Are you sick, Mr. Kephart?

Who's that coming in here?

Mary Wells from up the street. You remember me.

The old man started to sit up.

No. Don't move. She crossed to his bed. DJ says you seem like you're getting sick.

Well, I don't feel too good. But I ain't sick.

You look like you are. She felt his forehead and he looked up at her out of his watery eyes. You're hot. You feel feverish, Mr. Kephart.

It ain't nothing to talk about. I'll get over it.

No, you're sick.

He began to cough. She stood over him, watching his face. He coughed for a good while. When he was done he cleared his throat and spat into the handkerchief.

I want to take you to the doctor, Mr. Kephart. Let's see what he says.

No, I ain't going to no doctor.

Well, you can just stop that now. I'm going home to get the car. And while I'm gone you can get dressed. I'll be back in five minutes.

She left the room and they could hear the screen door slap shut. The old man stared at the boy. How come you ain't in school where you belong? Look here what you done. Now you got the neighbors all worked up.

You've got to get dressed, Grandpa. She's going to be here.

I know that, goddamn it. Meddling is what you been doing. Sticking your nose in.

Do you want me to help you get out of bed?

I can still do that myself. Goddamn it, give me a minute.

The old man came slowly out of the bed. The long underwear he wore was yellowed and dirty, the bottoms sagged in the seat and were considerably soiled in the front where he'd fumbled at the fly. He stood while the boy helped him into his blue workshirt and his overalls, pulling them on over the underwear, then he sat down on the bed and the boy brought him his high-topped black shoes and knelt and laced them. The old man stood again and went into the bathroom and swiped a wet comb across his white hair and rinsed his whiskered face and came out.

Mary Wells was honking at the curb. They went out and the old man climbed into the front seat and the boy got in back, and they drove out of the neighborhood over the tracks, going up Main Street. There were half a dozen cars parked at this noon hour at the curb along the three blocks of stores and a few more cars and pickups parked in front of the tavern at the corner of Third. The old man seemed lifted in spirit to be riding in the car on a bright day, heading up Main Street in the fall of the year with a young woman driving him. He seemed almost cheerful now that they were going.

Inside the clinic next door to the hospital they waited for an hour and Mary Wells decided to go home so she'd be in the house when the girls returned from school. She told DJ to call her if they needed a ride home. After she left, he and his grandfather sat without talking to any of the other patients who were waiting, and didn't talk to each other. They sat without reading or even shifting from their chairs. People came in and left. A little girl was whimpering across the room on her mother's lap. Another hour went by. Finally a nurse came out to the waiting room and called his grandfather's name. The boy stood up with him.

What are you doing? his grandfather said.

I'm going with you.

Well, come on then. But keep your mouth shut. I'll do the talking.

They walked back along the hall behind the nurse and were led into an examination room. They sat down. Across the room a diagram of the human heart was taped to the wall. All its valves and tubes and dark chambers were precisely labeled. Next to it hung a calendar with a picture of a mountain in winter, with snow on the trees and a cabin bearing up under the deep snow on its pitched roof. After a while another nurse came in and took the old man's pulse and his blood pressure and temperature and wrote the information in a chart, then left and closed the door. A few minutes later Dr. Martin opened the door and came in. He was an old man dressed in a blue suit and starched white shirt with a maroon bow tie and clear rimless spectacles, and he had blue eyes that were paler than his suit. He washed his hands at the little sink in the corner and sat down and looked at the chart the nurse had left. So what seems to be the trouble? he said. Who's this boy with you?

This here's my daughter's boy. He had to come along too.

How do you do, Dr. Martin said. I haven't seen you before, have I? He shook the boy's hand formally.

That boy's the cause of all this, the old man said.

How's that?

He decided I was sick. Then he goes over and gets the neighbor woman to drive me in here.

Well, let's see if he's right. Will you sit up here, please? The old man moved to the examining table and the doctor looked into his eyes and mouth, examined his hair-filled ears, and gently squeezed various spots along his stringy neck. Let me listen to your chest now, he said. Can you undo the tops of your pants there?

The old man unhooked the buttons on the shoulder straps of his overalls and let the bib fall. He sat forward.

Now your shirt, please.

He unbuttoned the blue workshirt and shucked it off, revealing the dirty long underwear top, with the white hairs of his chest showing at the open neck.

Could you pull up your top there? Yes. That'll do. That's far enough. Now I'll just listen for a moment. He pressed the cup end of the stethoscope against the old man's chest. Take a deep breath. That's right. And again. He moved to the back and listened there.

The old man sat and breathed with his eyes shut and puffed out his feverish cheeks. The boy stood beside him watching everything.

Well, Mr. Kephart, said Dr. Martin, it's a good thing your grandson brought you in here today.

Oh?

Yes, sir. You've got yourself a good case of pneumonia. I'll call the hospital and they'll admit you this afternoon.

The old man peered at him. What if I don't want to go to the hospital?

Well, you can die, I suppose. You don't have to do what's sensible. It's up to you.

How long would they have to keep me?

Not long. Three or four days. Maybe a week. It depends. You can go ahead and get dressed now. Dr. Martin stood back and gathered up the chart on the counter. He started to walk out, then stopped and looked at the boy. You did well to insist that your grandfather come in, he said. What was your name?

DJ Kephart.

And you're how old?

Eleven.

Yes. Well, you did fine. You did very well. You have reason to be satisfied that you made him come in to see me. I don't suppose that was very easy, was it.

It wasn't too hard, the boy said.

The old doctor went out of the room and shut the door.

The old man began to get dressed, but managed to put one of the buttons of his workshirt in the wrong hole so the front was looped forward. Here, he said. Fix this goddamn thing. I can't do nothing with it. The boy unbuttoned his grandfather's shirt and buttoned it again while the old man raised his chin and stared at the diagram of the heart that was taped to the wall.

You better not be getting a swelled head over what he told you, he said.

I'm not.

Well, see that you don't. You're a good boy. That's enough. Now help me get these overalls hooked up and we'll get out of here. We'll have to see what they're saying up front.

The boy fastened the shoulder straps of his grandfather's pants and the old man rose from the chair.

What'd I do with that handkerchief I was using?

It's in your back pocket.

Is it?

Yes. That's where you put it.

The old man took out the dirty handkerchief and cleared his throat and spat, then wiped the handkerchief across his mouth and put it back in his pocket, and then together he and the boy went out of the room down the hall to the front desk, to learn what next would be required of them.

17

IT WAS LATE AFTERNOON WHEN THE NURSE BROUGHT THE old man into the hospital room occupied by Raymond McPheron. She rolled his wheelchair in next to the vacant bed near the door and set the hand brakes and told the old man to get undressed and to put on the hospital gown that was laid out for him at the foot of the bed. It opens in the back, she said. Then I'll come back and get you settled in. She yanked the curtain partway closed around his bed and left. The boy had followed them into the room and stood now beside his grandfather, accompanying him as he had all the long afternoon.

Across the room Raymond lay in bed under the window, his leg in the cast and raised onto two pillows on top of the thin hospital blankets. Beside him sat Victoria Roubideaux with the little girl in her lap. They could see the old white-haired man and the boy beyond the end of the curtain, but they hadn't yet said anything to them. The old man had begun to complain in a high whining voice.

I can't change out of my clothes right here, he said. Do they expect me to take my pants off behind this goddamn curtain like I was in some kind of circus sideshow?

You have to, Grandpa. The nurse will be coming back any minute.

I ain't about to.

Raymond leaned up in his bed and spoke across the room: Mister, they put a bathroom in yonder through that door there. You can step in there if you'd care to. I don't guess they put it there just for me.

The old man pulled the curtain back. In there, you say?

That's right.

I guess I could do that. But look here, don't I know you? Aren't you one of the McPheron brothers?

What's left of them.

I read about you in the paper. I'm sorry to hear about your brother.

The woman that wrote that didn't even know the half of what she was saying, Raymond said.

My name's Kephart, the old man said. Walter Kephart. They tell me I got pneumonia.

Is that right.

That's what they're telling me.

You look like you got some good help there with you anyway.

Too good, the old man said. This boy here keeps telling me what to do all the time.

Well, it's nice having a young person around, Raymond said. I got awful fine help myself. This here is Victoria Roubideaux. And her little girl, Katie.

Hello, Mr. Kephart, Victoria said.

How do you do, young lady.

Grandpa, the boy said, you have to get changed.

You see there? the old man said. Right there's what I'm talking about.

You go ahead and use that bathroom, Raymond said.

The old man stood out of the wheelchair and shuffled slowly around the bed into the bathroom and shut the door. He was inside for ten minutes and beyond the door they could hear him coughing and spitting. When he came out he was wearing the striped hospital gown and carrying his clothes over one arm. The skirts of the cotton gown flapped about his old flanks. He had left the strings at the rear untied and all of his scrawny gray backside was exposed to view. He handed the clothes to the boy and sat down at the edge of the bed and settled the skirts of the hospital gown over his legs like an old lady. Go get that goddamn nurse that was in here, he said. Tell that woman I'm waiting on her.

The boy went out into the hall and they could hear the sound of his rapid steps going away on the tiled floor. The old man looked across at Raymond. It ain't even decent what they make you wear in this place.

No sir, Raymond said. I'll have to agree with you on that.

It's goddamn indecent is what it is.

The boy came back with the nurse. She was carrying a sterile tray that she set on the bedside table and then she looked at the old man. Are you ready, Mr. Kephart?

For what?

To get into bed.

I ain't planning on just setting here, he said.

No, I didn't think you'd want to do that.

She helped him swing his legs onto the bed and drew the sheet up and arranged the pillow under his head. Then she opened the sterile tray and wiped the back of his hand with a swab. This may sting, she said.

What's that you're doing?

I'm going to start the antibiotics now.

Is that what the doctor said?

Yes.

She poked the needle into the loose skin at the back of his hand and he lay in bed and looked up at the ceiling without moving. The boy watched from the foot of the bed, biting his lip when the needle went in. The nurse taped the needle to his hand, then hung the bags of fluid on a metal stand and connected the tubes and adjusted the steadily dripping fluid in the drip chamber and stood watching for a moment, and then inserted the thin oxygen prongs into the old man's nose. Now breathe in, she said. Take some deep breaths. I'll come back to check on you in a little while.

What good's this thing suppose to do me?

It'll help fill your lungs. Until you can breathe normally again on your own.

It don't feel right. His voice sounded high-pitched and unnatural, on account of the nose prongs. It tickles my nose.

Breathe, the nurse said. You'll get used to it. And when you need to spit, here's a box of Kleenex. Don't be spitting in that dirty handkerchief.

After she was gone the boy came forward and stood beside the bed. Did she hurt you, Grandpa? The old man looked at him and shook his head. He went on breathing and lifted his hand to adjust the oxygen tubes.

From across the room Victoria Roubideaux asked the boy if he didn't want to sit down. There's a chair over there, she said. You could bring it up next to the bed. But he told her he was all right, he said he wasn't tired. An hour and a half later when the orderly brought in the dinner trays, he was still standing beside the bed and the old man was asleep.

In the evening Guthrie and Maggie Jones came into the room together with Guthrie's two boys, Ike and Bobby. They all stood around the bed and talked quietly with Raymond. Victoria was still in her chair, with Katie sleeping in her lap. Guthrie explained what he and the boys had done out at the ranch that afternoon. The cattle in the pastures out south all seemed fine, and they had checked on the bulls and horses. The water levels were what they should be in the stock tanks.

I thank you, Raymond said. I don't like to have to bother you.

It's no bother.

Well I know it is. But I thank you anyway. He looked at Ike and Bobby. Now what about you two boys? How you doing these days?

Pretty good, Ike said.

I'm sorry you got your leg hurt, Bobby said.

I appreciate that, Raymond said. It's kind of a ugly thing, ain't it. But it was a bad thing that happened. You boys remember you got to be careful around animals. You won't never forget that, will you?

No, sir, Ike said.

I'm sorry about your brother, Bobby said softly.

Raymond looked at him and looked at Ike and nodded to them both, then he shook his head once very slowly, and didn't say anything. Ike gave Bobby a hard poke in the side when no one was looking, but in the awkward silence Bobby was feeling bad enough already and wished he had never said any word at all about the old man's brother.

Finally Maggie said: But how are you feeling this evening, Raymond? Are you feeling any better? You look a little more like yourself, I think.

I'm all right. He turned slightly under the bedsheet, adjusting his leg.

No he's not, Victoria said. He won't tell anybody the truth, not even the nurses. He's in a lot of pain. He just doesn't talk about it.

I'm all right, honey, he said. This ain't the worst of it.

I know it isn't. But you're in a lot of physical pain too. I know you are.

Maybe a little, he said.

Across the room DJ stood beside his grandfather's bed, listening to them all talking. He knew the Guthrie boys and didn't like them seeing him like this in the hospital room. His grandfather was dozing and he kept making noises in his throat and coughing and mumbling strangely. DJ had said nothing to Ike and Bobby when they came in but stood silently beside the bed, with his back turned to them, and his grandfather kept going in and out of his fitful sleep, with the nose prongs in his nose, the needle still taped to his hand, and then the old man would wake and look around in confusion until he remembered where he was, that he was still in the hospital, and the boy would lean over and ask quietly if he wanted something and the old man would shake his head and look away and drift off to sleep again, then DJ would stand and wait, listening to them talk across the room, waiting for them to leave.

AT EIGHT-THIRTY THE NURSE CAME IN TO ANNOUNCE THAT visiting hours were over. Guthrie and Maggie and the two boys told Raymond good night and went out. Victoria leaned over the bed, holding her thick black hair out of the way, and kissed Raymond on the cheek and gave him a hug, then he patted her hand and she carried the little girl out of the room.

DJ's grandfather was awake now. You better go too, he said to the boy. You'll do all right by yourself, won't you?

Yes sir.

You can come back tomorrow after school.

The boy looked at him and nodded and went out. Victoria was waiting in the hall, with Katie asleep in her arms. Is somebody expecting you at home? she said.

No.

Aren't you afraid to be by yourself?

No. I'm used to it.

Let me give you a ride anyhow. Will you do that?

I don't want to take you out of your way.

It'll only take five minutes. You don't want to walk home in the dark.

I've done it before.

But you don't want to do it tonight.

They went down the hall and out the front door onto the sidewalk. It was cold outside but there was no wind. The streetlights had come on and overhead the stars winked clean and hard. Victoria strapped the sleeping child into her car seat in the back and they drove off up Main Street. You'll have to tell me where to go, she said.

It's across the tracks. Then you turn left.

She looked across at him where he was sitting close to the door with his hand on the handle. I would've thought you knew the two Guthrie boys. They're your age, aren't they?

I know them a little. I know Bobby anyway. He's in the same class with me. Fifth grade.

Aren't you two friends? You didn't say anything to each other.

I just know him from school.

He seems like a nice boy. Maybe you could get to be friends.

We might. I don't know.

I hope so. You shouldn't be alone too much. I know what that's like, from when I was your age and later on in high school. This can be a hard place to be alone in. Well, I suppose any place is.

I guess, he said.

In the backseat Katie had begun to fuss, reaching her hands out, trying to touch her mother. Just a minute, sweetheart, Victoria said. She watched her daughter in the rearview mirror. It'll just be a few minutes. The little girl drew her hands back and began to whimper.

The boy turned to look at her. Does she cry all the time?

No, she almost never cries. She's not really crying now. She's just tired. There's nothing for her to do at the hospital. We've been there for three days.

Main Street was almost vacant as they drove along past the small individual houses and on north into the brief business district under the bright lights. Only two or three cars were out on the street. All the stores were closed and darkened for the night except the tavern. To the east when they crossed the railroad tracks the whitewashed concrete cylinders of the grain elevator rose up massively out of the ground, shadowy and silent. They drove on north.

Here, the boy said. This is where you turn.

They came into the quiet street and he pointed out the little house.

Is this where you live?

Yes, ma'am.

Really? I used to live near here. Before I had Katie. This was my old neighborhood. Do you like it here?

He looked at her. It's just where I live, he said. He opened the car door and started to get out.

Just a minute, she said. I don't know what you'd think of it, but maybe you could come out and stay with us tonight. So you wouldn't have to be here alone.

Out with you?

Yes. Out in the country. You'd like it out there.

He shrugged. I don't know.

All right, she said. She smiled at him. I'll just wait until you're inside and get the light on.

Thanks for the ride, he said.

He shut the car door and started up the narrow sidewalk. He looked very small and much alone, approaching the dark house with only the streetlamp shining from the corner illuminating the front of the house. He opened the door and went inside and then a light came on. She thought he would come to one of the windows and wave to her, but he didn't.

AT THE HOSPITAL THE NURSE ON NIGHTSHIFT CAME INTO the room and Raymond was still awake. She was a good-looking woman in her late forties, with short brown hair and very blue eyes. She bent over the old man in the bed next to the door, who was asleep on his side and still breathing the oxygen through the prongs in his nose, his face red and damp. She checked the level of the fluid in the plastic bags hanging from the stand, then came over to Raymond's bed and looked at him with his head raised up on the pillow, watching her. Can't you sleep? she said.

No.

Is your leg hurting you?

Not now. I reckon it'll start again directly.

How about your chest?

It's all right. He looked up at her. What's your name? he said. I thought I knew all these nurses in here by now.

I just came back on duty, she said. I'm Linda.

What's your last name?

May.

Linda May.

That's right. It's nice to meet you, Mr. McPheron. Is there anything I can get for you right now?

I could take some of that water there.

Let me get you a fresh pitcher. This isn't very cold. She left the room and came back with a pitcher filled with ice, and poured water in the glass and held it out to him. He drew on the straw and swallowed, then drew again and nodded and she set the glass on the bedside table.

He looked across the room. How do you think he's doing over there?

Mr. Kephart? All right, I think. He'll probably recover. Older people get pneumonia and don't do well sometimes, but he seems pretty strong. Of course I haven't seen him awake yet. But when we changed shifts they said he was doing okay.

She smoothed the blanket, making sure to keep it free of his casted leg. Try and get some sleep now, she said.

Oh, I don't sleep much, he said.

People are always coming in and waking you up for one thing or another, aren't they.

I don't like that light shining.

I'll shut the door so it's darker. Would that be better?

It might. He looked at her face. It don't matter. I'm getting out of here tomorrow anyhow.

Oh? I hadn't heard that.

Yeah. I am.

You'd have to ask the doctor.

They're burying my brother tomorrow. I won't be in here for that.

Oh, I'm sorry. Still, I think you'll need to talk to the doctor anyway.

He better get here early then, Raymond said. I'll be gone before noon.

She touched his shoulder and crossed to the door and closed the door behind her.

Raymond lay in the bed in the darkened room looking out the window at the bare trees in front of the hospital. Two hours later he was still awake when the wind started up, whining and crying in the higher branches. He thought about what the wind would be doing out south of town and he wondered if Victoria and the little girl had been wakened by it. He expected they hadn't. But out in the south pasture, the cattle would all be standing awake with their backs to the wind, and there would be dry little dust storms blowing up in the corrals, shifting across the dry clumps of manure and the loose dirt around the barn. And he knew if things were as they should be, he and his brother would step outside in the morning to begin work as usual and they would stop to smell the dirt in the air, and then one or the other of them would say something about it, and he himself might comment on the likelihood of rain, and then Harold would say that a blizzard would be more likely, this time of year, given the way things were going of late.

18

WHEN THE DOCTOR ENTERED THE ROOM IN THE MORNING
he was of a mind not to allow Raymond permission to leave the hospital, but when Raymond said he was going to leave regardless the
doctor relented and said he could go for half a day but would have to
return after the funeral. Just past noontime at the front desk Raymond signed the papers and they released him into the care of Victoria Roubideaux. She had put Katie with Maggie Jones, and earlier
that morning she'd brought him the clean clothes he'd asked for.
Now she pushed him in a wheelchair out to where her car was parked
at the curb in front of the hospital. One leg of his dark trousers was
slit to the knee to accommodate the cast, and he wore a blue shirt
with pearl snaps which she had pressed freshly that morning and he
had on his plaid wool jacket and the good Bailey hat that he wore
only to town. Balanced across his lap were the aluminum crutches
the hospital had loaned him.

When he came out of the hospital into the fresh autumn air he
looked at the sky and looked all around and breathed in.

Well, goddamn, he said. It feels about as good as church letting
out, to get shut of that damn place. Now you'll have to pardon my
language, honey. But by God, it does.

And it's a good thing to see you come out of there, she said. I
believe you look better already.

I feel better already. And I'll tell you another thing. I ain't going back in there. Not today, not ever.

I thought you agreed to go back this afternoon. That's why they let you out.

Oh hell, honey, I'd say anything to get them to release me from that place. Let's get going. Before they change their minds. Where's your car at?

Down the street here.

Let's go find it.

AT THE METHODIST CHURCH ON GUM STREET TOM Guthrie was standing at the curb in the bright sun waiting for Raymond and Victoria. They pulled up and Raymond opened the door and Guthrie helped him climb out. He stood up onto the sidewalk, but when Victoria opened the wheelchair behind him he refused to use it, telling them he would walk. And so with Victoria on one side and Guthrie on the other he fit the rubber cushions of the crutches under his arms and hobbled across the wide walkway into the church.

Inside, the organist hadn't started playing yet and there was no one in the sanctuary. They moved slowly down the carpeted center aisle between the rows of glossy wooden pews toward the altar and pulpit, Raymond stepping carefully with his head down watching his feet, and they reached the front and he shifted sideways into the second pew. Victoria went out to the nursery to see if she could find Maggie and Katie, and Guthrie sat down beside Raymond. Raymond appeared to be exhausted already. He removed his hat and set it next to him on the pew. His face was sweating, his face was even redder than usual, and for some time he only sat and breathed.

You all right? Guthrie said, looking at him.

Yeah. I will be.

You're not going to keel over, are you? Tell me if you feel like you're going to.

I ain't going to keel over.

He sat breathing with his head down. After a while he looked up and began to survey the objects in the high silent sanctuary—the outsized wooden cross attached to the wall behind the pulpit, the colored windows where the sun streamed in—and now he saw that his brother's casket was resting on a wheeled trestle at the head of the center aisle. The casket was closed. Raymond looked at it for some time. Then he said: Let me out of here.

Where you going? Guthrie said. If you need something, let me go get it for you.

I want to see what they done to him.

Guthrie stepped out of the way and Raymond grabbed the back of the pew ahead of him, pulling himself upright, and fit the crutches in place and hobbled out into the aisle up to the casket. He stood at the long smooth side of it. He set his hands on the dark satiny wood and then tried to raise the top half of the lid but couldn't manage to move it without dropping his crutches. He turned his head to one side. Tom, he said. Come help me with this damn thing, would you?

Guthrie came forward and raised the upper half of the polished lid and propped it back. There before Raymond was his brother's dead body, stretched out lying on his back, his eyes sunken in the waxy-looking face, his eyes closed forever under the thin-veined eyelids, his stiff iron-gray hair combed flat across his pale skull. At the funeral home they had called Victoria to ask her to bring them something appropriate for them to put on him, and she had located the old gray wool suit in the back of his closet, the only one he had ever owned, and when she had brought it to them they had had to cut the coat down the back seam to get him into it.

Raymond stood and looked at his brother's face. His thick eyebrows had been trimmed and they had dabbed powder and makeup on his cheeks over the scratches and bruises, and they had wound a tie around his neck under the shirt collar. He didn't know where they had gotten the tie, it wasn't anything he remembered. And they had folded his brother's hands across his suited chest, as if he would be preserved in this sanguine pose forever, but only the heavy callouses visible at the sides of his hands seemed real. It was only the callouses that appeared to be familiar and believable.

You can shut it again, he said to Guthrie. That ain't him in there. My brother wouldn't let himself look like that even for a minute if he was still alive. Not if he still had breath to prevent them from doing him like that. I know what my brother looks like.

He turned and hobbled back to the pew and sat down and laid his crutches out of the way. Then he shut his eyes and never looked at the dead face of his brother again.

PEOPLE BEGAN FILING INTO THE CHURCH. THE ORGANIST in the loft at the back of the sanctuary began to play, and Victoria and Maggie came in, with Katie in her mother's arms. Together they slid in beside Raymond. The mortician and an assistant in a matching black suit seated people in pews on both sides of the aisle, moving everybody up to the front, but there were not a great many mourners at the funeral, and only the first five rows were filled. Before the service began, the mortician came forward very somberly and opened the casket so that during the service people might view his handiwork, and then the minister came in from a side door and crossed to the pulpit and greeted them one and all in the name of Jesus in a voice that was laden with solemnity and import. Then there were prayers to be said and hymns to be sung. The organist played Blessed Assurance, Jesus Is Mine and Abide with Me: Fast Falls the Eventide, and people sang along, but not very loud. When the music was finished the preacher began to talk in earnest and he spoke about a man about whom he knew next to nothing at all, saying to those in attendance that he believed Harold McPheron must have been a good man, a Christian light among his fellows, else why would they be there marking his passing even if they were only a few in number, though they must all remember a man might be loved deeply even if he was never to be loved widely, and no one present should ever forget that. Sitting beside Raymond, Victoria cried a little despite the inadequacy and ignorance of what the man was saying, and Katie at one point grew so fussy that Raymond had to reach over and lift her onto his lap, patting her and whispering in her ear until she quieted down.

Then the service was over and Raymond and Victoria and Katie and Maggie and Guthrie went back up the aisle very slowly. Ray-

mond led them, his hat on his head again as before, limping and hob-
bling with his crutches. They went outside to the black cars waiting
in front at the curb in the sun. After some time, when the mourners
had filed past and looked at the body, the mortician and his assistant
rolled out the closed casket and slid it into the black hearse. Then
they all drove away in a slow procession with the headlights of all the
cars turned on in the broad daylight, heading out north and east to
the cemetery three miles outside of town. Beside the grave when
they were seated in the metal folding chairs under the awning, the
preacher said a few words more and read from scripture once again,
and he prayed for the safe translation of Harold's immortal soul into
everlasting heaven. Afterward he shook Raymond's hand. And by
that time the wind was blowing so hard that the caretakers had to
lean far over to do their work, and they lowered the dark casket into
the ground next to the plot in which the senior McPherons had been
buried more than half a century before.

Then they all drove back to town and Raymond climbed once
more into Victoria's car. Honey, you can take me home now, he said.

You're not going back to the hospital? You're sure?

I'm going back to the house. I won't be going nowheres else.

So she drove him through town and out south toward the ranch.
He dozed off before they had gotten far out of Holt and then he
woke when she stopped in front of the wire gate. She helped him into
the house, then went back and got Katie. I'll get supper pretty soon,
she said. You need to eat something.

I'm going to rest for a little bit, he said.

She took his arm and led him into the bedroom off the dining
room, where Maggie Jones had changed the sheets four days earlier,
and he lay down in what had been his parents' marriage bed so many
years before and until recently had been Victoria's bed. She propped
his leg on a pillow and spread a quilt over him. I'll have supper ready
when you wake up, she said. Try to get some rest.

Maybe I can sleep now, he said. Thank you, honey.

She went out to the kitchen and he lay in the old soft bed with his
eyes shut but soon he opened them again, sleep would not come to
him, and he turned to look out the window and then turned again to

look overhead, and he realized that this room he lay in was directly below his brother's empty bedroom, and he lay under the quilt staring at the ceiling, wondering how his brother might be faring in the faraway yet-to-be. There would have to be cattle present there somehow and some manner of work for his brother to do out in the bright unclouded air in the midst of these cattle. He knew his brother would never be satisfied otherwise, if there were not. He prayed there would be cattle, for his brother's sake.

19

IN THE WEEK AFTER HAROLD McPHERON'S FUNERAL, THE first-grade teacher in the elementary school on the west side of Holt noticed one morning, within the first hour of classes, that something was the matter with the little boy in the middle of the room. He was sitting peculiarly, almost on his backbone, holding himself slouched far back in his desk, and he was only playing with the worksheet she'd handed out. She watched him for some time. The other children were all working quietly, their heads bent over the sheets of paper like so many miniature accountants. After a while she rose from her desk and walked back between the rows and came to him and stood over him. He looked as undersized and ragged as ever, like some wayward orphan turned up by mere happenstance and misfortune in her class. His hair needed cutting, it stuck out behind against the collar of his shirt, which itself was not clean. Richie, she said, sit up. How can you work like that? You'll damage your back.

When she put a hand on his shoulder to urge him forward, he winced and jerked away. Why, what's wrong? she said. She knelt beside him. There were tears filling his eyes and he looked very frightened. What is it? she said. Come out in the hall a minute.

I don't want to.

She stood and took hold of his arm.

I don't want to.

But I'm asking you to.

She pulled him to his feet and led him toward the hallway door, but as they passed her desk he grabbed at it, dragging one of her books to the floor with a loud flat crash. The other students were all watching.

Class, she said. Keep working. All of you get back to work. She stood until their heads were bent again over their desks and then took him under the arms and pulled as he struggled against her and kicked and caught at the door. She got him into the hall and knelt in front of him, still holding him.

Richie, what's wrong with you? she said. Stop it now.

He shook his head. He was looking off along the hallway.

I want you to come with me down here.

No.

Yes, please.

She rose and took him by the hand in the direction of the office along the empty tiled hallway past the other classrooms, their doors all shut to the noises and murmurings rising from behind them. Are you sick? she said.

No.

But something's wrong. I'm worried about you.

I want to go back to the room, he said. He looked up at her. I'll do my work now.

I'm not concerned about that, she said. Let's just see the nurse. I think the nurse should look at you.

She took him into a small room next to the school office where a narrow cot was pushed close to the wall opposite a metal cabinet with locked doors. The nurse sat at a desk against the far wall.

I don't know what's wrong with him, the teacher said. He won't tell me. I thought you better have a look.

The nurse stood and came around and asked him to sit on the cot but he would not. The teacher left and went back to her classroom. The nurse bent over him and felt his forehead. You don't seem hot to the touch, she said. He looked at her out of his big wet eyes. Will you open your mouth for me, please? She put her arm around him and he squirmed away. Why, what is it? Are you afraid of me? I won't hurt you.

Don't, he said.

I need to look at you.

He leaned away but she pulled him close and examined his face and looked briefly in his ears and felt along his neck, and then she lifted his shirt to feel if he was hot and then she found the dark bruises on his back and below the belt of his pants.

She peered into his face. Richie, she said. Did somebody do this to you?

He looked frightened and he wouldn't answer. She turned him around and drew down his pants and underwear. His thin buttocks were crosshatched with dark red welts. In some of the places the welts had bled and clotted.

Oh, my God, she said. You stay right here.

She left and went next door and came back at once with the principal. She lifted the boy's shirt and showed the welts to the principal. They began to ask the boy questions but he was crying by now and shaking his head and he wouldn't say a word. Finally they called his sister out of her fifth-grade classroom and asked her what had happened to her brother. Joy Rae said: He fell off the slide at the park. He had a accident.

Would you go out? the nurse said to the principal.

All right, he said. But you let me know. We have to report this. We're going to find out what's going on here.

The principal went out and then the nurse said: Will you let me look at you too, Joy Rae?

I don't have anything wrong with me.

Then you'll just let me look, won't you?

You don't need to look at me.

Just for a moment. Please.

Suddenly the girl began to cry, covering her face with her hands. Don't, she said. I don't want you to. Nothing's wrong with me.

Honey, I won't hurt you. I promise. I need to look, that's all. I have to examine you. Won't you let me, please?

The nurse turned to her little brother. I want you to step into the hall for a minute, so we can be alone. She led him out and told him to wait there near the door.

Then she came back into the room and took the girl gently by the shoulders. This won't take long, honey, I promise, but I need to look at you. Slowly she turned her around. Joy Rae stood sobbing with her hands at her face, while behind her the nurse unbuttoned the back of her blue dress and drew down her underpants, and what she saw on Joy Rae's thin back and thin buttocks was even worse than what she'd seen on her brother.

Oh, honey, the nurse said. I could just about kill somebody for this. Just look at you.

An hour later when Rose Tyler from the Department of Social Services came into the nurse's room, the two children were still there, waiting for her. They had been given pop and cookies and two or three books to look at. And soon after Rose arrived a young sheriff's deputy from the Holt County Courthouse came in and began to set up a tape recorder. The two children watched him in terror. He talked to them but his efforts were of little use, and they watched him without blinking and when he wasn't looking they glanced at his thick leather belt and revolver and his nightstick. Rose Tyler was more successful in her attempts, the children knew her from before and she talked to them quietly and gently. She explained that they were not in any trouble but that she and the officer and the nurse and their teachers were all worried for their safety. Did they understand that they only needed to ask them some questions? Then she asked the deputy to go out of the room and she took photographs of their welts and bruises, and afterward when the deputy returned they began the interview, with Rose asking most of the questions. These were not meant to be leading questions, so as to avoid planting anything in the children's minds but to allow them to tell their story in their own words, but it didn't matter, the children were very reluctant to talk at all. They stood uncomfortably at the edge of the cot, standing side by side, and looked at the floor and played with their fingers, and it was Joy Rae who spoke for both of them, though she herself answered very few of the questions in the beginning. Instead she adopted a kind of bitter defiant silence. Gradually, though, she began to talk a little. And then it came out.

But why? Rose said. What would make him want to do this to you?

The girl shrugged. We didn't pick up the house.

You mean he expected you to clean the house.

Yes.

Yourselves? The two of you?

Yes.

And did you? The entire trailer house?

We tried to.

And was that all, honey? Was there anything else he was upset about?

The girl looked up at Rose, then looked down again. He said I talked back.

That's what he said?

Yes.

Do you think you talked back to him?

It don't make no difference. He says I did.

Rose wrote in her notebook, then finished and looked at the two children and looked at the sheriff's deputy and suddenly felt she might cry and not stop. She had seen so much trouble in Holt County, all of it accumulating and lodging in her heart. This today made her sick. She had never been able to numb herself to any of it. She had wanted to, but she had not succeeded. She looked at the two Wallace children and watched them for a moment and began again to question the girl. Honey, she said, where were your mother and father at this time, while this was happening?

They were there, the girl said.

They were in the room?

No. We was in the bathroom.

Were they in the room when he began talking to you?

Yes.

But they weren't in the bathroom when he whipped you?

No.

Where were they then?

In the front room.

What were they doing?

I don't know. Mama was crying. She wanted him to stop.

But he wouldn't stop? He wouldn't listen to her?

No.

Where was your father? Did he try to do anything?

He was hollering.

Hollering?

Yes. In the other room.

I see. And you and your brother were with him in the bathroom at the same time?

No.

He took you in there separately?

Joy Rae looked at her brother. He took him first, she said. Then me.

Rose stared at the girl and her little brother, then shook her head and turned away and looked out into the hallway, imagining how that must have felt, being taken toward the back of the house and hearing the other one screaming behind the closed bathroom door, being afraid of what was to come, and the man's face all the time getting redder and redder. She wrote in her notebook again. Then she looked up. Do you have anything else you might want to say to us?

No.

Nothing at all?

No.

All right then. I thank you for saying that much, honey. You're a brave girl.

Rose closed her notebook and stood up.

But you won't tell him, will you? Joy Rae said.

You mean your mother's uncle?

Yes.

The sheriff's office will certainly want to talk to him. He's in serious trouble. I can promise you that.

But you won't tell him what we said?

Try not to worry. You'll be safe now. From now on, you'll be protected.

ROSE TYLER AND THE YOUNG DEPUTY DROVE IN SEPARATE cars to the east side of Holt to the Wallaces' trailer on Detroit Street. The weeds surrounding the trailer were all dry now and dusty, dead for winter, and everything looked dirty and ragged. Still, the sun was shining. They went up to the door together and knocked and waited. After a while Luther opened it and stood in the doorway shielding his eyes. He was wearing sweatpants and a tee-shirt, but no shoes. Can we come in? Rose said. Luther looked at her. We need to talk privately.

Well. Yeah. Come on in, he said. We're in a terrible fix here. Dear, he called back into the house. We got company.

Rose and the deputy followed him inside. There was the sweetish-stale smell of sweat and cigarette smoke and of something spoiling.

Betty lay stretched out on the couch, sunken into the cushions and covered by an old green blanket that she kept wrapped about herself. I ain't feeling very good, she said.

Is your stomach still hurting? Rose said.

It hurts me all the time. I can't never get rested.

We'll have to make you another appointment with the doctor. But I wonder, is your uncle here?

No. He ain't here right now.

He's over to the tavern, Luther said. He goes over there most days. Don't he, honey.

He's over there every day.

We need to talk to him, Rose said. When will he be back, do you think?

You can't tell. Sometimes he don't come back till nighttime.

I think I'll just go find him, the deputy said. We'll talk later, he said to Rose, then let himself out.

After he was gone Rose sat down on the couch beside Betty and patted her arm and took out her notebook. Luther went into the kitchen for a glass of water and came back and lowered himself into his cushioned chair.

Do you know why the officer and I came here today? Rose said. Do you know why I need to talk to you?

My kids, Betty said. Isn't it.

That's right. You know what happened, don't you.

I know, Betty said. Her face fell and she looked very sad. But we never meant him to do nothing like that, Rose. We never wanted that, ever.

He wouldn't even listen to us, Luther said.

But you can't let him mistreat your children, Rose said. You must have seen what he'd done to them. It was very bad. Didn't you see it?

I seen it afterwards. I tried to put some hand ointment on them. I thought maybe that might help.

But you know he can't stay here if he does anything like that. Don't you see? You have to make him leave.

Rose, he's my uncle. He's my mother's baby brother.

I understand that. But he still can't stay here. It doesn't matter who he is. You know better.

I was trying to make him stop, Luther said. But he says he's going to break my back for me. He's going to take that kitchen table and throw it on me just as soons I turn my head.

Oh, I don't think he's going to do that. How could he?

That's what he says. And you know what I says?

What?

I says I can find me a knife too.

Now you better be careful about that. That would only make matters worse.

What else you want me to do?

Not that. You let us take care of this.

But Rose, Betty said, I love my kids.

I know you do, Rose said. She turned toward Betty and took her hand. I believe that, Rose said. But you've got to do better. If you don't, they'll have to be taken away.

Oh no, Betty cried. Oh God. Oh God. The blanket fell away from her shoulders and she jerked her hand free and began to snatch at her hair. They already taken my Donna away, she cried, and then she started to wail. They can't take no more.

Betty, Rose said. She pulled at her arms. Betty, stop that and listen to me. Calm down now. We are not taking your kids away. It shouldn't ever come to anything like that. I'm just trying to get you to see how serious this is. You have to do things differently. You have to change what you've been doing.

Betty wiped at her face. Her eyes were wet and miserable. Whatever you say, Rose, I'll do it. Just don't take my kids away from me. Please, don't do that.

What about you, Luther? Are you willing to make some changes too?

Oh yes, ma'am, he said. I'm going to change right now.

Yes. Well, we'll see about that. In any case you can start taking some parenting classes at night at Social Services. I'll arrange for it. And I'll come by here at least once a month to see how you're doing. I won't tell you when I'm coming, I'll just show up. This will be in addition to your coming to my office to collect your food stamps. But the first thing, the most important thing, is that you have to agree not to let him stay here anymore. You understand what I'm saying, don't you?

Yes ma'am.

Do you promise?

Yes, Betty said. I promise.

I just hope he don't break my back, Luther said. Quick's he hears what we been talking about here today.

WHEN THE SHERIFF'S DEPUTY WALKED INTO THE LONG dim stale room at the Holt Tavern on the corner of Main Street and Third, Hoyt Raines was at the back shooting pool for quarters with an old man, and he had already begun drinking for the day. A glass of draft beer stood on the little table near the pool table, with an empty shot glass beside it and a cigarette smoking in a tin ashtray. Hoyt was bent over the table when the deputy walked in.

Raines?

Yeah.

I need to talk to you.

Go ahead and talk. I can't stop you.

Let's go outside.

What for? What's this about?

Come out with me, the deputy said. I'll tell you at the station.

Hoyt looked at him. He bent over the cue stick, lined up his shot, and knocked the seven in and said to nobody: Hoo boy. Hot dog. He stood and rounded the table and took a sip of his beer and drew on his cigarette.

Let's go, Raines, said the deputy.

You ain't told me what for yet.

I said I'd tell you when we get there.

Tell me now.

You don't want other people to know about what I got to tell you.

What the fuck's that suppose to mean?

You'll know when we get there. Now let's go.

The old man leaned back against the wall, looking from the deputy to Hoyt, and the bartender stood watching from behind the bar.

Well, if this ain't the goddamn shits, Hoyt said. I'm shooting pool here. He drank from his glass. He looked at the old man. You owe me for this game, and the one before.

It ain't over yet, the old man said.

Yeah it is. It's close enough.

I was coming back on you.

You was coming back, my ass.

And this one would of put us even.

Listen, you old son of a bitch. There's no way you was going to win this game and you still owe me for the last one.

Let's go, the deputy said. Now.

I'm coming. But he still owes me. You all seen it. He owes me. I'll see you boys this afternoon.

He downed the rest of the beer and set the glass on the table and sucked on the cigarette once more before stubbing it out. Then he walked out ahead of the deputy. On the sidewalk he said: You got your vehicle?

Waiting on you, around the corner.

They went around to Third Street and got in and the deputy drove two blocks to the reserved parking lot on the east side of the county courthouse. He led Hoyt down the concrete steps to the sheriff's office in the basement, where they took him behind the front counter to a desk and charged him with misdemeanor child abuse and read him his rights. Then they booked and printed him, and afterward they led him back through a little corridor to a small windowless room. After they sat him down at a table, the deputy who'd picked him up switched on the tape recorder while another sheriff's deputy leaned back against the door, watching.

He claimed he was teaching them discipline. He did not try to deny it. He thought well of himself for it. He told them it was the right thing. He said he was putting order into their lives. Now when do I get out of here? he said.

There'll be a bail hearing scheduled within seventy-two hours, the deputy said. What did you whip them with?

What?

You whipped them with something. What was it?

Let me ask you something. You ever seen those kids? Walking around town? They need discipline, wouldn't you say? And you think their folks are ever going to do it? I don't think so. They don't know how. Wouldn't even know where to start. So I was doing them a favor. All of them. They're going to thank me someday. You have to have discipline and order in this life, isn't that right?

That's what you think? You believe that?

Goddamn right I do.

And you think an eleven-year-old girl and a six-year-old boy need to be physically abused to learn discipline?

It didn't hurt them. They'll get over it.

They're in pretty bad shape right now. They look real bad. We have pictures to prove it. How long have you been doing this?

What are you talking about? That was it. One time. It's not like I enjoyed it. Is that what you think?

You're sure about that.

Yeah. I'm sure. What have they been saying about me?

Who?

Those kids. You've been talking to them, haven't you?

What did you hit them with?

You're still on that.

That's right. We're still on it. Tell us what you used.

What difference does it make?

We're going to know.

All right. I used my belt.

Your belt.

That's right.

The one you're wearing right now?

I never used the buckle end. Nobody can say I used the buckle. Is that what they're saying?

Nobody's saying anything. We're asking you. We're not talking to anybody else right now. We're talking to you. You used something else too, didn't you.

I might of used my hands a couple of times.

You hit them with your hands.

I might of.

You used your fists, you mean. Is that what you're saying?

Hoyt looked at him, then at the other deputy. What if I smoke in here? he said.

You want to smoke?

Yeah.

Go ahead. Smoke.

I don't have my cigarettes. They're out there in the front. Let me borrow one off of you.

I don't think so.

Then let me buy one off you.

You got any money?

You mean on me? What the hell are you talking about? You emptied my pockets when you brought me in here. You know that.

Then I guess you can't buy any cigarette, can you.

Hoyt shook his head. Jesus Christ. What a asshole.

How's that? the deputy said, moving toward the table. Did you say something?

Hoyt looked away. I was talking to myself.

That's a bad habit to get into. You can get into a world of trouble doing that.

. . .

WHEN THE SHERIFF'S DEPUTIES AT THE HOLT COUNTY Jail finished questioning him that day, they led him back through the little corridor to the double row of cells. There were six in all, three on each side, and they were rank with the smell of urine and vomit. Hoyt stepped into the cell they'd indicated and sat down on the cot, and after a while he lay back and went to sleep.

The next day, upstairs in the courtroom, the judge set his bail at five hundred dollars. Hoyt had a little less than five dollars, no more than that. So they walked him back down to his cell in the basement and handed him orange coveralls that had HOLT COUNTY JAIL stenciled on the back in black letters.

It turned out the next docket day in this outlying district was a month away, since there had been one three days before, so Hoyt had to stay in jail waiting until then for his court date. When he heard about this state of affairs he cursed them all and demanded to see the judge.

One of the sheriff's deputies who was nearby said: Raines, you better shut your goddamn mouth. Or somebody is going to come in there and shut it for you.

Let him try, Hoyt said. We'll see how far he gets.

Keep it up, you smart son of a bitch, the deputy said. Somebody's going to do more than just try.

Part Three

20

So he was alone now, more alone than he had ever been in his life.

Living with his brother seventeen miles out south of Holt he had been alone since that day when they were teenage boys and they'd learned that their parents had been killed in the Chevrolet truck out on the oiled road east of Phillips. But they had been alone together, and they had done all the work there was to do and eaten and talked and thought out things together, and at night they had gone up to bed at the same hour and in the mornings had risen at the same time and gone out once more to the day's work, each one ever in the presence of the other, almost as if they were a long-suited married couple, or as though they were a pair of twins that could never be separated because who knew what might happen if they were.

Then when they had become old men, after a series of peculiar circumstances had transpired, the pregnant teenaged girl Victoria Roubideaux had come out to the house to live with them, and her coming had changed matters for them forever. And then in the spring of the following year she had delivered the little girl and her arrival had changed matters once again. So they had grown used to the presence of these new people in their lives. They had become accustomed to the way things had changed and they had got so they liked these new changes and got so they wanted them to continue day after day in the same way. Because it began to feel as if each succeeding day was good to them, as though all of this new order of things was what was pointed to all along, even if they could never have known or predicted it in any way or manner beforehand. Then the girl had finished high school and had gone off to Fort Collins to attend college, and they had missed her, missed her and her little daughter both terribly, because after they were gone it was as if they were suffering the sudden absence of something as elemental and essential as the air itself. But they could still talk to the girl on the telephone and look forward to her return at holidays and again at the start of summer, and in any case they still had each other.

Now his brother was buried in the Holt County cemetery northeast of town next to the plot where their parents lay.

IN THE DAYS AND WEEKS AFTER THE FUNERAL IT WAS nearly impossible to convince Victoria that she should return to college. She was not going to leave him, not the way he was. She said he needed her help now. This was the occasion for her to help him as he and his brother had helped her during that time two years ago when she was so alone and lost.

So she had stayed with him through the rest of October and through most of November. Then there came an evening, the Sunday after Thanksgiving, when they were sitting over the supper dishes at the square pinewood table in the kitchen, and Raymond said:

But you've got to have your own life, Victoria. You have to go on with it.

I have my own life, she said. I have it here. Because of you and Harold. Where do you think I would be without the two of you? I might still be in Denver or on the street. Or with Dwayne in his apartment, which would be even worse.

Well, I'm still awful glad you come back. I won't ever forget that. But you have to go on now and do what you said you wanted to.

That was before Harold was killed.

I know, but Harold would want you to go on. You know he would.

But I'm worried about you.

I'm all right. I'm still a pretty tough old bird.

No you're not. You just had your cast taken off. You're still limping.

Maybe a little. But that don't matter.

And Mr. Guthrie has stopped coming out to help you like he was before.

I told him not to. I can manage by myself now. He'll come out again when I need him. Raymond looked at the girl across the table and reached over and patted her hand. You just got to go on, honey. It's all right now.

Well, it just makes me feel like you're trying to get rid of me.

No. Now, don't you ever think that. You'll come back in the summertime and all the holidays between now and then. I expect you to. I'll be upset if you don't. You and me, we're bound together the rest of our lives. Don't you believe that?

She stared at him for a long moment. Then she drew her hand out from under his and stood up and began to clear the table.

Raymond watched her. You must be mad at me now, Victoria, he said. I just guess you are. Is that it?

You better not try to talk me out of coming home.

Why Jesus God, honey. I wouldn't be trying to talk you out of anything if there was some other way. Don't you see? I'm going to be about as lonesome as a old yellow dog around here, without you and Katie.

She took up the plates and the serving dishes and glasses and silverware and carried them to the sink and slammed them into the washbasin. One of the glasses broke. It cut her finger and she stood over the sink with tears brimming in her dark eyes. Her heavy black hair fell about her face and she looked slim and beautiful and very young. Raymond rose from his chair and stood beside her, his arm around her shoulders.

And I'm not crying about this broken glass either, she said. Don't you think that I am.

Oh, I guess I know that, honey, he said. But come on, let's get these dishes cleaned up here before we make any more mess out of things.

I don't like it, she said. I don't care what you say.

I know, he said. Where's that dishrag? I'm going to wash.

No. You go on and get out of here. At least I'm going to do this much. Go back to the parlor and read your paper. At least you can't stop me from doing the dishes.

But you know it's the right thing, don't you.

She looked up at him. Raymond was studying her face, his faded blue eyes regarding her with considerable kindness and affection. I suppose I don't have to like it, she said.

I don't like it myself, he said. We just both know it's got to be this way. It don't seem to matter at all what we like. It's how things are.

She began to wash the dishes and he went back to the parlor and sat down to read in one of the two recliner chairs, and the next day they packed her car and she returned to Fort Collins with her daughter. She moved into the apartment again and in the afternoon she went out to find her professors to see about her classes. She was farther behind in classwork than she had thought she would be. She decided to drop two of her courses and to attempt to catch up in the other three.

And now in Holt County Raymond was completely alone in the old gray house in the country. There was no one left for him to talk to. He missed the girl as soon as she was gone. He missed his brother. It was as if he didn't know where to look or what to think about. Every day he wore himself out working and he came in at night exhausted, too tired to cook anything, so he warmed up food out of cans. And all the while the wind blew outside and birdsong drifted up from the trees, and from time to time the calling of cattle and the sudden nicker of horses rose up from out in the pastures and the barnlots, and these noises carried up to the house in the evening. But that was all there was for him to hear or pay any attention to. He did not care for the radio. He only watched television for the ten o'clock news and the nightly prediction of tomorrow's weather.

21

SHE WANTED HIM TO COME INSIDE WITH HER AFTER school let out for the day, after they had walked home together through the park through the drifts of dead elm leaves and across the railroad tracks trailing off in the distance east and west in long silver ribbons, and when they got up to the house he said he would, and once they got inside, her mother was not herself. Mary Wells had gotten a good deal worse lately.

This afternoon when Dena went in to find her, she was sitting in her bedroom on the unmade bed, smoking cigarettes and drinking gin from a coffee cup, staring blankly out the window at the winter lawn and the dark leafless trees along the back alley. I'm home, Mom, Dena said.

Her mother looked up, her face lifted slowly as if she were waking from some dream. Are you? she said.

Yes. DJ's with me.

You better get yourselves something to eat.

What is there?

I think we have some crackers. Where's Emma?

She's here too.

Do something with her, please. It won't hurt you.

Mom, DJ's here.

I know. You said that. Go on now.

Mom, do you have to smoke?

Yes, I do. And shut the door on your way out. Don't forget about your sister.

She just gets in the way.

You heard me.

She went out and the three of them made peanut-butter crackers in the kitchen standing at the counter, and she found a single clean glass in the cupboard and they each drank milk from it, taking turns, and when they were finished she said: Let's go outside.

It's cold outside, DJ said.

It's not that cold.

What about me? said Emma.

You can stay in here and watch TV.

I don't want to watch TV.

You can't come with us. Come on, she said. Let's go if we're going.

IT WAS COLD AND ALREADY TURNING DARK IN THE SHED at the back of the alley. They lifted the latch and went inside and lit the candles. The candles cast a soft yellow light over the shelf at back and on the flowered carpet and it reached faintly into the chill dark corners. They sat down at the table opposite each other and draped old blankets over their coats.

I went last, she said.

I don't think so.

Yes, I did.

I thought I went last.

No, it was me.

He took up the dice and tossed them out on the board, then counted the moves and advanced his man seven places.

There, she said. You owe me five hundred dollars.

Let me see it.

She showed him the card with the details printed on the back, showing the figures in dollars if someone landed on the property.

All right, he said. He removed the rubber band from his bundle of pink and green and yellow money and counted the bills out on the table and handed them to her. When did she start smoking? he said. I didn't know she smoked.

Who?

Your mom.

She just started. She stinks up the house with them.

You ought to get some of her cigarettes sometime.

What for?

So we could smoke out here.

I don't want to. She looked across at him and then down at the board and gathered up the dice and rolled and went forward nine squares.

Count again, he said.

It's right.

You just missed me.

I know. I'm going to buy it. How much is it?

He looked among the cards and found the right one. Four hundred dollars, he said.

She counted out the money and he put it in the bank. Go ahead, she said.

He rolled. He moved his man around the corner and took out two hundred dollars from the bank.

You want to buy it?

I don't have enough money.

You want to borrow some from the bank? You could mortgage.

I don't like to mortgage.

What are you going to do then? Make up your mind.

I'm thinking about it. He looked across at her. Isn't your dad ever coming back?

I don't know. Maybe. But I might go up there.

Alaska?

Why not?

I'd like to go to Alaska, he said.

It's cold, she said. But it's different up there.

What do you mean?

It is. It's not like down here. My dad says you have to know what you're doing up there. You'll freeze if you don't. And they have Kodiak bears up there.

Are you going to roll or not?

She rolled and counted out her moves.

You landed on me this time.

I know that. How much?

Two hundred dollars.

Is that all? That's easy. She tossed the bills across to him. They floated out onto the board like yellow leaves and he took them up.

It gets dark all winter up there, he said. It hardly ever gets light up there in the wintertime.

Not all winter, it doesn't.

Most of it, he said. For about four months.

I don't care, she said. I might go anyway. It's your turn.

IN THE AFTERNOONS THEY WENT TO THE SHED AFTER school and sat and talked and played board games and contests of cards, and they lit the candles and wrapped up in blankets. And late one afternoon at the end of November they came back into the house in the cold early dark, and her mother was sitting with a man in the kitchen. They were drinking beer from green bottles and smoking cigarettes out of the same pack. Mary Wells had put on lipstick for the first time in weeks and half of the cigarettes in the ashtray were stained from her red mouth. She heard them come in at the front door. Come out here, Dena, she called. I want you to meet someone.

They came into the room and Mary Wells said: This is Bob Jeter. This is a friend of mine I want you to meet.

Bob Jeter had a thin face and a dark mustache and dark goatee. His blond hair was much lighter than his beard and she could see his pink scalp shining through his hair under the kitchen light.

Your mother didn't tell me you were such a beautiful young lady, he said.

She looked at him.

Aren't you going to say hello? her mother said.

Hello.

And who's this? Bob Jeter said.

This is our neighbor, DJ Kephart.

DJ. Well DJ, how are things at the radio station?

The boy glanced at him and looked away. I don't know what you're talking about.

Okay, Mary Wells said. That'll do. You two can go out now.

When they were out in the living room DJ whispered: Who's that?

I don't know, she said. I never saw him before. I don't know who he is.

IN THE EVENING AFTER SUPPER, AFTER BOB JETER HAD left the house, Dena said to her mother: What's that man doing here?

Her mother looked tired now. The bright glassy-eyed look she'd had before was gone. He's a friend of mine, she said.

What's he want here?

He's a friend, like I said. He's a vice president at the bank. He makes loans to people. I was talking to him the other day about our circumstances since your father isn't coming back.

He might come back.

I doubt it. I don't know anybody who even wants him to.

I want him to come back.

Do you?

Yes.

Maybe he will then. But tell me what you thought of Mr. Jeter.

I don't see why he had to stay for supper. Doesn't he have his own house?

Yes. He has his own house. Of course he has his own house. He has a very nice house.

LATER THAT NIGHT WHEN SHE WANTED TO CALL HER father, before she got on the phone, her mother said: If you get ahold of him, you tell him I had a friend here today. Tell your father that.

I'm not going to say that.

You are, or else you won't talk to him at all.

Mom, I don't want to.

Tell him I had somebody visiting here this afternoon. He's not the only one who knows people. That's something he ought to know, up there in hotshot Alaska.

22

THE PUBLIC DEFENDER ASSIGNED TO HIM WAS A YOUNG woman with red hair. She was three years out of law school and she'd been in possession of his police record for no more than an hour when she came to the Holt County Courthouse on the morning of the docket day to consult with him. She was carrying a stack of files under her arm, and they met in a little bare conference room down the hall from the courtroom, with a sheriff's deputy waiting outside the door guarding another inmate. Hoyt was wearing his orange jailhouse coveralls and he looked pale and seedy after a month of confinement. She set her files on the table and sat down across the table from him.

Hoyt watched her flip through his police record. You're about like the rest of them, ain't you, he said. You want to know what I want, bitch? My number one priority is to get the fuck out of this goddamn place.

She looked at him closely for the first time. You can't talk like that in here, she said. Not to me you can't.

What's wrong with the way I talk?

You know exactly what's wrong with it.

Hell, he said. I was just getting a little excited there. I'm out of the custom of having any company. He grinned at her. I'll try to contain myself.

She stared at him. Do that, she said. She closed his file. So, I don't expect you want to go to trial. Do you.

I don't know. You tell me.

I don't think you do.

Why's that now? I got things I might want to say. I have a right to be heard.

You're certain of that?

Why wouldn't I be?

Because your case probably wouldn't go to trial for two months. Maybe longer. Depending on when it could be heard. Which means in the interim you'd go back to jail. You don't have bail money, do you?

No, I don't have no bail money. Where would I get money? They've had me locked up for twenty-nine days.

Then you don't want to go to trial.

I said I didn't.

When did you say that?

I'm saying it now, Hoyt said. How old are you anyway?

What?

How old a woman are you? You're pretty good-looking for a lawyer.

She stared across the table at him. She took up a pen and began tapping it on the table. Listen. Mr. Raines.

Yes ma'am, he said. You got my entire attention. He grinned at her and leaned forward.

You know what, she said, I don't think I do. Because you need to stop playing these stupid games. I don't need this from you. I've got seven other cases to deal with this morning besides yours. You keep this up and we don't get this resolved today, I'll see you next month and you can go back downstairs and sit in jail till then. Now do you think you heard that?

Hell. He sat up straight and pulled down the cuffs of his coveralls onto his thin wrists. Take it easy, will you? You're all strung up here. I never meant nothing. You're just a good-looking woman, that's all I'm saying. I haven't even seen a woman for a month.

That's only one of your problems, isn't it.

Yeah, he said. But not for long. Soon as I get out of here I'll take care of it.

She studied the expression on his face. She thought of saying something to him but then just shook her head. All right, she said. I've already spoken to the district attorney and I've negotiated the option of two plea agreements on your behalf.

What am I pleaing to?

What do you plead?

Yeah. What do I plead.

You plead guilty to a charge of misdemeanor child abuse. As stated in the police report. With the stipulation that there would be no additional jail time. You agree to have no more contact with the two children and to stay away from their parents' house. Do you accept all of these conditions?

You think I want to go back to that place after all the trouble they got me into?

That's not what I asked you.

All right, yes, I accept them. Yes, I'm not going back there again and I won't contact those kids no more. Does that suit you? What else have you got to say?

Before you're released the judge will set a period of probation.

How long is that going to be?

A year, maybe two. That's one possibility. The positive for you in this option is that you'll be getting out of jail today. The negative is that if you violate your probation you'll potentially receive a flat jail sentence because of it. Do you understand what I've said so far?

Yeah. What else?

Then there's the other possibility. The charge could be reduced to attempt to commit child abuse. If you accept this option you leave the sentencing to the judge. The positive here for you is that if you violate your probation you'd probably have less jail time in the future. The negative is that you might not get out of jail today. Depending on what sentence the judge hands down.

She stopped and looked at him.

What? he said.

You understand what I've just told you.

It's not that difficult. I got it.

Which option do you want me to negotiate?

I already said what I want. I want out of jail today.

Then you enter a plea of guilty. And you sign this form I'll give you.

I have to sign something?

You need to commit yourself before we go into court.

She removed two sheets of paper from his file and turned the top sheet so they could both see it, then leaned over and began to read each section aloud, looking up at him frequently as she went through them. The Advisement Per Colorado Rule of Criminal Procedure, Rules Five and Eleven, Plea of Guilty stated his rights and the terms he would agree to in waiving his right to a trial, made sure that he understood the elements of the offense, that he was entering a guilty plea voluntarily, and that he wasn't under the influence of drugs or alcohol.

Those are the terms, she said. If you understand the terms and agree to them, you sign it.

What's that other paper you've got there?

Standard Conditions.

What's that?

It's a list of conditions you'll be expected to adhere to while you're on probation.

Like what?

She read through these aloud too. Sixteen conditions saying he would not violate any law or harass any prosecution witness, that he'd maintain a permanent residence, that he wouldn't leave the state of Colorado without permission, that he'd get a job or at least try to get one, that he wouldn't use alcohol to excess or other dangerous drug.

I don't have to sign that?

No, there's nothing here to sign. This is simply for your information, so you can make an informed decision. You only have to know about it and understand it.

Okay.

Then you're ready to sign this form of Advisement?

If it gets me out of here, I'll sign anything.

No. Now wait a minute, she said. You're not signing just anything. You have to understand exactly what you're signing.

I understand that. Give me your pen.

You're sure.

You want me to sign this thing, don't you.

That's entirely up to you.

You going to let me use that pen or not? I don't have one of my own. They're afraid I'm going to stab somebody.

She handed him the pen and he looked at her and then ducked his head over the paper and printed and signed his name on the two lines and wrote the date beside them. There you go, he said. He pushed the paper across the table.

She took up both sheets of paper and put them in his folder.

What am I suppose to do now?

You wait with the sheriff's deputy in the courtroom until you're called.

She rose from the table and took her stack of case files under her arm and went out the door. He watched her leave, looking at her skirt and legs. The deputy waiting outside in the hallway came in, accompanied by the second inmate, and put the cuffs on Hoyt's wrists again and walked the two of them down the wide corridor to the courtroom to wait for their cases to come up. The second inmate wore shackles on his ankles in addition to his handcuffs, and shuffled along slowly.

There were several people in the courtroom already, sitting and talking. The deputy led Hoyt and the other inmate to a bench near the back, and they sat and watched as more people entered and filed into the rows of benches.

After a while Hoyt leaned toward the sheriff's deputy. I got to take a piss, he said.

How come you never thought of that earlier?

I never had any reason to think of it earlier.

Get up then, the deputy said. Let's go. You too, he said to the other inmate. Before they get this thing started.

How come I got to go?

Because I said so. I ain't about to leave you here.

They went out into the corridor past the lawyers talking to clients and past other people standing in groups below the tall narrow windows. They went down the wooden stairway to the main floor, the other inmate turning sideways taking one step at a time, then the deputy led them into the public rest room behind the staircase. Try not to piss yourself, he said to Hoyt.

Ain't you going to unzip me? Hoyt said. I know you been wanting to.

I wouldn't touch you with a goddamn cow prod, you sorry son of a bitch.

You're missing your chance here.

I'm going to tell you something, Raines. Not everybody in Holt County thinks you're real cute.

There's some that do. Some of these women I could name.

Nobody I know of.

You don't know the right ones.

That must be it. Now hurry the fuck up there.

The other man used the urinal too and they went back upstairs to the courtroom and sat down and waited. The D.A. came in and the young red-haired public defender took her place opposite him at the table in front of the benches where some of the other lawyers were already seated. The bailiff came in and checked the thermostat, tapping the little cage with his finger and peering at it before he sat down. Finally the clerk entered from a side door and called: All rise, and the judge came in, a short heavy dark-haired man in a black robe, and everybody stood until he was seated behind his high desk, then the clerk said: Be seated, and the judge called the first case.

Hoyt's case came about an hour later. He sat beside the sheriff's deputy, barely able to stay awake, while various Holt County defendants rose as their names were called and stood at the lectern between the lawyers' tables and listened to the judge. A boy came forward and the judge motioned for him to take his cap off. The boy removed his cap. The judge asked him if he had acquired auto insurance since the last time he'd appeared in court. The boy said he had and held up a paper. All right, you can go, the judge said. A woman in jeans and a pink shirt was next and her lawyer rose beside her and told the court that one of the causes of her current stress was in custody in Greeley now and that she herself was ready to go to jail today at five o'clock. The judge sentenced the woman to seven days in the county jail and ordered that she abstain from alcohol for two years and informed her that she was to serve one year of supervised probation and do forty-eight hours of public service. When he finished speaking the woman turned and went out into the hall with two girlfriends. Her face had turned red and she had already begun to cry. Her friends put their arms around her waist and whispered softly to her whatever encouragement they could think of.

Then the sheriff's deputy led the inmate next to Hoyt up to the lawyers' lectern. The man's name was Bistrum and he moved forward in his little shuffling steps. He was charged with possession of marijuana and the bouncing of checks, but due to a complication in his case the judge ordered him to return to court on the eighteenth of January. The man swung around to look at a tall girl sitting in the third row and mouthed words to her, and she whispered back to him, then he shook his head and shrugged his shoulders and the deputy led him shuffling back to their bench.

When the judge announced *People of the State of Colorado vs. Hoyt Raines*, the deputy nodded at him and said: You're up, asshole. Hoyt gave him a grin and stepped forward. The young public defender stood up beside him and addressed the court.

Your Honor, we wish to advise the court that Mr. Raines has decided to enter a plea of guilty to the charge of misdemeanor child abuse. He is fully aware of the charges and he has been advised of his rights. We submit to the court this copy of the Advisement signed by the defendant.

She stepped to the bench and handed the judge the form. He reached down and took it, then she returned to her place beside Hoyt.

The judge looked at the form. Mr. Raines, do you understand your rights in this courtroom?

I understand them, Hoyt said.

And you understand the charges against you?

Yeah. But that don't mean I like them.

You don't have to like them. But you do have to understand them. And you're telling the court that you do want to plead guilty to the charge of child abuse?

I guess so.

What do you mean you guess so.

I mean yeah, I do.

The judge looked at him for some time. He glanced at the papers in front of him, then addressed the district attorney: You agree that there is a factual basis for this case?

Yes, Your Honor.

What is your recommendation regarding Mr. Raines here?

Your Honor, we believe that since Mr. Raines has already served a month in jail, no further jail time is required. We recommend that there be a period of not less than a year of probation and that Mr. Raines accept without dispute whatever the probation officer reasonably recommends for treatment. We further recommend that the defendant refrain from any contact with the children in question and that he not be permitted to live in the Wallace household any longer.

The judge turned to the young lawyer. Do you concur with all we've just heard?

Yes, Your Honor.

Mr. Raines, have you yourself got anything to say?

Hoyt shook his head.

Am I to take that as a no?

No. I haven't got anything more to say. What good would it do me anyhow.

That might depend upon what you said.

There ain't nothing to say.

Then you will be remanded over to the sheriff and he will release you from custody today. You will contact the probation officer within twenty-four hours. The court orders you to serve one year of supervised probation. Further, you are ordered to pay full court costs, plus a fine of two hundred dollars, and to do ninety-six hours of public service. You will refrain from any contact with the Wallace children and you will no longer reside in the Wallace household. Any question?

Hoyt looked at the young public defender beside him and when she shook her head he looked at the judge. I heard you, he said. I haven't got any question.

Good, the judge said. Because I don't want to see you in here again. This court has seen all it ever wants to see of you, Mr. Raines.

The judge signed the Advisement and handed it to the clerk, then pulled another file out and called the next case.

Hoyt turned and walked to the rear of the courtroom. The deputy rose and escorted him and the other inmate into the hall and on downstairs to the sheriff's office, where the other man was returned to his cell.

The deputy stood before Hoyt and unlocked his handcuffs. You can gather up your belongings now, he said. And report to the probation officer.

I have twenty-four hours till I have to see him.

That's the way you're going to do this, is it? Make it difficult for everybody, like you been doing all along.

It's none of your fucking business anymore what I do, Hoyt said. The judge released me. I'm free to go. And you're free to kiss my ass.

23

On a Saturday morning in December Tom Guthrie and the two boys, Ike and Bobby, drove out to the McPheron place just after breakfast. It was a clear cold day. Only a little wind was blowing up out of the west.

They got out of Guthrie's old red faded Dodge pickup and entered the horse lot where Raymond was waiting for them next to the barn. The two boys, twelve and eleven, were slim and lank, dressed for the cold day in jeans and lined jackets and wool caps and leather gloves. In the horse lot Raymond already had the horses brushed and saddled, and they stood loose-tied at the pole fence, swinging their heads to look as the Guthries approached.

You fellows are right on time, Raymond said. I'm about ready for you. How you boys doing this morning?

They looked at each other. We're okay, Ike said.

Hell of a deal having to come out here on a Saturday morning so early, isn't it.

We don't mind.

Did he feed you any breakfast before you left town?

Yes sir.

That's good. It's going to be a long time till noon dinner.

How do you want to go about this? Guthrie said.

Oh, about like always, I guess, Tom. We'll just ride out amongst them and bring them all in together to the holding pen there and start separating them. How's that sound to you?

Sounds fine to me, Guthrie said. You're the boss.

They mounted the horses and rode out into the pasture. The horses were fresh and a little skittish, a little high in the cold weather, but soon settled down. Far across the pasture the cattle and two-year-old heifers and big blackbaldy calves were spread out in the sagebrush and the native grass, their dark shapes visible over a low wind-blown rise. As they rode on, Guthrie and Raymond talked about the weather and the lateness of the snow and the condition of the grass, and Guthrie thought to inquire about Victoria Roubideaux. Raymond told him she had called the night before. She sounded pretty good, he said. Seems like she's doing real well in her studies there in Fort Collins. She'll be coming home for Christmas.

The two boys rode alongside the men, not talking. They looked around at all there was to see, glad to be out of school doing anything on horseback.

When the four riders drew near, the old mother cows and heifers and calves all stopped grazing and stood as still and alert as deer, watching them approach, then began to move away across the grass toward the far fence line.

You boys go turn them, Guthrie said. Don't you think, Raymond?

That's right. Head them back this way.

The boys touched up their horses and loped off after the cattle, riding like oldtime cowboys out across the native grass on the treeless high plains under a sky as blue and pure as a piece of new crockery.

THEY GATHERED THE CATTLE AND DROVE THEM BACK TO the home corrals and then shut them up in the holding pen east of the barn. Then they dismounted and loosened the cinches and watered the horses and tied them at the pole fence. The horses stood and shook themselves, resting with one back leg cocked. They each were dark with sweat at their necks and flanks and lathered between their back legs.

Raymond and the two boys began to work the cows and calves now, pushing one cow-calf pair at a time out of the holding pen into the high plank-sided alley where Guthrie stood at the far end ready with the swing gate. One of the boys would trot behind with a herdsman's whip, heading them down the alley. The calves stayed close to their mothers, but when they reached Guthrie he shoved the head of the gate between them and closed it, sorting the cow out to pasture and the calf into a second big pen. As soon as they were separated both cow and calf began to bawl, crying and calling, milling in a circle. The dust rose in the air out of the unceasing noise and commotion and hung above them in a brown cloud that drifted away only gradually in the low wind. And all the time the cattle kept stirring, shoving against one another, then standing still to set up to bawl, and the calves in the pen kept raising their heads and bawling and crying, their mouths thrown open, showing pink like rubber and roped with slobber, their eyes rolled back to rims of white. Now and then a cow and its calf would locate each other along the plank fence and stand breathing and licking at the other through the narrow spaces between the rough boards. But when the cow would move away, milling along the fence, the calf would lift its head to bawl once more. It all grew louder and dirtier as the morning hours passed.

In the holding pen Raymond said: Here now, you want to watch this one. She tends to be a little snorty. Stay back from her.

A tall black cow came trotting out from the pen with her calf close behind. The boys succeeded in turning them both into the alley and got them headed toward Guthrie. At the end of the alley she came rushing at him, tossing her head as if to hook him. He climbed quickly up the fence two or three boards, and when she reached for him with her horns he kicked at her head. Then she and her calf dodged into the pasture before he could jump down and swing the gate. Ike called: You want me to go get them, Dad?

No, I'm going to leave her. We'll get a rope on the calf later. That all right, Raymond?

That's exactly right, Raymond said.

They went on working cattle in the bright day in the dust-filled pens. The day had warmed up a little, the wind had stayed down and they grew warm in their lined jackets. By half-past noon they were finished.

You better come up to the house for some dinner now, Raymond said. I believe these boys here could use something to eat.

Oh, we'll just go into town, Guthrie said. We'll get us something to eat at the café. But let us get that calf in first.

No, you better come up to the house. We'll get the calf later. I got some of that good ground beef thawed out from the locker. It's going to waste if you don't come in. I ain't going to eat all of it by myself.

They left the corrals and walked across the gravel drive to the house and porch where they slapped the dust off their jeans and stomped their boots and went inside and took off their warm jackets and hats, and Raymond washed his hands and face at the sink and started to cook at the old enameled stove. Guthrie and the boys washed up at the sink after him and dried off on the kitchen towel. You boys can help me set the table, Guthrie said.

They got down plates and glasses from the cupboard and set them on the table and laid out silverware, then looked in the old refrigerator and took out bottles of ketchup and mustard. Anything else? Guthrie said.

You can open this can of beans, Raymond said, so I can heat it up. Maybe one of you boys can find some milk.

They stood about in the kitchen watching him cook, and when he was finished at the stove they sat down at the table to eat. He carried the big heavy frying pan to the table and forked two hamburgers onto each plate, the meat was badly overcooked, black and hard as something poked out of a campfire. Then he set the pan on the stove and sat down. Go on ahead and eat, he said, unless somebody wants to pray. No one did. He looked around at them. What are you waiting on? Oh hell, I forgot to buy hamburger buns, didn't I. Well shoot, he said. He got up and brought a sack of white bread to the table and sat down again. You boys can eat these hamburgers without buns, can't you?

Yes sir.

Okay then. Let's see if any of this is worth our attention.

They passed the dish of heated beans around the table and poured ketchup on the hamburgers. The ketchup soaked through and made pink circles on the bread. The bread turned soggy and came apart in their hands so that they had to lean over and eat above their plates. There was not much talking. The boys looked once at their father, and he nodded toward their plates and they ducked their heads and went on eating. When the beans came around again they each spooned out a second large portion. For dessert Raymond got down four coffee cups and opened a big can of grocery-store peaches and went around the table to each place and spooned out bright yellow quarters into each of the cups and poured out the syrup in equal quantities.

Meanwhile Guthrie was looking about the kitchen. There were pieces of machinery and bits of leather and old rusted buckles collected on the chairs and in the corners.

Raymond, he said, you ought to get out of the country now and again. Come into town, have a beer or something. You're going to get too lonesome out here.

It does get kind of quiet sometimes, Raymond said.

You better drive into town one of these Saturday nights. Have a little fun for yourself.

Well, no. I can't see what I'd do with myself in town.

You might be surprised, Guthrie said. You might find some manner of interesting trouble to get into.

It might be some kind of trouble I didn't know how to get out of, Raymond said. What'd I do then?

AFTER LUNCH THEY WENT OUTSIDE AGAIN AND THE TWO boys mounted their horses and rode into the pasture among the cows and located the tall black cow and dropped a rope on her calf and dragged the stiff-legged calf back into the big pen with the rest. The cow made a run at them there, but they were able to turn her away and take the calf inside.

The cattle were all still bawling as before. They would go on bawling and milling for three days. Then the cows would grow hungry enough to move farther out into the pasture to graze and their bags would dry up. As for the calves, Raymond would have to fork out brome hay in the long row of feed bunks in the holding pen and bucket out ground corn on top of the hay, and he'd have to watch them carefully for a while or they might turn sick.

WHEN GUTHRIE AND THE BOYS DROVE OUT TO THE county road to return to Holt, they could still hear the cattle from a mile away.

They're all right, aren't they? Bobby said.

Yeah, they're all right, Guthrie said. They're going to have to be. It happens every year like this. I thought you knew that.

I never paid it any attention before, Bobby said. I never was a part of it before.

Those cows and heifers are already pregnant with their next year's calves, Guthrie said. They'd have to wean these calves themselves if we didn't do it for them. They've got to build up their strength for next year's crop.

They make an awful lot of noise, Ike said. They don't seem to like it much.

No, Guthrie said.

He looked at his sons riding beside him in the pickup, headed down the gravel road on this bright winter afternoon, the flat open country all around them gray and brown and very dry.

They never do like it, he said. I can't imagine anything or anybody that would like it. But every living thing in this world gets weaned eventually.

24

THE RAILROAD PENSION CHECK HAD COME AND THE OLD man wanted to go out despite the bitter cold. The temperature had begun to drop every night into the teens and below. You don't have to come, he said. I can manage without you.

You can't go by yourself, DJ said. I'm coming with you.

He went back to his bedroom and got into heavier clothes and returned to the front room and took down his mackinaw and mittens from the plank closet in the corner and put them on and then stood at the door holding his stocking cap in his hand. You better dress warm, Grandpa. You remember last winter when you got frostbite.

Don't you worry about that. I been out in more freezing weather than you ever heard of. Goddamn it, boy, I worked out in this cold all my life.

He put on his old heavy black coat and pulled a corduroy cap down over his white head, the flaps hanging loose beside his big ears. Then he slipped on leather mittens and looked around the room. Turn that light off.

I will, as soon as you go out. I'm waiting on you, DJ said. Have you got your check?

Course I got my check. It's right here in my wallet. He patted the chest pocket of his overalls under the heavy coat. Let's go, he said.

They stepped out and immediately the south wind blowing down on them was enough to take their breath away. Above the lights of town the sky was hard and clear. They walked along the street toward downtown. There was no traffic. The lights were on in Mary Wells's house but all the blinds were pulled down tight. Patches of snow lay scattered in the yards and ruts of ice were hardened in the road.

At Main Street they turned south into the wind and walked along on the sidewalk. A car drove by, its exhaust as white and ragged as wood smoke, before the wind snatched it away. They crossed the railroad tracks and the red signal light shone at the west. The grain elevators loomed over them.

In Holt's small business district their paired images walked beside them in the plateglass storefronts. The old man went limping bent over in his heavy coat, his head down, and the boy was a good deal shorter in the windows.

At the corner of Third Street they crossed Main and stepped into the tavern, entering the long hot smoky room with its clamor of loud talk and country music and pool games going on in the back and the television playing from the bracketed shelf above the bar. His grandfather peered about while he stood beside him, waiting. Old men were sitting against the wall at a round wooden table, and they went over there.

Who's that you got with you? one of them said. Is that DJ? Cold enough for you, boy?

Yes sir. Just about. He took a chair from the next table and sat behind his grandfather.

Just about, he says. Hah.

Don't tell me you walked over here, another old man said. Walt, you must of about froze your tail off coming down here.

I've seen colder, he said.

Everybody's seen colder. I'm just saying it's cold.

It's December, ain't it, the old man said. Now where's that waitress? I need something to drink here. I want something to heat up my insides.

She'll be here. Give her a minute.

Watch her when she comes over, said a red-faced man across the table.

Who is she?

Her name's Tammy. She's new.

Who is she?

Reuben DeBaca's ex-wife from over by Norka. Look her over. Here she comes.

The barmaid came over to the table. She was blonde and good-looking, with wide hips and long legs. She had on tight faded jeans, a deliberate hole in the front of one thigh showing tanned skin underneath, and she wore a white low-cut blouse. When she bent forward to remove two empty glasses from the table, all the old men sitting there watched her closely. Didn't you just come in? she said to the old man.

Just now, he said.

Why don't you take your coat off and make yourself at home? You're going to get too hot, then you'll catch cold when you go back out. What can I bring you?

Bring me, the old man said. He looked toward the bar. Bring me some kind of drinking whiskey.

What kind? We have Jack Daniel's and Old Grand-Dad and Bushmills and Jameson's.

Which is your bar whiskey?

That's Old Crow.

It's cheaper, ain't it.

Is that what you want?

That's it.

And what about you? she said to DJ.

He glanced at her. A cup of coffee, please.

You drink coffee?

Yes ma'am.

He does, his grandfather said. I can't stop him. He's been drinking it ever since he was little.

All right then. Anything else?

Bring the boy some corn chips, one of the men said.

Coffee, corn chips, whiskey. Is that it?

Could you wipe this off over here? the red-faced man said. There's a spot over here.

She looked at him and bent over and wiped the table with a wet rag, and they all looked down the front of her blouse. Will that do? she said.

It sure helps, he said.

You old bastard, she said. You ought to be ashamed of yourself. Acting that way in front of this boy. She went off to get their drinks.

I believe she's warming up to me, the red-faced man said.

She'd warm up to your bank account a lot faster, one of the others said.

Maybe she would. But a woman like her, you wouldn't mind spending a little money on her. You got to.

What about her ex-husband?

That's what I'm talking about. She's older now. She's not going to just fold her hands up and sit at home. She wants something better out of life. She knows there's something more coming her way than a dryland farm out south of Norka.

And you could give it to her.

Why not.

Well, I kind of remember you complaining just last week about how you couldn't get something in your undershorts to cooperate no more. After that operation you had, where the doctor cut on you.

Well, yeah, he said. There is that. The men at the table all laughed. But a woman like her, he said, she might put some new life in you. She might even manage to raise the dead.

The man next to him slapped him on the back. You just keep thinking that way.

DJ looked toward the bar where the woman was setting out glasses on a tray. Under the blue lights she appeared tall and pretty.

She brought the coffee and corn chips and the whiskey to the table, and his grandfather reached inside the chest pocket of his overalls and drew out his old soft leather wallet and removed his pension check.

What's this? she said.

My check. From the railroad.

She turned it over and looked at the other side. You want me to cash this?

That's the usual custom.

You'll need to sign it, she said.

She handed him a pen, and the old man leaned over the table and stiffly signed his name and gave the pen back together with the check.

I'll have to see if they will accept this, she said.

They will. I been cashing checks here for years.

I'll just see, she said, and walked away toward the bar.

What the hell's a-wrong with her?

She's just doing her job, Grandpa, DJ whispered.

The old man lifted his tumbler of whiskey and took a long drink. Drink your coffee there, he said to the boy. It won't do you no good once it gets cold.

The woman came back with a handful of bills and some change and handed the money to the old man. He drew out a dollar bill and gave it to her. Thank you, she said. I never should of questioned you, should I?

No, ma'am, he said. I've been coming in here a long time. Longer than you, I imagine. I plan on coming a while yet too.

And I hope you do, she said. Can I bring you anything else?

You can bring me another one of these after a while.

Of course, she said. DJ watched her walk away to another table.

As the old men around the table began to talk, the boy drank some of his coffee, then set the cup beside his chair on the floor and ate a few of the corn chips and took his math assignment from his coat pocket and got out a pencil and laid the sheets of paper on his lap. One of the old men said: Speaking of people getting cut on, and began to tell a story about a man he knew who couldn't get his equipment to work anymore, so he and his wife went to the doctor. The doctor examined him and then presented him with a sterile needle and vial of fluid to inject into the skin alongside his business, just before he and his wife tried again, and told them to come back afterwards and say how it all went. The couple came back a week later. How'd it go? the doctor said. The man said: Pretty good, it stayed up for forty-five minutes. So what'd you do, the doctor said, and the man said: Well, we did what you're suppose to, you know. Then after we was finished I went out to the front room and set down on the couch, watching TV and eating salted popcorn, waiting for it to go down again so I could go to bed. The doctor turned to the man's wife. That must have been pretty good for you too, he said. Like hell, she said. He only had enough wind for five minutes.

DJ listened until his grandfather began telling the story of the Korean War veteran working on the railroad tracks one winter in the cold country south of Hardin Montana. DJ had already heard this one, and he went to work on the math papers he held in his lap. His grandfather's story was altogether different from the one he'd just heard, and he wasn't much interested in hearing about some vet chasing his foreman around with a shovel.

THE BARMAID CAME BACK AFTER A TIME AND BROUGHT another glass of whiskey to his grandfather, then left and came back with another round for the others. After the old men paid her, she leaned close to the boy and said softly: Why don't you come up here with me?

Up where?

Up to the bar. That way you'll have a place to work on your papers. You can write better up there.

Okay, he said. He stood up next to his grandfather. I'm going up to the bar, Grandpa.

Where?

To the bar. Where I can do my problems.

You behave yourself up there.

I will.

DJ followed her through the room past the men and women who were all talking and drinking, and at the bar she had him climb onto one of the high stools at the corner and he spread his math assignment out on the polished surface. She set his coffee cup and the corn chips beside him.

The bartender came over. Who's this we got here?

My friend, she said.

He's a little young to be drinking at a bar, don't you think?

You leave him alone.

I'm not bothering him. Why would I bother him? I just don't want him getting us into trouble.

He won't get us into any trouble. Who's going to complain?

They better not. But it's your responsibility, if they do.

Don't worry about it.

I ain't going to worry. They don't pay me enough to worry about shit like this. The bartender looked at her and moved away.

She smiled at DJ and went around behind the bar and brought a steaming glass coffeepot and refilled his cup. Don't pay any attention to him, she said. He always has to talk.

I don't want you to get in trouble.

This? she said. This isn't trouble. I could tell you what trouble is. Don't you want some sugar in your coffee?

No thank you.

No milk either?

No. I like it this way.

Well, I just expect you're sweet enough. I have a boy myself, only a little younger than you, she said. He's a sweet thing like you are. I'll see him tomorrow. She stood across the bar, holding the coffeepot.

Doesn't he live with you? he said.

He lives with his daddy. It was better that way. You know, until I got settled.

Oh.

But I sure do miss him.

DJ watched her face. She smiled at him.

But now what about you? Where's your daddy and mama?

I don't know who my dad is, he said. I never met him.

Didn't you? What about your mother? Where's she?

She died a long time ago.

Oh hell, she said. Listen to me. I'm sorry to hear that. Well, I'm sorry I ever said anything.

DJ looked past her into the backbar mirror, where he saw himself reflected above the ranks of bottles, and he saw her blonde head and the back of her white shirt in the mirror. He looked down and picked up his pencil.

You go on and do your schoolwork, she said. You just have to call if you need something. Will you be all right up here, do you think?

Yes, ma'am.

I'll be right here if you need something.

Thank you.

You're very welcome. She smiled. You know what? You and me could get to be good friends, do you think we could?

I guess so.

Well, that's good enough. That's being honest. She set the coffeepot on the hotplate and moved out from behind the bar again to work among the tables.

LATER A WOMAN WITH SHORT BROWN HAIR AND VERY blue eyes came to the end of the bar and stood beside DJ. Don't I know you? she said. I've been watching you for half an hour.

I don't know, he said.

Isn't that your grandfather? Sitting over there with those other men?

Yes.

I took care of him at night. Don't you remember? I saw you when you came in early before school one time. Before I went off duty.

Maybe so, he said.

Yes, I'm sure I did.

Then while she was standing beside him at the end of the bar, Raymond McPheron came in at the front door of the tavern.

Well, look at that, she said. This must be hospital reunion night. I didn't think that man ever came out.

RAYMOND STOOD AND TOOK HIS GLOVES OFF AS HE looked around. He was wearing his silver-belly Bailey hat and his heavy canvas winter coat. He moved out of the doorway and stood behind the men sitting on the stools, waiting until the bartender noticed him.

What's it going to be?

I'm deciding, Raymond said. What have you got on tap?

Coors and Budweiser and Bud Light.

Let me try a Coors.

The bartender drew the beer and handed it to him past a seated man and Raymond reached him a bill. The bartender made change at the cash register below the mirror and brought it back. Raymond took a drink and turned to look at the people sitting at the tables. He drank again and wiped his mouth with the palm of his hand, then unbuttoned his heavy coat.

The woman who had been standing beside DJ came up and tapped him on the shoulder and Raymond turned to look at her.

There's room down here, she said. Why don't you come join us? Raymond took off his hat, holding it in one hand. You remember me, don't you? She smiled at him and took two little steps, as if she were dancing.

I'm starting to, he said. I'm going to say you must be Linda May from the hospital.

That's right. You do remember. Come join us down here.

Where?

At the end of the bar. There's someone else I think you know.

Raymond put his hat back on and followed her along the bar. The men turned on the barstools to look at him as he went by, watching him with the woman. She stopped beside DJ. How about this young man here? she said. Do you remember him?

I believe I do, Raymond said. This must be Walter Kephart's grandson. I never got his name though.

DJ, the boy said.

How you doing, son?

Pretty good.

Is your grandfather here with you?

DJ pointed to the table against the far wall.

I see him now. How's he doing? Is he doing pretty good too?

Yes sir. He got over his pneumonia.

Good, Raymond said. He looked at the boy again and noticed his papers on the bartop. Looks like we're interrupting your schoolwork there. Maybe we better leave you to it.

I'm done. I'm just waiting on Grandpa, till he's ready to go.

How soon you reckon that's going to be?

I don't know. He's talking.

Old men like to talk, don't they, Raymond said. He drank from his glass and glanced at the woman standing next to him.

I'm surprised to see you out here, she said. I didn't think you ever came out at night.

I don't, Raymond said. I can't say what I'm doing out here this time.

You need to get out once in a while. Everybody does.

That must be it.

They do. Believe me. It's good you came out.

Aren't you working tonight?

No, she said. This is one of my nights off.

Well. That would explain how one of us came to be here any-ways.

The boy's grandfather stepped up to bar next to DJ. You staying out of trouble?

Yes.

It's about time we get on home.

How you doing there? Raymond said.

Who's that? Is that you, McPheron?

More or less. Yes sir.

Look who else is here, the old man said, looking at the woman. Aren't you from the hospital?

That's right, Linda May said.

Well. Okay then. It's good to see you. He turned to DJ. Let's go, boy. Here's your coat.

DJ stood down from the barstool and put on his coat and stuck his papers in the pocket. I want to tell her good-bye first, he said.

Who?

That lady who was nice to me.

The old man looked into the back. She's working, he said. She don't need you bothering her.

I'm not going to bother her.

He walked back toward the pool tables at the rear of the long smoky room where she was talking to some men sitting at a table.

They were all laughing and he waited behind her until one of the men said: I believe there's somebody here wants to say something to you.

The barmaid turned around.

I'm going now, DJ said.

She reached toward him and pulled his coat collar up. You stay warm outside now.

Thank you for all the— He motioned behind himself. For the place to work on my papers.

That's all right, sweetheart. She smiled at him. I was just glad to see you. Now you come again sometime. Okay? He nodded and went back to his grandfather.

You think you're ready to go now? the old man said.

Yes.

Let's go then.

Just a minute, Raymond said. Are you walking?

We walked over here.

You'd better let me drive you home.

You don't need to do that. We got over here all right.

Sure, but it's colder now.

Well. The old man glanced toward the door. I don't like this boy being out like this, I'll say that.

Linda May looked at Raymond. You haven't finished your beer. Why don't you go ahead and run them home and I'll keep your glass here for you. Then you can come back.

I might, he said.

Do, she said.

They went outside and got into Raymond's old battered pickup, and he backed away from the curb and turned north up Main Street and followed Walter Kephart's directions across the railroad tracks and then west into the quiet neighborhood, pulling up in front of their house. The old man and the boy got out. We thank you kindly for the ride, the old man said.

Don't you take no more sickness, Raymond said.

I don't plan on it.

The old man shut the pickup door and it didn't catch, so Raymond leaned across and pushed it open, then slammed it hard. When he looked up they were already halfway to the door of the house. He drove to the end of the block and made a U-turn at the intersection and drove back to Main Street and parked down the block from the tavern. For a while he sat in the cold cab looking at the darkened storefront in front of him. What in hell's sake do I think I'm doing? he said. His breath smoked in the cold air. I don't have the first idea. But I guess I'm doing it.

He got out and went back into the warmth and noise once more and walked to the end of the bar where Linda May stood. When he came up to her she smiled and held out his beer glass.

Well, here you are, she said. I didn't know if you'd come back or not.

I said I might, Raymond said.

That doesn't mean you would. Men say I might, and it doesn't mean a thing.

I thought it did, he said.

Maybe it does for you.

He took the glass from her hand and drank the rest of the beer. He looked around and all the people nearby appeared to be having a good time.

Let me buy you another beer, she said. This'll be my round.

Well, no, he said. Ma'am, I don't believe I could do that. I better buy you one. Wouldn't you let me do that?

But the next one's on me. This is a new day, she said.

Ma'am?

I mean women are different now than they used to be. It's all right for a woman to buy a man a drink in a barroom now.

I wouldn't know a thing about that, Raymond said. I don't believe I ever did know anything about women. There was just my mother and then this young girl that lived with us lately.

You mean the girl with the little child I saw visiting you in the hospital.

Yes ma'am. That would be her. That was Victoria Roubideaux. And her little daughter, Katie.

Where are they now? Don't they still live with you?

No ma'am, not all the time. They're off at school. In Fort Collins. She's taking a course of study at college.

Good for her. But don't you think you could call me something else? Ma'am makes me sound so old.

I might try, he said.

Good, she said. Now why don't you tell me about them.

Victoria Roubideaux and Katie?

That's right. They seem to mean a great deal to you.

Well yes, they do. They mean just about everything to me.

He began to talk to Linda May about the girl and her child, and he told her how it was that they had come to live with him and his brother in the country two and a half years ago, and after a while a table was vacated and they sat down across from each other and he allowed her to buy him a drink, though he insisted on buying the next round himself. He sat there in his hat and winter coat until the place closed, talking to this woman. He had never done such a thing before in his life.

It was late when he drove into the graveled drive and stopped at the gate in front of the old gray house. The temperature had fallen to zero and a pale half-sided moon was coming up in the eastern sky. He got out of the pickup and walked up the sidewalk onto the porch. Inside, the house felt empty and quiet. He hung his coat on its peg and went into the bathroom, then climbed the stairs to his bedroom. He turned the light on and everything there seemed quiet and desolate too. He looked around and finally sat down on the bed and pulled his boots off. He got undressed and put on his flannel striped pajamas and lay awake under the heavy blankets in the cold room, unable to sleep yet, thinking about the woman at the bar and about the old man and the boy, and he began to remember the time his brother was courting the woman in town and how that turned out. The moonlight was showing in the room, silver on the wall, and after a while he went to sleep, and in his sleep he dreamed of Victoria and Katie, knocking at the door of some house he didn't recognize situated in some town he had never seen before in his life.

25

THERE WAS SNOW FALLING WHEN THEY CAME OUTSIDE
Holt County Social Services at the rear of the courthouse in the
evening. They had been in the long conference room for an hour,
attending a class in the practice of parenthood, while Joy Rae and
Richie played with the scarred tedious brightly colored toys in the
waiting room and read the little broken-backed books, and during
the hour they were all inside it had begun to snow. It was snowing
hard now, piling up in the gutters along the street curbs and blowing
up against the dark brick walls of the courthouse.

When they came outside, the children were wearing the cheap
coats that were too big for them they had bought at the racks at the
thrift store, and Betty had on an old calf-length red wool winter coat
that was fastened in front with big safety pins. Luther wore only a
thin black windbreaker, but he was warm even in that.

Hoo doggie, he said when they stepped out the door. Look at this
snow.

We better hurry, Betty said. These kids is going to get cold.

They walked out away from the old high redbrick courthouse.
Above them the tiled roof was obscured by the falling snow. They
crossed Boston, and, as yet, there were no tracks in the street from
any passing cars. The snow came down thickly under the corner

streetlight and they went on. The children scuffed their feet, making long dragging marks, and began to fall behind.

Betty turned to look at them. You kids, come on now, she said. Hurry up. Catch up with us.

You ain't allowed to talk that way, Luther said. You suppose to be nice to them.

I am. I don't want them to catch cold. We never should of took them out here in this.

How was we going to know it would come on snowing while we was in there in that room?

Well, they ain't suppose to be out in something like this. Come on.

The children kicked and scuffed along the sidewalks. The atmosphere in the silent town seemed all blue around them. The snow muffled any sound and no one else was out walking. A single car went by, without noise or commotion, a block away, moving at the intersection, stately and quiet as a ship sailing on some silent ghostly sea. They crossed Chicago, then turned up Detroit toward home.

At the trailer they climbed the snow-filled steps and entered the house and removed their shoes at the door and walked out into the room in their stockings. Richie's had gathered in damp wads around his toes, and his thin heels were scarlet.

You kids get on to bed now and get warm, Luther said. Tomorrow's school.

Here, Betty said. What was you just telling me about how to talk to these kids right? That teacher said you got to ask them what they want, not just say it.

Oh, yeah, Luther said. Joy Rae, honey, you want anything? You want you a bedtime snack before you go off to sleep?

I want some hot chocolate, Joy Rae said.

What about you, Richie?

I want some pop.

Is he suppose to have pop at night?

I don't know what he can have, Betty said. She never said nothing about no pop. You just suppose to ask him.

I asked him. He said he wants pop.

What kind of pop?

What kind of pop you want, Richie? You want strawberry? We got black cherry.

Strawberry, Richie said.

Betty brought the drinks and they sat down at the kitchen table. Luther took a package of lasagna from the freezer and put it in the microwave, and it came out steaming and he set it on the table, and Betty got down paper plates left over from a birthday party and they began to eat.

When they were finished, Luther and Betty walked the children back to their bedrooms and left the door open at Richie's room so he could see the light in the hall. Then Luther went into his and Betty's room, and he undressed and got into bed in his underwear and stretched out. The bed sagged and complained under his weight. Dear, he called, ain't you coming to bed?

In a minute, Betty said. But she had stayed in the front room and was sitting on the couch now, watching the snow falling in the front yard and out in Detroit Street. After a while she took up the phone, set it in her lap, and made a call to a house in Phillips. A woman answered.

I'd like to speak to Donna, please, Betty said. I want to talk to Donna Jean.

Who's calling? the woman said.

This is her mother.

Who?

Her mother. This is Betty Wallace.

You, the woman said. You're not supposed to call here. Don't you know that?

I want to talk to her. I ain't going to do nothing.

It's against the regulations.

I won't hurt her. I wouldn't hurt her for nothing in the world.

Listen to me. You want me to put her on the phone and have her tell you herself you're not her mother anymore? Is that what you want me to do?

I am too her mother, Betty said. You ain't suppose to say something like that to me. I'm always going to be her mother. I give birth to her, out of my own self.

Oh no, the woman said. That's not what the court order says. I'm her mother now. And don't you ever call here again. I'll call the police. I got enough trouble on account of her without you making it worse.

What kind of trouble? Is something the matter with Donna?

That's none of your business. The Lord will guide me. I don't need any help from you. The woman hung up.

Betty put the receiver down and sat motionless on the couch, and presently she began to cry.

Outside the trailer house the snow continued to fall. It fell thickly in the yard and in the street in front and it kept falling until midnight, then it began to diminish and by one o'clock it had stopped altogether. The sky cleared and the cold brilliant stars came out.

Betty woke then, lying on the couch. It was cold in the room and she rose and walked back to their bedroom and pulled off her thin dress and stepped out of her underwear and unfastened her bra. She put on a tattered yellow nightgown and lay down beside Luther in the sagging bed. Shivering and cold, she pulled the blankets up and moved closer to him. Then she began to remember what the woman had said to her. How her voice had been. You want me to put her on the phone and have her tell you herself you're not her mother anymore. Betty lay in bed beside Luther, remembering. Soon she began to cry again. She cried quietly for a long time and at last fell asleep against his great warm wide bare back.

26

CHRISTMAS EVE OBSERVANCE WAS GENERAL IN HOLT. There were candlelight services at the local churches and family gatherings in the front rooms of the houses overlooking the quiet streets, and out on the east side of town on US Highway 34 the bartender Monroe kept the Chute Bar and Grill open until two o'clock in the morning.

Hoyt Raines was sitting in a back booth with a middle-aged divorcée named Laverne Griffith, a fleshy maroon-haired woman twenty years his senior. She was buying and they were sitting close together on the same side of the booth, their drinks before them next to the ashtray on the scarred wooden table.

The Chute had been decorated for the season. Loops of red and green lights were festooned above the bar and silver tassels hung from the mirror. A half-dozen men were sitting at the bar, drinking and talking, and an old woman was asleep with her head in her arms at a far table. From the jukebox Elvis Presley was singing I'll have a blue Christmas without you. A man who had been at the bar earlier had put in enough quarters to play the same song eight times over, but then had gone outside and driven off in the night in his pickup.

One of men at the bar turned to look balefully at the jukebox. He turned back to the bartender. Can't you do something about that?

What do you want me to do about it?

Well, can't you turn it off or something?

It'll stop pretty soon by itself. It's Christmas. You got to enjoy yourself.

I'm trying to. But I'm sick of that goddamn thing.

It'll run out pretty quick now. Forget it. Let me get you another drink.

Are you buying?

I could.

Make it a double then.

I said it was Christmas. I never said it was old home week.

The man looked at him. What in hell's that suppose to mean?

I don't know. It just come to me. Let's say it means I'll get you a single drink.

I'm waiting.

You know what? Monroe said. You ought to cheer up. You're starting to make everyone around here feel bad.

I can't help it. It's the way I am.

Well try, for christsake.

In the back booth Hoyt had circled his arm around Laverne Griffith. She picked a cigarette from the pack on the table and put it in her mouth, and he reached the lighter with his free hand and took it and lit it for her. She blew a cloud of smoke and squinted her eyes shut and rubbed them, then she opened her eyes again, blinking, and stared unhappily across the table.

You all right? Hoyt said.

No, I'm not all right. I'm sad and blue.

Why don't you and me go over to your place when they close up here. That'll make you feel better.

She inhaled and blew a long thin stream of smoke away from her face. I've been down that old road before, she said. I know where it comes out.

Not with me, you haven't.

She turned to stare at him. His face was only inches away, his cap pushed back on his thick head of hair. You think you're that much different?

I'm like nothing you ever knew before, Hoyt said.

What makes you so different?

I'll show you. I'll give you a little demonstration.

I'm not talking about that, she said. That's available to a woman anytime. What about in the morning when we wake up?

I'll make you breakfast.

What if I don't eat breakfast.

I'll make one you will.

She smoked again and looked out into the room. It doesn't close here for two more hours, she said. She turned and lifted her face toward him. You can give me a kiss anyhow.

AT THE STROKE OF MIDNIGHT MONROE CALLED: MERRY Christmas, you sons of bitches. Merry Christmas, everybody. The men at the bar shook hands and one of them said they should wake the woman sleeping at the far table and ask her if she could guess what day it was.

Let her sleep, one of the others said. She's better off sleeping. Here, he said to Monroe, give me one of those decorations. Monroe took down a piece of silver tassel from the bar mirror and the man walked over to the woman and leaned over and draped it across her head and shoulders. How's that look? he said. The woman groaned and sighed, but didn't wake.

In the booth, Hoyt and Laverne kissed a long time at the announcement that it was Christmas. Oh hell, she said finally. Let's get out of here. We might as well go back to my place. They stood up out of the booth.

Monroe called: You two have yourself a merry little Christmas now. Drive careful.

Hoyt waved at him and they went outside. It was very cold in the parking lot, the air dry and hard on their faces. They got into her car and she drove them along the ice-rutted empty streets to her apartment on the second floor of a house on Chicago Street, a block south of the grain elevators. They walked around to the back of the house in the frozen grass and he followed her up the plank stairs that were built up outside the house, climbing to a little porch that was roofed over with tin above the landing. She found her key in her purse and unlocked the door. Inside, the apartment was stifling hot but neat and tidy, with almost no furniture. She locked the door and he at once turned her around and began to kiss her face. Jesus Christ, she said, shoving him back, let me get my coat off first. I have to use the bathroom.

Where's your bedroom at? Hoyt said.

Back there.

She went through the kitchen, and he walked a few steps across the room and entered the bedroom. There was a red comforter over the bed and a mirrored dresser against the bare wall. The mirror reflected the room at an odd angle, including a little closet with a naked lightbulb hanging from a cord. He switched on the lamp beside the bed and got out of his clothes, then dropped them on the floor and got in bed and pulled the cover up. He stretched out comfortably looking at the ceiling and put his hands under his head.

Laverne stepped into the room. Well, why don't you make yourself at home?

I'm just waiting on you.

You didn't wait long.

Come on to bed.

Don't look at me, she said.

What?

Don't watch me. She turned her back and removed her blouse and her slacks and hung them in the little closet and stood in the doorway facing away from him, and took off her black bra and black silky underwear. Are you looking?

No.

Yes you are.

I'm just doing what you want me to.

Like hell. Shut your eyes.

He looked at her and shut his eyes and she turned toward the bed. She was very pale and soft-looking, with a thick stomach and large fallen breasts and heavy legs, and she seemed saddened in the dim light. She crossed to the bed and crawled in under the covers. She switched off the bedside lamp.

You have to be nice to me, she said. I don't like to be hurt.

I'm not going to hurt you.

Kiss me first.

He raised up on his side and put one hand to her face and kissed her, then he kissed her again and she lay back quietly and closed her eyes, and beneath the sheet he began to move his hand over her flattened breasts and across her soft stomach, and she said nothing more to him but seemed content just to breathe, and he went on kissing and after a while he lay on her and began to move.

When he was finished he saw that she had gone to sleep beneath him. Laverne, he said. Darlin. Hey. He looked into her sleeping face and rolled off and lay back beside her under the warm covers, and soon was asleep himself.

THE NEXT DAY HE GOT UP LATE AND MADE A BREAKFAST of eggs and coffee and buttered toast, and he sprinkled paprika on the eggs and arranged everything on a large white plate and brought all of it to her in the bedroom. She sat up with the blankets drawn around her shoulders, her maroon hair all matted and disheveled, but she seemed to be cheered now in the morning. What have you got here? she said.

Didn't I say I'd make you breakfast?

At noon they rose from bed and spent the afternoon and the evening watching the holiday parades on television and viewing the old sweet movies that were shown at Christmastime. And in the succeeding days and weeks in the heart of winter she allowed him to stay with her in the upstairs apartment on Chicago Street while she went off to work as an aide at the Holt County Twilight Nursing Home and he took a job riding cattle pens at the feedlot east of town. He reported to the probation officer at the courthouse as the judge had ordered, and he and Laverne Griffith were still together at the middle of February, and during all that time things stayed satisfactory for Hoyt in the little apartment upstairs.

27

IN THE WEEK BETWEEN CHRISTMAS AND NEW YEAR'S they passed the long afternoons in the shed beside the alley. It was very cold in the shed and the sunlight came in only thinly from the single window. They lit candles on the table and the back shelf, and they had the blankets. For greater warmth they took to lying beside each other on the carpet in the patch of sunlight that fell in through the window.

They lay under the blankets on their backs and talked. Frequently now she talked about her mother. He recalled a memory of his own mother, how she once wore a sleeveless red blouse in the summertime, sitting in the shade on the back porch of a little house in Brush Colorado, and how she was wearing shorts and would stretch her toes in the dirt below the porch step. There was red polish on the nails of her toes and the dirt was soft like powder.

In return, she remembered how her father picked her up one time when she was a little girl and carried her on his shoulders, ducking through a doorway into the kitchen. Her mother was making white flour gravy at the stove, and she turned and smiled, looking at them both. Then her father said something funny, but she couldn't recall what it was. It had made her mother laugh, she remembered that.

ONE AFTERNOON THEY WERE LYING ON THE FLOOR IN THE shed when she turned toward him and looked at his face in the weak sunlight. What happened to you here?

Where?

This little curved scar.

I ran into a nail, he said.

There was a white scar the shape of a quarter moon beside his eye.

I have a scar too, she said. She opened the blanket and put her shirt neck down for him to see.

SOME AFTERNOONS HE BROUGHT CRACKERS AND CHEESE from his grandfather's house together with a thermos of coffee. He also brought them books, though he read more than she did. For some time now he'd been checking books out of the old limestone-block Carnegie Library on the corner of Ash Street, where the librarian was a thin unhappy woman who took care of her invalid mother when she wasn't at work and who during the day conducted the library as if it were a church. He had found the shelves of books he liked and brought the books home every two weeks, summer and winter, and now he took to bringing them to the shed to read lying on the floor beside her.

She took more and more to the practice of daydreaming and wishing, more so now in the absence of her father and in the new desolation that filled the house since her mother had turned so sad and lonely. An hour might go by in the shed with little or no talking, and then watching him read she would eventually begin to tease him, tickling his cheek with a piece of thread, blowing thinly in his ear, until he would put his book down and push her, and then they would begin to push back and forth and to wrestle, and once it happened that she rolled on top of him, and while her face was so close above his she dropped her head suddenly and kissed him on the mouth, and they both stopped and stared, and she kissed him again. Then she rolled off.

What did you do that for?

I felt like it, she said.

AND ONCE HER LITTLE SISTER OPENED THE DOOR OF THE shed in the afternoon, late in that week of Christmas vacation, and found them reading on the floor with the blankets over them. What are you doing?

Shut the door, Dena said.

The little girl stepped inside and shut the door and stood looking at them. What are you doing there on the floor?

Nothing.

Let me under too.

You have to be quiet.

Why?

Because I said so. Because we're reading.

All right. I will. Let me in.

She crawled under the blanket with them.

No, you have to be over here, Dena said. This is my place next to him.

So for a while the two sisters and the boy lay on the floor under the blankets, reading books in the dim candlelight, with the sun falling down outside in the alley, the three of them softly talking a little, drinking coffee from a thermos, and what was happening in the houses they'd come from seemed, for that short time, of little importance.

28

WHEN RAYMOND CAME UP TO THE HOUSE IN THE AFTER-
noon of New Year's Day after feeding in the winter pasture, shoving
hay and protein pellets onto the frozen ground in front of the shaggy
milling cattle, he removed his overshoes and canvas coveralls at the
kitchen door and went back through the house to shave and wash up,
then mounted the stairs to his bedroom and put on dark slacks and
the new blue wool shirt Victoria had given him for Christmas. When
he came downstairs into the kitchen, Victoria was cooking chicken
and dumplings in a big blued pot for their holiday dinner and Katie
was standing on a chair at the table stirring flour and water in a red
bowl. Each had a white dish towel tied about her waist, and Victoria's
heavy black hair was pulled away from her face and her cheeks were
flushed from the cooking.

She turned to look at him from the stove. You're all dressed up,
she said.

I put on your shirt.

I see that. It looks good on you. It looks just right.

So what can I do? he said. What else needs to be done here to get
ready for dinner?

You could set the table.

So he spread a white tablecloth over the formal walnut table out in the dining room, where it was centered under the overhead light, and got down the old rosebud china his mother had received as a wedding gift so many years ago and arranged the plates and glasses and silverware about the table. The low afternoon sun streamed in onto the dishes from the unshaded windows. The sunlight was brilliant in the glassware.

Victoria came into the room to see how he was faring and looked closely at the table. Is somebody else coming? she said.

He looked at her briefly and turned to peer out the window toward the horse barn and corrals beyond the graveled drive. I guess you could say there is, he said.

Who is it?

It's somebody I met.

Somebody you met?

You met her too.

Her? A woman's coming to dinner?

It's a woman from the hospital.

What's her name?

Her name is Linda May. She was working nights when I was in the room there with my leg.

The middle-aged woman with short dark hair?

That sounds about right. Yes, I guess that would have to be her.

Victoria looked at the dishes and glasses ranged in order on the white tablecloth. Why didn't you tell me?

Raymond stood with his back to her. I don't rightly know, he said. I guess I was kind of scared to. I didn't know what you'd think of it.

It's your house, she said. You can do what you want.

Now that ain't right, he said. Don't say that. This here is your house as much as it is mine. It's been that way for a good while.

I thought it was.

Well it is. He turned to face her. I can tell you that much.

But I don't understand you not telling me about somebody coming for dinner.

Oh hell, honey, can't you lay it to an old man's mistake? An old man that don't know how to do something he's never done before?

He stood before her in the new blue shirt, with an expression on his face she had never seen or even imagined. She moved up beside him and put her hand on his arm. I'm sorry, she said. It'll be all right. It's just fine. I'm glad you asked her.

Thank you, he said. I hoped you wouldn't take no offense. I just got the idea to ask her to dinner, that's all it was. I never saw the harm in it.

There isn't any, Victoria said. What time did you tell her to come?

Raymond looked at his watch. About a half hour from now.

Did you tell her how to find us out here?

She told me she already knew. She'd been asking around about us, she said.

Oh?

That's what she told me.

THAT AFTERNOON SHE DROVE UP TO THE HOGWIRE FENCING in front of the house in a ten-year-old cream-colored Ford convertible. She got out and surveyed the gray house and the patches of dirty snow and the three leafless stunted elm trees in the side yard, then came up through the wire gate onto the screened porch. Before she could knock, Raymond opened the door. Come in, he said, come in.

I see I got the right place.

Yes ma'am.

Now you'll have to call me Linda today, she said. You have to remember that.

You better come in. It's cold out here.

She entered the kitchen and looked across the room at the girl holding her child at the stove.

This here is Victoria Roubideaux and little Katie.

Yes. I remember them from when you were in the hospital. How do you do.

Victoria stepped forward and they shook hands. Linda May tried to touch Katie but the little girl turned away, pointing her face into her mother's shoulder.

She'll be more friendly after a while.

Let me take your coat, Raymond said.

He hung it next to his coveralls and his canvas work jacket on the peg beside the door. Linda May wore black slacks and a red sweater and there were bright silver hoops suspended from her ears. Something sure smells good, she said.

It's just about ready, Victoria said. Why don't you go ahead and be seated and I'll bring it in.

Is there anything I can do to help?

I don't think so.

Raymond led his guest into the dining room.

What a beautiful table, she said. It all looks so pretty.

This table was my mother's table. It's been in that same spot for as long as I can remember.

May I look at it?

Well, how do you mean?

Just underneath, at the table itself.

It's going to be kind of dusty under there.

She lifted the white cloth and examined the polished surface and then peered below at its massive center pedestal. Why, this must be real walnut, she said. An antique.

It's old anyhow, Raymond said. Older than me even. Why don't you sit here.

He pulled out a chair and held it for her and she sat down.

Thank you, she said.

I'll be right back.

He went into the kitchen, where Victoria was dishing food at the stove. What's next? he said.

Will you take Katie in and get her settled?

Course I will. Come on, little darlin. Are you ready for some dinner? He bent over to pick her up, then leaned back to take in her round dark eyes that were exactly like her mother's, and brushed the shiny black hair out of her face. He carried her into the dining room and sat her on a wooden box on the chair opposite Linda May. The little girl looked across the table at her, then picked up her napkin and studied it with great interest.

Victoria came in with the steaming bowl of chicken and

dumplings and another of mashed potatoes and went back for a plate of hot rolls and a dish of green beans flavored with bacon. Raymond stood at the head of the table until she sat down and then took the seat across from her, with Linda May and Katie on either side.

Would you say grace? Victoria said.

Raymond appeared startled. What?

Would you say grace, please?

He glanced at Linda May and back at Victoria. I suppose I could take a run at it. It's been a hell of a long time, though. He dropped his iron-gray head. His cheeks were chafed red and his white forehead shone. Lord, he said. What we're going to do here, we're just going to say thank you for this food on the table. And for the hands that prepared it for us. He paused for a long time. They all looked up at him. He went on. And for this bright day outside we're having. He paused again. Amen, he said. Now do you think we can eat, Victoria?

Yes, she said, and passed Linda May the chicken and dumplings.

LINDA MAY DID MUCH OF THE TALKING WHILE VICTORIA and Raymond listened and answered her questions. Victoria tended to the little girl. After dinner they helped her clear the table, then she took Katie back to the downstairs bedroom they'd been sharing since Raymond had moved up to his old room again, and she put the little girl into bed and lay down with her and read to her until she was asleep, and afterward lay in the darkened room listening through the opened door to Raymond and the woman talking.

They'd already done the dishes together at the kitchen sink and had retired to the parlor. Around them the old flowered wallpaper, stained in places and darkened in one corner from some long-ago rain, was dim and gray. When Linda May entered the room she'd seated herself in Raymond's chair and he had looked at her and hesitated, then he sat in the chair that had always been his brother's.

My, she said, that was a wonderful dinner.

That was Victoria's doing. We never taught her any of that.

Yes. She looked through the doorway into the dining room. The ceiling light made a bright glare over the white tablecloth. I don't know how you two stand it out here, she said. It's lonely, don't you think?

I've always been out here, Raymond said. I don't know how it'd be other places. There's a neighbor a mile and a half down the road if you need something.

A farmer like you?

Well, I wouldn't say we was farmers exactly.

What would you say?

I guess you'd have to call us ranchers. We raise cattle. Poverty-stuck old cattle ranchers, more like it.

You make it sound like you're close to starving.

We've done that a time or two. Or pretty near to it.

How big a ranch do you have?

How much land?

Yes.

Well, we have about three sections. All counted.

How much is that? I don't know what a section is.

There would be six hundred forty acres to a section. It's mostly grass pasture, what we have. We put up a lot of brome hay every summer but we don't do any real farming. Well, I keep saying we. I mean me now. I haven't figured out what I'll do about haying next summer.

How will you manage?

I'll think of something. Hire somebody I expect.

It must be terribly hard without your brother here anymore.

It's not the same. It's not anything like it. Harold and me, we was together all our lives.

You just have to go on, don't you.

He looked at her. People always say that, he said. I say as much myself. I don't know what it means, though. He looked out the window behind her where the night had fallen. The yardlight had come on and there were long shadows in the yard.

She sat watching him. I was surprised to see you come into the tavern the other night, she said.

No, it ain't like me, he said. I was surprised to be there myself.

Do you think you might come in again?

I imagine it's possible.

I hope you do.

She sat with one foot folded up under her in his big recliner chair. Her red sweater looked very bright against her dark hair.

And I want to thank you again for inviting me to dinner today, she said.

Well, yes, ma'am. Like I say, Victoria is the one that did all that.

But you're the one who asked me. I've lived in this area long enough to know quite a few people, but I don't think I've ever been invited into one of these old ranch houses before.

Our grandfather homesteaded this place. Him and our grand-mother. They come out in eighty-three from Ohio. But where do you come from yourself, can I ask you that?

From Cedar Rapids.

Iowa.

Yes. I was ready for a change.

Don't they have good hospitals back there?

Oh, sure. Of course they do. But my life kind of fell apart, so I thought I'd come out here. I thought I'd start over, try out life in the mountains. But I only got this far and kind of broke down. I think I may go on to Denver yet, though.

When do you reckon on doing that?

I don't know. I guess it depends. I've only been here a year.

Sometimes a year can be a long time, Raymond said.

Sometimes it can be too long, she said.

WHEN LINDA MAY WAS GETTING READY TO LEAVE, VICTORIA came out from the bedroom to say good night. They stood in the kitchen and Raymond took down Linda May's coat and held it as she put it on, then he walked her out through the wire gate to her car. Outside in the cold air everything seemed brittle and the ground was frozen down as hard as iron.

Thank you again, she said. You make sure you come into town one of these days.

Be careful out there on that road, he said.

She got into her convertible and turned the key, and the engine turned over but wouldn't catch. When she tried again it only whined and clicked. She rolled the window down. It's not going to start, she said.

Sounds like it's your battery. Is it a old one?

I don't know. The battery was in it when I bought the car a year ago.

I better give you a push. Let me get my coat.

He went back into the house and pulled his coat and hat from the pegs in the kitchen. Victoria was putting the clean dishes up in the high cupboards. What's wrong? she said.

I need to give her a push.

You better stay warm out there.

He walked back out past the Ford, where Linda May was still sitting behind the wheel, and crossed the rutted gravel to the garage and climbed into his pickup. He let it run for a minute, then pulled it behind her car and got out to see how the two bumpers would meet. When he walked up to the side of the car and opened the door, she was shivering and hugging herself.

Are you all right? he said.

It's really cold.

You want to go back in the house?

No. Let's go ahead.

You know what to do, don't you?

Pop the clutch once we get going, she said.

And have the key turned on. But don't try it till I get you out on the county road where we can go a little faster.

He shut the door and got back in his pickup and eased it forward. The bumpers touched and he pushed her slowly out the drive onto the lane and then onto the dark road, his headlights shining very bright on the rear of her car. He went faster, the gravel kicked up under the fenders, and with a lurch her car leapt forward and she pulled away and her headlights and taillights came on. She sped up, the dust was boiling under them from the dry road, and he followed her for half a mile to be sure she was all right, then he slowed and stopped and watched the red taillights going away in the dark.

Victoria was sitting at the kitchen table when he came inside. She had made a fresh pot of coffee. He took off his coat and hat, and she stood up when she saw his face was so dark and red.

Why you're just freezing, she said.

It must be down around zero out there. He cupped his ears with his hands. It's going to turn off pretty cold tonight.

I made you a pot of coffee.

Did you, honey? I thought you'd be in bed by now.

I wanted to make sure you got back all right.

Were you worried?

I just wanted to be sure, she said. Were you able to get her car started?

Yes. She's gone on toward town. Well, I expect she's almost back to her own home by this time.

29

On a bright cold day in January Rose Tyler parked unannounced in front of the trailer and got her purse and notebook and walked up the snow-muddied path to the faded trailer house. Dead stalks of cheatgrass and redroot stuck up through the snow beside the path like ragged stands of tiny gray trees. The plank porch had been swept clean, that much had been done. She knocked on the metal door and waited. She knocked again. She looked out into the empty street. Nothing was moving. She turned to knock once more and waited a while longer. She had started down the steps when the door opened behind her.

Luther stood in the doorway wearing sweatpants but no shirt. Is that you, Rose? he said.

Yes. Weren't you going to let me in?

I didn't hear you knock. He stood back from the door so she could pass inside. Betty ain't up yet.

It's past ten o'clock. I thought you'd both be up by now.

Betty never slept good last night.

What's wrong?

I don't know. You'd have to ask her.

I came to talk to both of you this morning. To see how things are going.

Things is fine, Rose. I guess we been doing pretty good.

Why don't you go put on a shirt and tell Betty to come out. We'll have a little visit.

Well, I don't know if she'll want to get up.

Why don't you ask her.

He disappeared into the hall and she surveyed the front room and the kitchen. There were dishes and pizza cartons on every flat surface, and the black plastic bag of pop cans leaned against the refrigerator. A morning game show was playing on the television in the corner.

Luther came out of the hallway in a tee-shirt, with Betty shuffling barefooted behind him, looking tired and haggard in a pink bathrobe. She had brushed her hair and it hung down stiff on both sides of her face. She looked at Rose and looked at the television. Is something wrong, Rose? she said.

Nothing that I know of. I said before that I'd come by now and then. It's part of the court order. Don't you remember?

I ain't feeling very good.

Is it still your stomach?

My back too. It's been gripping me bad this past week.

I'm sorry to hear that.

I can't sleep no more. I have to rest during the day.

Yes, but you know I'm going to visit you at any time, don't you. You remember we talked about that.

I know, Betty said. You want to sit down?

Thank you.

Rose seated herself on a chair near the door and glanced at the television. Luther, would you turn that off, please?

He clicked the television off and sat down on the couch close to Betty.

So. How are things? Rose said. You said they were going fine, Luther.

Everything's pretty good, he said. We're doing okay, I guess.

How are Joy Rae and Richie?

Well. Richie he still has him some trouble at school. Like before.

What kind of trouble?

It's hard to say. He don't talk about it.

It's those other kids picking on him all the time, Betty said. They won't never let him alone.

Why do you think that is?

He don't do nothing to them. Richie's a good boy. I don't know what they got against him.

Have you tried talking to his teacher?

That wouldn't do no good.

But you might at least try. Maybe she knows what's going on.

I don't know.

What about Joy Rae?

Oh, now she's doing real good, Luther said. She can already read better than me.

Can she?

Better than Betty too. Can't she, Betty.

Betty nodded.

Better than both of us put together, Luther said.

I'm glad she's doing so well, Rose said. She's a smart girl. Rose looked around the room. Snow was melting outside on the roof, dripping down in front of the window. Now I have to ask you about Hoyt, she said. Has he been over here?

No ma'am, Luther said. We don't want him here. He ain't welcome with us no more.

You need to insist that he stay away. You understand that, don't you. He cannot be here.

We don't want to have nothing to do with him. We ain't even seen him. Have we, Betty?

We seen him that one time in the grocery.

We seen him that one time in the grocery, but we didn't talk to him. We never even said how you doing. Just went around the other way, didn't we?

And we ain't never going to talk to him again, Betty said. I don't care what he calls us.

Yes, Rose said. That's right. She studied them both but couldn't be sure they were telling the truth. Luther's great red face was damp with sweat, and Betty looked merely dull and sick, her lifeless hair hanging about her face. Rose looked out into the kitchen. That's fine, she said, I'm glad Hoyt hasn't been here, but it has to stay that way. Now I want to talk to you about something else. It's important for you and for your children that you live in a clean and safe environment. You know that. So you need to do a little better in the house here. Things are not as clean and orderly as they might be. You can do better, don't you think you can?

I told you I been sick, Rose, Betty said.

I understand that. But Luther can help too, can't you, Luther.

I already been helping, he said.

You need to do a little more. You can start by keeping the dishes washed. And by emptying the trash. You need to take that bag of pop cans out. They'll attract bugs.

In winter? Luther said.

It's possible.

Well somebody might steal my cans if I put them outside.

You can keep them on the porch.

I can't see how they're going to collect no bugs in winter.

In any case, they shouldn't be in your kitchen. They shouldn't be near where you eat.

Luther looked at her, and then he and Betty stared out the front window, their faces stony and obstinate.

Rose watched them. How're you doing with your money? she said. Are you still separating it into envelopes and paying your bills on time?

Oh, yes ma'am.

That's fine, then. Do you have any questions for me?

Luther looked at Betty. I don't have no questions. Do you, dear?

I don't, Betty said.

And I've been told you've been going to the parenting classes.

Luther nodded. There's only two more left, the teacher said.

Yes. Well, it appears that you're doing okay. I'm glad to see that. So I think I'll go now. But I'll come back again before long.

Rose slipped her notebook into her purse, and Luther opened the door for her, and outside in the car when she glanced back in the rearview mirror he was still standing barefoot on the porch, watching her drive away, and Betty was out of sight, somewhere in the house.

30

IN THE NEW YEAR VICTORIA ROUBIDEAUX RETURNED TO Fort Collins with Katie to begin the second semester of classes, and a week after she left Raymond called Linda May on the telephone in the mid-afternoon. When she answered he said: Are you likely to be home for a hour or so?

Yes. Why do you ask?

I wanted to stop by for a minute.

I'll be here.

The address in the phone book says eight thirty-two Cedar.

Yes. That's right.

He hung up and drove in to Holt to the Co-op Implement Store on the highway and went past the racks of tools and the box drawers of nuts and bolts and the spools of electrical wire and on to the back, where the snow shovels were hung from hooks like medieval weapons collected in some castle or armory. He looked among the metal shelves of car batteries, reading the brief tags attached to the sides, and finally selected one and carried it to the cash register. The clerk said: Raymond, this ain't hardly big enough for your pickup.

It ain't for my pickup.

The man looked at him. Okay then. I didn't know you had you a car. I just didn't want you to get the wrong battery and have to come back. You want to charge it or pay cash?

Put it on the ranch account, Raymond said.

The man punched in the numbers on the register and stood waiting, looking at nothing, and drew out the receipt when it appeared and spread it forward on the counter. Raymond signed it and folded away his copy, then hefted the battery onto his hip and went outside and pushed the battery across the front seat and got in. At the stoplight where the highway crossed Main Street he looked left toward the Gas and Go at the solitary car parked in front and looked to the right up Main Street, where just a few cars were moving at this time of day. When the light changed he drove ahead three blocks and turned north on Cedar. Her small white frame house was in the middle of the block, and the Ford convertible at the curb was crowded by snow from when the snowplow had gone through. There was more snow piled up along the walkway in mounds that had melted and hardened overnight, with winter grass showing dry and brown along the edges. He went up to her door and knocked. She came out at once, in a bright blue sweatshirt and sweatpants and her short dark hair was combed neatly. I've been standing at the window watching for you, she said. You sounded so mysterious on the phone.

I just brought you something. Could I ask to borrow your car keys?

What are you going to do?

I got something for your car.

Well, come in, she said. The keys are in the house. But I still can't tell what you're up to.

He stood in the front hall as she went back to the bedroom to get her purse. He looked in through the doorway. Above the couch in the living room was a framed print of a hazy lavender garden containing a rock bridge and a mist-shrouded pond of water lilies. It looked green and lush, unlike any place in Holt County. She came out and handed him the keys. It won't start, she said, if that's what you're thinking. I tried it just yesterday.

He put the keys in his pocket and went outside to her car and reached inside to pop the hood latch. Then he got a screwdriver and a pair of wrenches from the toolbox in his pickup and carried the new battery back to the Ford, balancing it on the fender as he raised the hood. He lifted out the old battery and put in the new one. After cleaning the battery clamps with his pocketknife, he attached the cables to the posts and tightened them down.

Linda May came out and stood beside him in the street in her coat and scarf. He hadn't seen her coming and looked up from under the hood.

Why, what in the world? she said.

Get in, he said. Give it a try. He held out her keys.

She took them. You replaced the battery?

Let's see if this one works.

She climbed into the car and Raymond stood beside her, at the open door. The engine ground and turned over and tried to start. She looked up and he nodded. When she tried again it ground and sputtered and popped and finally started, a burst of black smoke blowing out from behind the car.

Give it a little gas, he said. It needs to idle a while.

Thank you, she said. Thank you so much. What a nice thing for somebody to do. What do I owe you?

You don't owe me a thing.

Of course I do.

No, he said. Well, how about just making me a cup of coffee? We'll call it one of these after-Christmas bargain deals. I just thought you might want to run around town someday. I'll take this old battery back to the co-op and they'll get rid of it for you.

He shut the hood and put the dead battery in the bed of his pickup while she stood in the street watching him.

Won't you come in now? she said. It's cold out here.

If it isn't no bother.

Good Lord. Of course it isn't.

They went inside and he followed her into the kitchen where the late afternoon sun was streaming through the back window. He took off his hat and set it on the countertop, then pulled out a chair from the table and sat down. His iron-gray hair was dented at the sides where the hatband had pressed it. She moved to the stove and put the kettle on. Would tea be all right? she said. I only have instant coffee.

Whatever you got'll be fine.

She took down a variety from the cupboard. Red containers and little square boxes decorated with pictures and round canisters of loose tea. What would you care for? she said.

Oh. Just something regular.

I've got green tea and black tea and all of these herbal kinds.

It don't matter. You pick it out.

But I don't know what you want. You have to decide.

Just one of them. I don't hardly drink much tea.

I could make you instant coffee.

No, ma'am, tea's fine.

Now don't start calling me that again, she said.

The kettle started whistling and she poured boiling water into a large brown mug and put in a bag of black tea. He watched her at the counter, her back to him. She made herself a cup of green tea and put spoons in the mugs and brought them to the table. Do you use sugar?

I don't believe so.

You sound so tentative. She sat down across from him.

No. I don't reckon I'm too tentative.

But is something wrong?

Raymond looked around and fixed on the window over the sink. I just never been in a woman's kitchen before. Only my mother's.

Haven't you?

Not that I can recall. And I believe I'd recall it too.

Well. You just have to relax. It's okay, you know. You've done me a great favor. This is the least I can do.

He stirred the tea with his spoon though he had put nothing in it, then put the spoon on the table and sipped at the mug. The tea bag came up and burned his mouth so he fished it out with his spoon and put the spoon back on the table. He sipped again and looked at it and set the mug down.

She was watching him. You don't like it, she said.

No, ma'am, he said. I'm just going to let it cool a little. He looked at the pictures displayed on one of the walls, there was a young girl standing beside an oak tree. Who's that you got captured in the picture there?

That one?

Yes.

Well, that's my daughter. Rebecca.

Oh. I didn't know. You never mentioned a daughter before.

Oh yes. That's one of my favorite photographs of her. It was taken when she was much younger. We don't talk much anymore. She doesn't approve of me.

Doesn't approve of you. How do you mean?

Oh, it was something between us back in Cedar Rapids. After her father left.

Did you two have a fight?

You mean with Rebecca?

Yes, ma'am.

Sort of. Anyway she left the house and wouldn't come back. That was two years ago. I don't think about it much lately. She laughed sadly. Not too much anyhow.

Is that how come you to move out here?

That, and other things. Are you sure you don't want me to make some instant coffee? You're not drinking your tea.

No. But thanks just the same. This here's fine. He drank some of the tea and set the mug down and wiped at his mouth. He looked out the window and then at her. I don't believe Victoria and me's ever had a fight. I don't know what we'd have to fight about.

She's a lovely girl.

Yes. She is.

But you've only just gotten started with her, haven't you.

How do you mean?

We'll, she's only been with you for a short time, isn't that right?

She come out to us two years ago. About two and a half years ago now. We had a little bit of a rough time at first but things have worked out. At least I think so on my side. I can't speak for her.

She's very lucky to have you.

If she is, Raymond said, it goes both ways.

She smiled at him, then stood and carried the tea mugs to the sink and dropped the tea bags into the trash.

I'm afraid I'm keeping you, he said.

I would offer you supper. But I've got to get ready for work.

This is one of your work nights.

Yes.

I better get on towards home anyway.

He stood and walked to the counter and picked up his hat and looked inside the crown, then glanced at her and started toward the front door. She followed behind. As he passed through he looked about the rooms once more. In the front hall he put on his hat. You want me to shut off your car when I get out there?

Yes, if you would. I forgot all about it.

I'll just leave the keys on the seat.

Thank you again, she said. Thank you so much.

Yes, ma'am. You're welcome.

He cut off the ignition in the car and set the keys on the seat, then climbed into his pickup and drove around the block onto Date Street and turned south toward the highway. It was growing dark now, the early darkening of a short winter's day, the sky fading out, the night coming down. The streetlamps had flickered on at the street corners. When he came to the highway he sat for a moment at the stop sign. There was no one behind him. He was trying to decide. He knew what awaited him at home.

He turned right and drove to Shattuck's Café at the west edge of Holt and went in and sat at a little table by himself at the window, watching the big grain trucks and the cars going by on US 34, their headlights switched on in the evening dark, the exhaust trailing off in the cold air.

When the high-school girl came to take his order, he said he'd take a hot roast beef sandwich and mashed potatoes and a cup of black coffee.

Don't you want anything else? she said.

Not that I can get here.

Pardon?

Nothing, he said. I was just thinking out loud. Bring me a slice of apple pie. And some ice cream on the side too, vanilla if you got it.

31

VALENTINE'S FELL ON A SATURDAY AND HOYT WORKED from six in the morning until six in the evening at the feedlot east of town, riding pens in the blowing dirt and cold and doctoring cattle in the sick pen next to the barn, where a blackbaldy steer with bloody scours kicked him in the knee, then loosed itself on his jeans while he was trying to push it into the chute. At the end of the day he caught a ride into town with Elton Chatfield in Elton's old pickup.

They decided to stop for a beer at the Triple M out on the highway to wash the dust out of their throats, and an hour later they were invited to sit in on a game of ten-point pitch at the card table in the back room. In the following two hours the four old men playing at the table managed to take from Hoyt twenty-five dollars and from Elton nearly fifteen, and afterward bought them each a shot of whiskey out of their own money.

In the meantime Laverne Griffith had been waiting for Hoyt since five-thirty, and she had passed through a number of emotions by the time he arrived at home. She had been sad and blue, and for a while she had worried something might have happened to him, but for much of the time she had simply felt sorry for herself, so by nine o'clock she was mad. She was waiting in the kitchen, drinking gin with the lights off, when she heard him climb the outside stairs and open the front door.

Laverne, you ready, girl? he called.

You son of a bitch, where have you been?

Where are you? How come you haven't turned any lights on?

I'm out here in the kitchen. For all you care.

He walked back to the kitchen in the dark and felt for the light switch, then looked at her. She was sitting at the table already dressed in her party clothes, a black blouse and white jeans, and her face was rouged and her eyes were made up thickly with mascara. The glass of gin sat before her.

Damn, girl, Hoyt said, you're looking good. He leaned over and kissed her on the side of the face.

Well, you're not, she said. And you stink of cow shit.

A steer emptied on me this morning while I was trying to head him. I'll just grab a shower, then I'll be ready.

Don't bother. She looked at him and turned away. I'm not going.

What do you mean you're not going?

You didn't even bring me a box of chocolates, did you.

Chocolates?

It's Valentine's Day, you son of a bitch. You didn't even know that. I'm nothing to you. I'm just a place to stay and somebody to fuck in bed when you feel like it. That's all I mean to you.

Oh hell. You're all upset. I'll buy you chocolates tomorrow. I'll buy you five boxes of chocolates if that's what you want.

He bent and kissed her again and put his arm around her and poked his hand down into the loose front of her blouse. She slapped at his hand.

Don't, she said.

Why what's wrong here?

What do you think is wrong.

Hell, I'm ready to go. Soon as I take a shower.

I'm not going anywhere with you. I told you. You can just get the hell out of here too.

Honey, now this ain't like you, he said. This don't sound like my girl.

She took up her glass and took a long drink. He watched her.

You got to quit that drinking. That's what it is. You're already drunk and we ain't even got out of the house yet.

He took her glass away and walked across the kitchen and poured the gin into the sink. Laverne came up out of her chair. She stumbled toward him and slapped him hard in the face.

Don't ever tell me what I can do in my own goddamn house. Her eyes were wild. She brought her hand up and slapped him again.

You crazy bitch, he said.

He hit her smartly in the face with his open hand, and she spun half around and sat down all at once on the floor.

I'm going to go shower, he said. And you can calm your ass down. Then we'll get out of here for the night.

When he went back to the bathroom, she stood and grabbed a long metal cooking spoon she'd been stirring their chili with, and lurched after him. He was sitting on the toilet, pulling off his boots, and she began hitting him over the head and about the shoulders with the heavy spoon, spattering chili on his face and shirt and jacket.

Goddamn it, Hoyt shouted. You stupid bitch. Quit it.

He rose up and took hold of her shoulders, spinning her around in the little bathroom, neither of them saying anything at all but both panting furiously, and he grabbed her hand and bent it back until she let go of the spoon. The spoon clattered on the floor. Then he released her, but immediately she scratched desperately at his face, and he shoved her away and she fell backward into the shower curtain, grabbing wildly at anything, and tore the curtain loose from the rod and crashed into the bathtub.

Look what you done, he said. Are you satisfied now?

Help me out of here, she whimpered. Her eyes were wet with tears. She was half wrapped up in the curtain.

You going to quit?

Help me out of here.

Tell me you're going to quit.

I quit. All right? I quit. You son of a bitch.

You better behave.

He pushed the curtain aside and pulled her by the hand and stepped back, waiting, but she only looked at him. Her makeup had run and her eyes were awash with mascara. Without a word she hurried out of the bathroom and ran through the apartment to the bedroom closet where she grabbed an armful of his shirts, hangers and all, and then rushed back into the front room. He was standing in the kitchen doorway and, when he saw what she was doing, came forward to stop her, but she'd already thrown the door open and flung his shirts through the door out across the stair landing into the night, his flannel work shirts and his good western shirts alike, all drifting and sailing to the ground as in some dream or fantasy.

There, she cried. I did it. Now get out. Get out, you filthy bastard. I'm done with you.

Then Hoyt hit her in the face with his fist.

She fell back against the door and he wrenched it open and went leaping down the stairs to collect his shirts, ducking and bobbing across the yard as he picked them up.

Laverne pulled herself up and shoved the door closed, locked it, and stood looking out the narrow window, panting. She wiped at her nose with her shirt cuff, leaving a smear across her cheek. Her soft woman's face looked like a Halloween fright mask now. The mass of her maroon hair was all undone.

Hoyt came pounding back up the stairs with his shirts under his arm and tried to turn the knob. Bitch, he said. You better let me in.

Never.

You goddamn bitch. You better open this fucker.

I'll call the police first.

He hammered on the door, then stepped back and rammed it with his shoulder, glaring back at her through the little window.

You're going to be sorry for this, he said.

I already am. I'm sorry I ever met you.

He spat at her face in the window and it dribbled slowly down the glass. He stood and watched it for a moment, then walked back down the stairs. He looked around but the houses along the street were all quiet and dark. He walked toward downtown as far as Albany Street, and hid the shirts under a bush across from the courthouse, then went on to the tavern at Third and Main. He was still wearing his work clothes, his flannel shirt, the denim jacket spattered with chili, and his manure-stained jeans. He entered and went directly to the bar.

BY MIDNIGHT HE WAS WEAVING DRUNKENLY ON THE STOOL next to an old local man named Billy Coates who had long dirty white hair and lived alone in a tarpaper house north of the railroad tracks. Hoyt had been telling him his tragic story for an hour and Coates finally said: They's the davenport if you want it. If you don't got nowheres else to go.

I don't have no place else, Hoyt muttered.

I got a dog but you can just push him off. He won't bother you any.

When the tavern closed, they walked to Albany Street to collect Hoyt's shirts. The shirts were frozen stiff and Hoyt gathered them up and carried them like boards under his arm, then followed Billy Coates across the tracks to his house, and immediately fell to sleep on the davenport in the front room. The old mongrel dog whined for a while but finally curled up on the floor next to an old coal oil heater, and they each—man and man and dog—slept soundly until Sunday noon.

32

WHEN THE CALVES CAME IN FEBRUARY, RAYMOND ROSE two and three times in the freezing night to check on the cattle he had noticed were showing springy and had begun to bag down, having moved the cattle into the corrals and loafing shed next to the barn in the days before. Once he was there he would check that the nose and the front feet were exposed and started out as normal, or he would catch the laboring cow and pull the calf with the calf-chain, ratcheting the calf out, and sew the cow up afterward and doctor her with antibiotics. So, for weeks of these indistinguishable days and nights, he was exhausted, he was worn out almost beyond thinking. He still had the ordinary daily chores and the hay-feeding to do as always, which by themselves would have been almost too much for one man to do and keep up with, but he was doing all of it alone now, since his brother had been killed in the previous fall. He went on regardless. He went on in a kind of daze. He found himself falling asleep at the kitchen table, noon and night and sometimes, though he'd just risen, in the mornings too when he sat down to his meager solitary hurried meal. Then he would wake an hour or two later, with his neck stiff and his hands numb and his tongue as dry as paper from having breathed through his open mouth for too long with his head lolled back against the chair back, and with the food before him already long gone cold on his plate and the black coffee on the table no longer even tepid in his cup. Then he would sit up and rouse himself and look around, study the light or the lack of it in the kitchen window, and push himself up from the old pinewood table and get into his canvas coveralls and overshoes again and pull on his wool cap and step outside into the winter cold once more. And then walk across the drive to the corrals and calving shed to begin it all again. This routine, day and night, lasted for something over a month.

So it was already the start of March before he felt rested enough to think he might allow himself a single night's vacation in which to drive to town once again to the tavern on Main Street.

HE SET OUT ON A COOL FRESH NIGHT, DRESSED AGAIN IN his town clothes and his Bailey hat. He had shaved and washed up and had put on some of the cologne that Victoria had given him at Christmastime. It was a Saturday night, the sky overhead clear of any cloud, the stars as clean and bright as if they were no more distant than the next barbed-wire fence post standing up above the barrow ditch running beside the narrow blacktop highway, everything all around him distinct and unhidden. He loved how it all looked, except he would never have said it in that way. He might have said that this was just how it was supposed to look, out on the high plains at the end of winter, on a clear fresh night.

In Holt he parked at the curb in front of the *Holt Mercury* newspaper offices, closed and darkened for the night, and walked up the block past the unlit stores to the corner. Inside the tavern it was just as before. The same noise and desolate country music, the men shooting pool at the tables in the back and the TV blaring over the bar, the long room just as crowded and smoky as it had been in December—all of it the same, except maybe a little more of it now, a little more gaiety, since it was a Saturday night.

He stood at the door and saw no one that he might sit down with, so he went up to the bar as he had that other time and ordered a draft beer and got it and paid for it and then turned to survey the room. He drank from his glass and wiped the palm of his hand across his mouth. And then he saw that she too was there again, sitting by herself in a booth, looking off to the side. Her short dark hair had grown out a little, but it was Linda May.

He took his glass of beer and walked back past the tables of patrons toward her booth, stopping once to let somebody pass in front of him, then she saw him coming toward her and she sat looking at him without moving, without anything showing in her face. He stood at the booth and removed his hat and held the hat in one hand at his side.

Raymond, she said. Is that you? She spoke too loudly. She was wearing a red blouse that was unbuttoned deeply at the neck, and above the throat of the blouse she wore a silver necklace and there were silver hoops in her ears. Her eyes looked too shiny.

Yes ma'am, he said. I reckon so.

What are you doing?

Well. I come out for a night. I thought I would. Like I done that other time.

She seemed to study him. Have you been here long? she said.

No. Not long.

How have you been?

Okay, I reckon. I guess I've been pretty good. I've been kind of busy. He looked at her dark hair and shining eyes. How about yourself?

She started to say something but turned to peer toward the back, and then turned forward again and took up her glass and drank.

Ma'am, he said. You okay?

What?

I said, are you okay? You seem a little disturbed.

I'm all right.

How's your car running?

She looked at him. My car.

Yes ma'am. It wouldn't start that other time.

Oh, that. No, it's fine. I thank you for getting me the battery. It starts every time now. She made a little gesture with her glass. Why don't you sit down.

If you wouldn't mind.

No. Please do.

He sat opposite her and set his glass of beer on the table and laid his hat on the seat beside him.

How's that young girl and her baby? she said.

Victoria? They're both doing pretty good, I believe. They're back in Fort Collins.

She looked around again, peering toward the back of the room, and this time her eyes changed. Raymond followed her gaze and saw a tall red-haired man with a considerable stomach approaching the booth. He stopped and stood for a moment, then slid in beside Linda May and rested his arm on her shoulder. You attracted you some company while I was gone, he said.

This is a friend, she said. Raymond McPheron. I took care of him at the hospital one time.

I hope you took good care of him.

I did.

How you doing, old buddy?

Raymond looked at him across the table. I don't believe I know your name, he said.

Why hell, don't you know me? I thought everybody knew me around here. I'm over at the Ford dealership.

I drive a Dodge, Raymond said.

That would explain it, the man said. Cecil Walton, he said. He lifted his hand into the air above the table and Raymond looked at it and then shook it once, briefly.

Can I buy you a drink—what'd you say your name was?

His name is Raymond, Linda May said. I told you.

That's right, you did. But I forgot. Is that all right with you?

I didn't mean it that way.

Okay then. So Ray, can I buy you a drink?

I have one, Raymond said.

How about another? I need one myself. And I know this little lady does. Don't you. He looked at her.

Yes, she said.

The man looked out across the room and began waving his hand. He kept looking and he waved and whistled once through his teeth.

Linda May was sitting close beside him, leaning against the shoulder of his green corduroy shirt. There. She seen me, the man said. She's coming over.

The young blonde barmaid walked up carrying a bar tray with empty glasses balanced on it. She looked tired. You ready for another round, Cecil? she said.

Does the bear shit in the Vatican?

I don't know. I'm too wore out. So what's it going to be?

The same for me and her. And whatever our buddy here wants.

I wouldn't care for anything, thank you, Raymond said.

Have a drink, Ray.

I don't think so.

You sure?

Yes.

The blonde woman left and went back through the crowded room toward the bar. The man across from Raymond watched her walk away in her tight jeans, then bent and kissed Linda May on the side of the face. I'll be right back, he said. I want to talk to this guy over here. He come in the other day looking at new cars and I'm going to sell his ass one of them yet. You go ahead and get caught up with your friend here.

He got up and walked to a nearby table where a fat man was sitting with two women and drew out a chair and sat down. He said something and they laughed. Linda May was watching him closely.

You sure you're all right? Raymond said.

She turned back. Yes. Why?

No reason, I reckon. I think I'll head on home.

You just got here.

Yes ma'am, I know.

But is something wrong?

There ain't nothing wrong. This is the best of all possible worlds, ain't it.

I don't understand. What did you come here for? What did you think was going to happen?

I don't think I had any clear idea about that. I just kind of thought I'd come in and have a drink and see if you was here.

But where have you been? It's been almost two months.

I got kind of busy.

But my God, did you think I was waiting for you? Is that what you thought? Don't you know anything?

No ma'am. I don't believe I do. He stood up out of the booth. Anyway, you take good care of yourself now.

Raymond?

It's been nice to see you, he said.

He reached for his glass and his hat and walked away. He drank down the rest of the beer and set the glass on the windowsill next to the front door and pulled his hat down tight over his head as though he were expecting high winds and stepped outside. He'd been in the tavern for no more than fifteen minutes.

He walked up the wide sidewalk along the dark storefronts and climbed into his pickup and drove south out of town. There was no car or other vehicle out on the highway. At home he parked in the garage and walked back across the graveled drive.

When he reached the wire gate he stopped and stood looking back toward the horse barn and the cow lots. Then he raised his head and peered up at the stars. He spoke aloud. You dumb old son of a bitch, he said. You dumb old ignorant stupid son of a bitch.

Then he turned again and went through the gate up into the dark quiet house and pulled the door shut behind him.

Part Four

33

SHE WAS SIXTEEN NOW AND BETTY NOR LUTHER HAD
seen her in the twelve years since she was taken away by court order
and placed in a series of foster homes in Phillips. A tall ripe-looking
blonde girl with a loose-boned body and blue eyes like her mother's,
she had her father's long thin nose and square face. Her father was
not Luther. She had never known her father and had no desire to. He
was living in the Idaho State Prison, serving a ten-year sentence for
assault and armed robbery. Betty had met him in that long-ago summer when she was just twenty-two and still loose-boned and ripe
herself, and he'd disappeared after spending only a single month
with her. No one in Holt County had seen or heard from him since.
Betty had given their daughter her maiden name, Lawson, and her
own dear dead mother's two first names, Donna Jean.

The girl showed up one night toward the end of March at Luther
and Betty's trailer house three hours after they'd gone to bed. She
stood at the door in the cold until Luther came out in his ragged
underpants. What you want? he said.

I'm Donna, she said.

Who?

Donna. Don't you even know me?

She stood looking at him, wearing only a thin black raincoat against the cold and no scarf or gloves. She smelled of cigarette smoke and cheap wine.

Donna, he said.

Yeah.

How do I know that's you?

Well fuck yes, it's me. Who else would it be? Let me in. It's freezing out here. Isn't my mama at home?

She's here. She's trying to get her sleep.

Wake her up. I ain't going to do nothing. I got kicked out. I have to find a place to stay for the night.

I guess you can come in.

He stood back and allowed her to pass and the tall blonde girl stepped into the front room and peered about. Luther went back to the bedroom and woke Betty.

What is it? she said.

You better get up and come look.

What for?

Come out here and see.

Betty rose from bed and put on her robe and walked out sleepily to the front room. Don't tell me, she said, looking at the girl. Is that you?

It's me, the girl said.

Oh Lord. Oh my little girl. Betty rushed across the room and threw her arms around her and hugged her neck. The girl stood stiffly in her arms. Betty began to sob, patting her head. Oh my God. Oh my God. She leaned back to look at her. I ain't seen you in so long. And look at you. So growed up. I just been hoping. Praying every day. Ain't I, Luther.

Yes, ma'am, he said. Sometimes more than once.

What happened? Betty said. I tried calling you but that last woman you was with, she wouldn't even let me talk to you.

I got kicked out, the girl said. She stepped back away from Betty's arms.

She got kicked out, Luther said. That's how come she showed up here. Looking for her mama.

I need a place to stay, the girl said. That's why I come here.

You still ain't said what happened, honey.

It's that woman, the girl said. She's just a total bitch. It's all she is. She wouldn't let me do nothing. I had to go to church with them all the time and then she tried to stop me from seeing Raydell.

Who's he?

This boy I know.

What's wrong with him?

There ain't nothing wrong with him. She's just prejudiced. He's half black and half white. She didn't appreciate his black half.

Where's he at now? Is he here?

Here? What would he be doing here? He's back in Phillips. He lives there.

Then how'd you get over here, honey?

I got a ride from this man in a truck. I was out there on the high-way waiting for a ride, freezing my ass off.

I don't think you should be out this time of night. Something could happen to you.

What's going to happen?

Something.

Oh, he never tried nothing. I wouldn't even let him get started.

It's still dangerous like that to be out in the cold this time of night.

What else was I going to do? I thought you'd let me stay for a while.

Oh honey, course you can stay. It's just so good to see you. Are you hungry? You want me to make you a bite to eat?

I want to smoke one of my cigarettes.

You smoke?

Sure.

Betty looked around. But we don't usually let nobody smoke in here, she said. On account of Joy Rae and Richie.

Who're they?

You don't even know, do you. Your own half sister and half brother.

I never even heard their names before.

Well, that's who they are. You got family you didn't even know about.

That's right, Luther said. You got all kinds of family here. He grinned. But you two going to want to stay up and talk. Me, I'm going back to bed.

When he left the room Betty took the girl's hand and led her to the kitchen table. Why don't you sit down here a minute. At least let me make you something hot to drink. I know you got to be thirsty.

The girl looked around the kitchen. This is a mess, she said.

I know that, honey. But you'll hurt my feelings if you talk like that. I been sick.

Well, it is.

I'm going to clean it up. Betty removed a few dirty dishes to the counter and stacked some in the sink, then she set a jar lid in front of the girl.

What's that for?

You go ahead and smoke if you only going to smoke a little. It's your first night, honey. I'm just so glad you come home.

SHE MOVED IN AND SLEPT THAT FIRST NIGHT ON THE couch in the front room. In the morning they introduced her to Joy Rae and Richie. The two children looked at her with suspicion and said nothing to her. After they left for school, she went back to sleep until noon, and then took a shower while Betty made lunch.

The girl soon grew bored in the trailer and went out and walked downtown in the bright cold windy afternoon in her black raincoat and wandered into the stores. She loitered in Weiger's Drug and at Schulte's Department Store she looked at clothes hanging from the metal pipe racks. She tried on a long pink evening gown with a low-cut bodice while a nervous clerk watched her. The dress suited her tall body and made her look older and more sophisticated. For a long time she studied herself in the mirrors, turning to see how the dress looked from the side and the back, holding her hands as she had seen women do in magazines, then she took off the dress and put it back on the hanger and handed it to the woman. I changed my mind, she said. I wouldn't care for it. She went outside again and crossed Second Street and walked up to the middle of the block to Duckwall's.

In Duckwall's she wandered back into the aisles and picked up various items and examined them, and after about fifteen minutes, while the salesclerk at the cash register was ringing up a sale, she pocketed a tube of lipstick and a small tin container of mascara and eye shadow, then drifted slowly away to look at hand mirrors and purses and came up to the front of the store to the stands of greeting cards, and stood there for a while reading the messages, and finally walked out of the store onto the broad sidewalk.

The children had come home on the bus by the time she returned to the trailer, and Betty then told Joy Rae to let her big sister move into her bedroom. Both of you can sleep in the same bed. You have to get to know one another sometime.

Joy Rae was upset and frightened but the girl said: I got something to show you.

What is it?

The girl turned to her mother. We'll be all right, she said.

Because you're sisters, Betty said.

They went down the hall to Joy Rae's orderly bedroom. Sit down, the girl said, and shut the door.

What are you going to do?

I ain't going to hurt you. Sit down. I want to show you something. Joy Rae sat on the bed as the girl took the lipstick and the mascara from Duckwall's out of her purse. I'm going to show you how to make up your face, she said. How old are you?

Eleven.

Well, shit. I was already kissing boys and wearing Make a Promise lip dew by then. You're way behind. You're awful young-looking, aren't you. Kind of skinny.

Joy Rae looked away. I can't help it. It's just the way I am.

Well, don't worry about it. We'll fix you up. The boys in this little shit-ass town are going to go nuts over you. They're going to want to eat you up. She smiled. Or wish they could.

What are you going to do?

I'll show you. Lift up your face. That's it. Well shoot, you're kind of pretty too, did you know that?

No.

You are. I can see it. You're going to get prettier too. Like me.

The girl bent over her half sister and brushed mascara on her eyelashes and penciled on eyeliner. Stop blinking, she said. You want to fuck this up? You can't blink your eyes while I'm doing this. She angled the younger girl's chin a little and brushed on eye shadow, then stood back to inspect her and twisted open the lipstick tube and outlined the top lip and dabbed a quick deft spot on the bottom. Smooch them together, she said. Yeah, like that. But not so much.

How do I?

Like this. She showed her, then stood back again. Don't you want to see what you look like?

Yes.

She stepped across the room and took a hand mirror from the dresser and held it in front of her. Well?

Joy Rae studied herself in the mirror, lifting her head and turning her face. Her eyes opened wider. It don't even look like me.

That's the point.

Can I keep it on?

Why not? I ain't going to stop you. Girl, you're ready to go. Then she lit a cigarette and sat down beside her on the bed.

When Betty called them to supper, Joy Rae came out with the makeup still on her face, and she sat down in her customary chair, looking steadily across the room, waiting.

Hey now, Luther said. Who's this? Look at my little girl.

Betty looked at her and said: Oh, I don't know if she's old enough for that.

She's got to learn, the girl said. Who's going to teach her if I don't?

They sat at the table and ate packaged salisbury steak and french-fried potatoes and bread, with ice cream for dessert, and Joy Rae said very little to anyone while they ate but only looked at them out of her strange new eyes.

After supper when everyone had gone to bed, the girl telephoned Raydell in Phillips and talked to him for a long time. You miss me? she said. Tell me what you'd do if you was allowed to see me. And what he answered her made her laugh.

The next morning Betty allowed Joy Rae to wear the lipstick to school, but it wasn't until recess that anyone said anything about it. Then three of the girls crowded around her and asked if she had the lipstick tube with her, and she told them it belonged to her big sister. They wanted to know since when had she gotten a big sister and Joy Raè said she had always had one, except she had never seen her before. They wanted to know when they could meet her. Maybe she could do their faces too.

THE FOLLOWING DAY SHE WAS BACK IN DUCKWALL'S wandering the aisles in the late afternoon. When she was satisfied nobody was watching, she slipped a woman's clasp purse from a display table into the pocket of her raincoat. Then she drifted again through the aisles and after a while she started out of the store. But the lady clerk stepped in front of her. You plan on paying for that?

For what?

That purse in your pocket. I saw you take it. She pulled the purse out and held it up.

Oh. I forgot I put it in there.

You were going to steal it.

Like hell I was.

The hell you weren't.

The lady called the manager out of his office in the back, a tall stringy man with a hard little paunch. What's going on? he said.

This girl here stole this purse.

I wasn't going to steal it.

Yes she was.

Do you know shoplifting's a crime? the manager said.

I wasn't shoplifting, you dumb asshole. I forgot I had it in my pocket.

You better just watch that dirty language. And you can sit right there. He pointed to a chair near the door. Call the police, Darlene, he told the clerk.

The lady made the call and the girl sat on the chair and glared and waited. The manager stood over her. After a while a patrol car drew up to the curb in front of Duckwall's, and a sheriff's deputy in a dark blue uniform with a leather belt and revolver came inside, where the manager explained what happened. Is that right? the deputy said.

No, the girl said.

What's your side of it then?

I wasn't stealing nothing. I forgot to pay, that's all. I forgot I had it in my pocket.

You have the money to pay for it?

From her coat pockets she drew out cigarettes and matches and a little plastic purse that contained only coins.

He looked at her. I haven't seen you before, he said. Who are you?

Donna Lawson.

Where do you live?

I'm staying with my mama and her husband on Detroit Street.

Who's that?

Luther and Betty Wallace.

The deputy studied her. All right, he said. He turned to the store manager. I'll take care of this.

I don't want her back in this store.

She won't be back in this store. Don't worry.

She better not.

The deputy led her by the arm out to the car and opened the back door and she got in. He came around and got in behind the wheel and backed away from the curb and drove to Detroit Street and stopped in front of the trailer. This is it, isn't it?

Yeah, the girl said. She started to get out.

Where you going? he said. Did I tell you to get out?

No.

You wait till I tell you. Shut the door.

She pulled it closed. What do you want?

I'm going to tell you something before we go in there. I'll give you a break this time. But you better watch yourself. You're going to end up in more trouble than you can even imagine, more trouble than you ever thought there was in this world.

I didn't do anything.

Yeah. I heard you before about that. That's just bullshit. But you and me both know that's what it is. Because I know what a girl like you can do. I've seen it over and over again. And I bet you've never been in the backseat of a car before either.

What do you mean?

You know exactly what I mean.

Go to hell.

That's right. Just keep that up. But you better mind me. Hear?

The girl sat looking at his face in the mirror.

I said, did you hear me.

Yes, she said. I heard you. All right? I heard you.

Okay. Let's get this over.

They got out of the car and walked up the dirt path to the trailer. Inside, the officer told Betty and Luther what the girl had been accused of. He said that she shouldn't be wandering around the streets and that they had to be more careful and keep better control of her. And why isn't she in school? he said.

She just got here, Luther said. We ain't had no time to put her in her classes yet.

Well, she better start going. As it is, she's got too much time on her hands. I'll be checking back with you on this.

After he left, Betty and Luther tried to talk with her, but within five minutes she got fed up. Oh, fuck you, she said, and went back and lay down on Joy Rae's bed. She didn't come out for supper, but instead took the phone into the room and called Raydell to tell him to come get her. Raydell said it was too late. You better come over here, goddamn it, she said. You better come get me.

She stayed in the bedroom with Joy Rae until eleven that night. Then Raydell drove up in front of the trailer and honked the horn, and she came out to the front room where Betty and Luther were sitting on the couch. Don't try and stop me, she said.

Betty began to cry and Luther said: You can't go. Think about your mama.

Fuck you, you fat fucker. And I'm sick of my mama. Look at her. She makes me sick. This ain't my family. I don't have no family.

Then she slammed the door and ran out the path to the car. She slid in beside the boy and the car roared away, headed up Detroit Street, pointed toward the highway and out of town.

Hearing the car speed away, Betty threw herself on the floor and began to thrash about and wail and kick. She kicked over the coffee table. Luther bent over trying to quiet her. It's going to be all right, honey, he said. It'll turn out okay. She didn't mean them things she said. The two children Joy Rae and Richie came out of their rooms and stood in the hall, watching their parents, not at all surprised by what they saw, and after a while they turned and went back to bed.

In her bedroom Joy Rae went through the items on her dresser but the lipstick and mascara were gone now. She looked at her face in the hand mirror. Only a faint trace of red still showed on her mouth.

34

IN THE NIGHT SHE WAS LYING IN THE BACK BEDROOM with the blond man from the bank. Dena and Emma were asleep in their room up the hall, and it was a springlike night and the window was open to the fresh air and Mary Wells and Bob Jeter were talking softly in the dark. You don't have to leave, she said. I don't care about the neighbors. There's just the two old widow women next door. They'll talk anyway.

I better go, he said.

Please, she said. She was lying on her side facing him, her arm across his chest. Isn't it nice here? Stay with me.

What about your daughters?

They're beginning to get used to you. They like you already.

No they don't.

Why do you say that?

They don't care for me at all. Why would they?

Why wouldn't they? You're nice to them.

I'm not their father.

Stay, she said. Just for a while longer.

I can't.

Why not?

Because.

Because you don't want to.

That's not it, he said. He slid out from under her arm and turned away and rose from the bed, and in the dark he began to collect his clothes. Moving about the room he hit his foot against the leg of a chair. He cursed.

What happened? she said.

Nothing.

I'll turn the light on. She switched on the bedside lamp and watched him dress. Unlike her husband in Alaska, this man was very careful about his dressing. He stepped into his underwear, settling the waistband and drawing out the seat, and pulled on his shirt and pants and stood spreading his knees to support his pants while he tucked in the shirttail, then he buckled the leather belt with its thin brass clasp and afterward sat on the bed and pulled on his dark socks and dark shoes. His hair was disordered and he stood bent-kneed before the mirror at her dresser and combed his thin blond hair neat again and combed through his mustache and goatee. Then he put on his suitcoat and shot his shirt cuffs.

She was lying on her side with the sheet over her, watching him. One of her shoulders was exposed, it gleamed and was very pretty in the light. Give me a kiss before you go, she said.

He stepped to the bed and kissed her, then walked noiselessly down the hall and out through the front room into the cool night air. She got up from bed with the sheet around her and followed him, watching him drive away on the vacant street, seeing him pass under the corner streetlamp, then onto Main and out of sight. Shadows from the lamp were like long stick figures thrown out behind the trees and all along the street were the quiet mute fronts of houses. She sat down in the dark room. An hour later she woke shivering and went back to her bed.

AFTER THAT NIGHT A WEEK PASSED WITHOUT HIS CALLING in the evening as he had before. She waited until the middle of the following week and he still hadn't called, and then she called him twice in one night from her dark bedroom, but he made excuses about why he couldn't talk, and the second time she called he hung up without waiting for her to say anything more than his name. The next day at mid-morning she went to see him at the bank.

His office was in the back corner, with a glass window that looked out into the lobby. She could see him sitting at his desk talking on the phone when she stepped inside. A woman at the reception desk asked if she could help but Mary Wells said: No, you can't help me. I came here to see him. Then he was off the phone and she went into his office and sat down as if she had come to see about a loan or a second mortgage.

What are you doing? he said.

I came to see you.

I can't talk now.

I know that. But you won't talk to me on the phone. So I had to come here. You're through with me, aren't you.

He took up a long silver pen from his desk and held it in his fingers.

You are, aren't you. You ought to at least be able to say it.

I think we ought to slow down for a while, he said. That's all.

Slow down, she said. What chickenshit.

He stared at her and leaned back in his chair.

You're very timid, aren't you, she said.

No.

Yes. Yes, you are. I understand that now. You want your fun but you don't want any complications. You're still a little boy.

I think you'd better go, he said. I've got work to do. I'll call you later.

You'll call me later?

Yes.

No you won't. You won't call me. You think I'm that stupid? That pathetic? She stood up. And you have work to do now, don't you.

Of course. This is my office. This is where I work.

That's very interesting, she said. And you'd like me to leave, wouldn't you. You'd like me to walk out and not make any fuss. Isn't that right? She looked at him. He didn't say anything. Okay, she said. Then she bent over his desk and swept all the papers onto the floor.

He rose up and caught her wrist. What in the hell do you think you're doing?

She wrenched her wrist free and shoved the phone onto the floor. That's what I think of you and your work. You little chicken-shit. You timid little boy.

Are you going to go now?

You know, I think I am. Because you know what? I'm through with you. I'm dumping you. I'm the one this time. And don't call me. Some night you're going to get lonely and start remembering what it was like in bed with me and how nice I was to you and then you're going to want to call, to see if you can come over for a little while, but don't do it. I'll be over you by that time, you scared little chicken-shit boy. I won't answer the phone. I don't ever want to talk to you again.

She walked out of his glassed office into the lobby. The cashiers and the people in line at the counters and the woman at the reception desk were all watching her, and she looked at them and then she stopped. She stood in the middle of the lobby to address them.

He's not a very good fucker, she said. I don't know if any of you knew that. He never was much good in bed anyway. I deserve better. Then she went outside to the street and got in her car and drove home.

And at home she went to pieces. She scarcely got up to make the girls breakfast or to see them off to school in the morning, and she was often still lying in bed in the back room, drinking gin and smoking, when the girls came home in the afternoon. They would come to her room and stand in the doorway and look at her. Sometimes they would lie down on the bed beside her and go to sleep in that place that used to be so pleasant and comfortable. More often now the two sisters would fight with each other when they were at home and she would call to them to stop, but other times she would simply get up and shut the door and light a cigarette and lie down again.

Outside, the trees beyond her window along the alley began to bud into leaf in the warm advancing days of early spring. But she lay in bed, smoking and drinking, staring at the ceiling as the light moved across the white flat surface as evening descended, and all the time she was lost in her troubled thoughts. The only thing she felt proud of herself about was that she had not called Bob Jeter again. She took some satisfaction in that. And she hoped very much that he too was suffering in some important way.

35

WHEN VICTORIA ROUBIDEAUX CAME HOME TO RAYMOND at spring break she had a boy with her. He was a tall thin boy, with wire glasses and close-cropped black hair, and he had a little gold earring hooked through one of his ears. They came up to the house in the evening in the blue shadows under the yardlight and she was carrying Katie in her arms. When they entered the kitchen Raymond moved away from the window where he'd been watching them, and Victoria kissed him as she always did and he hugged her and the little girl. I want you to meet Del Gutierrez, she said.

The boy came forward and shook Raymond's hand. Victoria's told me a lot about you, he said.

Is that so? Raymond said.

Yes, she has.

Then you got me at a disadvantage. I don't believe I've heard the first thing about you.

I did too tell you about him, Victoria said. The last time we talked on the phone. You're just trying to be obstinate.

Maybe you did. I can't recall. Anyway, come in, come in. Welcome to this old house here.

Thank you. It's good to be here.

Well, it's pretty quiet. Not like in town. Where you from, son?

Denver.

From the city.

Yes sir. I've been there all my life. Until I went to college.

Well, things are a little different out here. Kind of slow. Anyhow, if you're a friend of Victoria's you're welcome.

They went back to the car and brought their bags in and afterward Victoria made a light supper. It was a quiet awkward meal. Victoria did most of the talking. Afterward Raymond took the little girl into the parlor and sat her on his lap in the recliner chair and read the paper and talked to her a little while her mother and the boy did the dishes. Katie had been shy of him at first, but warmed up over supper and now was asleep, curled against his shoulder. Raymond peered out into the kitchen above the top of his newspaper. He couldn't make out what they were saying but Victoria looked to be happy. Once the boy leaned over and kissed her, then looked up and saw Raymond was watching them.

Victoria made up the bed for Del Gutierrez in Harold's old room upstairs, and Raymond watched the ten o'clock news and weather on television, then said good night and went up to bed. He lay awake for a time listening for what he might hear, but he couldn't hear anything from downstairs and after a while he went to sleep, and then he woke when the boy entered the room across the hall and shut the door. He lay there thinking how long it had been since he'd heard anyone moving about in his brother's room.

The next morning the boy surprised him. He was drinking coffee at the kitchen table when Raymond came downstairs in the slanted light of early morning. I never expected to see you at this hour, Raymond said.

I thought you might let me help you do something, the boy said.

Do something.

Outside. Whatever you have to do.

Raymond looked around the kitchen. Did you make this coffee?

Yes.

Were you planning on sharing it?

Yes sir. Can I get you a cup?

Oh, I believe I know where we keep the cups. Unless they got moved since last night.

He took down his usual cup and poured some coffee and stood

looking out the window with his back to the boy. Then he finished and set the cup in the sink. All right, he said. You can come out with me if that's what you think you want to do. I've got to feed out, then we'll come back in for breakfast later on.

All right, the boy said.

You have any warm clothes?

I brought a jacket.

You'll want something warmer than that.

Raymond handed him his brother's lined canvas chore jacket from the peg by the door. There's gloves in the side pocket. You got a hat?

I don't usually wear one.

Here, wear this. He handed the boy Harold's old red wool cap. I don't want to think what Victoria would say if I got your ears froze off the first day you got here.

The boy pulled on the old cap. In his wire glasses and with the earflaps hanging loose beside his head, he looked to be some manner of nearsighted immigrant farmhand from an era much earlier.

Well, Raymond said. I guess you'll do. He put on his coat and cap and gloves and they went outside.

They walked out through the wire gate and crossed to the haylot east of the barn where the ancient red sun-faded Farmall tractor was hooked up to the flatbed hay wagon next to the stack of bales. A cold wind was blowing out of the west, the sky obscured by streams of cloud. Raymond told him to climb onto the stack and throw down the bales while he stacked them on the wagon. We might as well do a good load, since you're here, he said.

They worked for most of an hour. The boy threw down one bale after another, each one bouncing on the worn plank floor of the wagon, and Raymond set them in place, stacking them in tiers. After a while the boy took his coat off and they went on working. Then Raymond called a halt and climbed down from the wagon and got up into the seat of the tractor. Let's go to it, he said.

Where should I ride? the boy said.

Stand here on the draw bar. And hang on. You don't want to get yourself dumped off and mashed under these iron wagon wheels.

The boy put his coat back on and stepped up behind Raymond, holding on to the back of the metal seat, and they went clattering and bouncing out of the haylot into the pasture, rocking across the rough ground on a track through the sagebrush and soapweed, and on out to where the mother cows and calves were milling about and shoving into one another, waiting for their morning feed.

Raymond braked to a stop. You think you can drive this tractor?

I don't know. I've never driven one before.

Climb up here and I'll show you.

They traded places and Raymond showed him which gear to use so the tractor would creep along, and indicated to him the two foot brakes and the clutch and the hand throttle.

I expect you've drove a stick shift before.

I've done that much.

There isn't anything to it. Just keep it in compound and let it crawl. Give it a little gas when you need to, going up any rise.

The boy sat in the metal seat and they started out, the tractor rocking and heaving.

You want to head out this way, Raymond said. Follow that trail of worn ground there where I been feeding.

Along there?

You think you can do that?

Yes.

All right then. Let's feed these cattle.

Raymond climbed onto the hay wagon and pulled the twine from the first bale, draped the twine over an upright, and broke the bale open and shoved it off the side onto the ground, and they went creeping ahead as he broke and scattered the next bale, and the hungry cattle and calves began to bunch and feed, strung out in a long line behind the lurching wagon, their heads all lowered, a fog of steam and hot breath above them. From the tractor the boy looked back to see how things were going and he saw the old man working steadily, shoving the loose hay out on the ground. Then he looked forward again and noticed a deep dip in the ground ahead of them where the sand was hollowed out. He turned sharply to miss it and the corner of the hay wagon rode up the cleats of the tractor wheel as far as the first stringer, tilting the wagon bed at a sharp dangerous angle and lifting the bed four feet off the ground. Raymond hollered at him. The boy turned to look and slammed on the brakes, then turned back again. Raymond was holding on to the upright.

The boy's face had turned to ash. Oh shit, he said. What'd I do?

You turned too sharp. You can't turn that sharp pulling something behind you. Turn it hard the other way now.

Did I hurt the wagon?

Not yet. But turn it hard and go slow.

Maybe you better come up and do it.

No. Go ahead. You'll do all right. Just take it slow.

I don't know about this.

Go on now. Try it.

The boy sat forward in the seat and cranked the steering wheel to the left and slowly let out the clutch. The tractor made a sharp turn and the corner of the wagon bumped down the tractor wheel's big cleats, splintering the wood a little, and then the wheel was free and the hay wagon stood flat on the ground again.

Straighten it out, Raymond hollered. But real slow or you'll have her up on the wheel again.

The boy drove forward and the wagon swung around behind the tractor, and when he looked back Raymond waved for him to go on. He drove very slowly, staring straight ahead past the exhaust stack as they crossed the cold worn ground. After a while Raymond hollered for him to stop, then stepped down from the wagon and climbed onto the back of the tractor. That'll do for today. Take us up to the haylot.

I think you better drive.

How come? You're doing okay. But shift up. We don't want to stay in grandma all the way home.

What about what I did back there?

That happens. You just don't have to do it twice. Pay attention next time and it'll be all right. Let's go have us some breakfast.

The boy shifted gears and they moved bumping and rocking out of the pasture. Raymond climbed off to shut the gate and the boy parked inside the fence at the haylot and turned the tractor off, and together they walked up to the house under the thin clouds.

I don't see how you manage to do all this by yourself, the boy said.

You don't?

No sir. It seems like too much for one person to do.

Raymond looked at him. What else you going to do?

The boy nodded and they went on.

IN THE KITCHEN THE LITTLE GIRL WAS SITTING AT THE table over a coloring book and Victoria was standing at the stove. When she saw Del Gutierrez in Harold's canvas chore coat and old wool cap, with the earflaps dangling free beside his red cheeks, she said: Now wait. Stand right there till I get my camera.

No you don't, Raymond said. You leave him alone. Del and me, we been outside working, feeding cattle. We don't need no pictures.

I got to keep warm, don't I? the boy said.

You look warm all right, Victoria said. Just look at you. Then she laughed and they stood looking at her, seeing how white and straight her teeth were, how her thick black hair fell across her shoulders, how her black eyes shone, and they both felt at once awkward and speechless in the presence of such beauty, to see her in this way, having themselves come in from the cold and the wind and the blowing dirt, to find her waiting for them, laughing and amused by something they'd done. It made Raymond think suddenly of his brother and he was afraid he might embarrass himself and begin to weep. So he said nothing. He turned away and he and the boy hung up their coats next to the door and washed at the sink.

Victoria had breakfast ready for them. She brought the platters of eggs and bacon and buttered toast and poured out cups of coffee and they all sat down at the pinewood table in the kitchen. The little girl reached her arms out and said: Poppy, so Raymond took her onto his lap and they began to eat.

You think you could make a rancher of him? Victoria said.

Raymond stopped eating. I don't know, he said. He looked at her. I guess he might make one. He did pretty good this morning.

Did you have him drive the tractor?

Yes, ma'am. He did pretty good at it too. He turned to look at the boy. Course I can't say much for that earring he's wearing. I guess that hole in his ear might grow in after a while, but I haven't had no experience with that kind of thing.

The boy's face went red and he touched his ear. He grinned across the table at Victoria.

I think he should just keep it the way it is, she said. I like it.

ON FRIDAY OF THAT WEEK VICTORIA AND DEL GUTIERREZ decided to go to the movie in Holt. They didn't care what was being shown, they wanted only to get out of the house and to do something on their own, and Raymond encouraged them to have dinner at the Wagon Wheel Café before the show, and he gave the boy forty dollars for helping him with the ranch work. Before they went out, he drew Victoria into her bedroom and pulled the door closed. What's wrong? she said.

Not a thing, he said. Then he told her in an old man's loud whisper: He's a pretty good hard worker, isn't he.

What are you talking about? she said.

That boy's been doing pretty good this week. Working pretty hard.

Do you think so?

Yes I do.

He told me about the trouble he had driving the tractor that first time.

He didn't have to tell you that.

He said you weren't much upset about it. That you didn't yell at him or anything.

Well, it didn't break nothing, and everybody has to do that once. He did all right. Anyway, you just might want to think about keeping him around.

Victoria looked at Raymond. He was watching her closely. Now what is it you're saying? she said.

I just mean you might want to keep this one. He's okay with me. I kind of like him.

That sounds like you're trying to rush me, she said.

I'm not rushing you, he said. Hell, I ain't rushing a thing. He looked a little hurt at such a suggestion. I'm just saying he's not a bad young fellow. I ain't saying anything else. Now you two go on out for dinner and I'll take care of Katie. It'll be my pleasure. All I'm saying is this boy and me, we might get on together. And I'll tell you something else. It looks to me like he flat thinks the world of you too.

Maybe he does, she said. But I've already made a fool of myself once. I'm in no hurry to do it again.

I know, honey. You'd have to feel that way. Of course you would. But that don't mean you got to end up like me, either.

What about that woman you were seeing?

What woman?

Linda May. The woman that was here for New Year's dinner.

That's what I'm talking about, Raymond said. I don't know nothing about this kind of thing. Maybe I sort of thought I was seeing her, but she sure as hell had no idea she was seeing me. No, all I want is for you to be happy.

I am happy, she said. Don't you know that? And so much of that is because of you. Now do you suppose I ought to get ready so Del and I can go out tonight?

Yes, ma'am, I believe you should. I'm just going to get out of here and leave you to it.

VICTORIA PUT ON THE SOFT BLUE CASHMERE SWEATER that set off her black hair and put on a short gray skirt, and the boy was wearing a pair of good black jeans and a plaid shirt, and they drove out in her car to Holt to eat dinner and to attend the movie. After they were gone Raymond and Katie were busy in the kitchen. He warmed up some leftover ham and gravy, with mashed potatoes and creamed corn, and the little girl sat on her box on a chair at the table, and while they ate he looked across at her and listened. She was taking regular bites as she talked, and she went on without stop, talking about whatever came into her mind, with no need for Raymond to remark on any of it at all, though he paid heed to all she said, whether it was about a girl he didn't know at her day care in Fort Collins or about some black-and-white dog that barked in the yard below their apartment. For dessert he got out a quart container of chocolate ice cream and they ate some of that too while she continued to talk, sitting on her box at the table like some miniature black-haired black-eyed church woman at some basement bazaar, like some tiny Presbyterian female starved for the sound of her own voice. Then they cleaned up the kitchen, and she stood on a chair beside him to help rinse the dishes, still talking, and afterward they went into the bathroom and she climbed onto a little wooden stool in front of the sink and brushed her teeth. Then he took her into the downstairs bedroom and she put on her pajamas and they both lay down in the ancient double bed and Raymond began to read. He didn't read long. Three pages into the book he was already falling asleep. She poked him and touched his weathered face with her hand, feeling along his stubbled chin and the loose skin at his neck. He woke and turned to look at her, then squinted and cleared his throat, and read another page before drifting off again, and now she lay close beside him and went to sleep herself.

When Victoria and Del Gutierrez came home at midnight, the old man and the little girl were lying in bed under the bright overhead light. Raymond was snoring terrifically, his mouth wide open, and the little girl was burrowed into his shoulder. The book he had started reading lay off to the side among the quilts.

36

EARLY ON SATURDAY EVENING MARY WELLS GOT HERSELF out of bed and she and the girls drove to the Highway 34 Grocery Store at the edge of town to do the shopping that had not been done in days. There was nothing to eat in the house and Mary Wells was indifferent whether she had food or not, but the girls were hungry.

On the highway east of Holt a man from St. Francis Kansas was pulling a gooseneck stock trailer behind his Ford pickup, hauling five purebred Simmental bulls. He'd meant to sell the bulls in the fall, but his wife had been so sick that he had never gotten around to it, because of the daily care and the hurried trips to the hospital and finally the wearying bitter arrangements for her funeral. Now he was hauling the bulls to the sale barn in Brush for the auction on Monday, planning to feed and rest the bulls on Sunday, and make sure they drank enough that their weight was up so he could get all he could for them though it was not an opportune time to sell bulls.

He was not driving fast. He never did drive fast when he was pulling a stock trailer, and he made a particular point of slowing down because of the increase in traffic at that hour and more especially because of the glare of the setting sun shining in the windshield. He entered Holt and then a car suddenly pulled out in front of him from the grocery store parking lot.

Mary Wells was driving the car. Ten minutes earlier she had seen Bob Jeter standing at the refrigerated meat case in the Highway 34 Grocery Store beside a blonde woman, and Bob Jeter had had his arm wrapped around the woman's waist.

Her older daughter, sitting in the passenger seat beside her, saw the pickup coming toward them and shouted: Mama! Look out!

The man from St. Francis did what he could to stop, but he had all that weight behind him and the pickup crashed into the side of the car and drove it skidding across the highway into a light pole that broke in half and fell over, dragging the wires down.

The younger girl, Emma, sitting in the backseat behind her mother, was thrown against the back door and knocked unconscious. Mary Wells's head was slammed against the driver's-side window and when her head cleared she discovered she could not move her left arm. It had already begun to throb. Next to her, Dena had been hurled forward and sideways, and a piece of the windshield had made a long deep gash through her right eyebrow and cheek. When the car rocked to a stop she cupped at her face with her hands. And then her hands filled with blood and she began to scream.

Honey, Mary Wells cried. Oh my God. She brushed the girl's hair away from her face. Look at me, she said. Let me see. Oh Jesus. Blood was streaming down her cheek onto her shirt, and her mother wiped at it, trying to stop it.

Across the street a man in the parking lot ran back into the grocery store and called for an ambulance, and it came roaring up within minutes and the attendants jumped out and pried open the doors on the one side of the car and lifted Mary Wells and the two girls into the ambulance and raced them to the emergency room at Holt County Memorial Hospital on Main Street, just a few blocks away.

THE PICKUP, THE STOCK TRAILER, AND THE CAR WERE still blocking traffic, and the five tan-and-white bulls had stumbled out of the trailer when the tailgate had crashed open. Men from other cars and pickups were trying to herd them into a makeshift pen of vehicles at the edge of the road, but one of the bulls was lurching about, slipping on the blacktop, bellowing, its left hind leg severed almost in two at the joint, with the lower half flopping and dragging behind. The bull kept stumbling, trying to put his back foot down, while the blood pumped steadily out onto the pavement. The man from St. Francis kept following the bull, shouting: Somebody shoot him. Goddamn it, somebody shoot him. But no one would. Finally a man produced a rifle from the rack in the cab of his pickup and handed the rifle to him. Here, he said. You better do it yourself.

A patrolman who was directing traffic saw the rifle and came running over. What do you think you're doing? You can't fire off a gun out here.

By God, I'm going to, the man from St. Francis said. You want to let him suffer like that? I've seen all the suffering I'm going to see for a while.

You're not going to shoot off that gun.

You watch me. Get out of the way.

He walked up to the bull, shouldered the rifle and shoved the end of the barrel point-blank at the bull's head, then pulled the trigger. The bull dropped all at once to the pavement, rolled over on its side and quivered and finally lay still, its black eyes staring at the streetlamp. The man from St. Francis stood looking down at the dead bull. He handed the rifle back to the man who owned it, then turned to the patrolman. Now go ahead and arrest me, goddamn it.

The officer looked at him sideways. I ain't going to arrest you. How am I going to arrest you? I'd have a goddamn riot on my hands. But you never should of done that. Not in town.

What would you of done?

I don't know. Probably the same damn thing you just did. But that don't make it right. By God, there's a law against shooting a gun off inside city limits.

AT THE HOSPITAL THE DOCTOR SEDATED THE OLDER GIRL and put seventeen stitches in her face while Mary Wells waited outside in the emergency room with her limp arm hanging painfully, supported in the palm of her hand. She cried quietly and wouldn't let anyone attend to her arm until they had completed the surgery on her daughter. In the bed near the wall the younger girl was now coming awake. She had a severe headache and there were abrasions on her arm and a blue knob forming on her forehead. Though they would have to watch her through the night, it appeared she would recover well enough.

The doctor finished sewing up the older girl's face and they wheeled her out and brought her into the emergency room. She was still asleep and her face was bruised and yellow where it wasn't bandaged. Mary Wells stood looking down at her.

That will all heal, the doctor said. It was a clean cut. She's fortunate it didn't involve the eye.

Will it scar? Mary Wells said.

He looked at her. He seemed surprised. Well yes, he said. It usually does.

How much?

We can't tell that yet. Sometimes it turns out better than we think. She'll probably want to have a series of treatments with a cosmetic surgeon. That would take some time.

So she'll have to go through life until then, looking like this?

Yes. The doctor looked down at the girl. I can't predict how long that will take. She'll have to heal completely before they can do anything more.

Oh God, what a fool I am, Mary Wells said. What a stupid little fool. She began to cry again and she took up her daughter's hand and held it to her wet cheek.

THEY KEPT ALL THREE OF THEM IN THE HOSPITAL overnight for observation. In the evening one of the police who had been out on the highway came to the hospital and left a traffic ticket, for reckless driving and the endangerment of life, and he informed Mary Wells that her car had been towed away.

The next morning a nurse drove them home. Mary Wells's arm was in a sling, and she and the girls each walked up to the house with great care. Inside the house it was quiet. It felt as if they had been gone for days. Will you come out to the kitchen, please? Mary Wells said. Please, both of you. I want you to help me say what we're going to do now. I don't know what that will be. But we have to do something.

They sat down at the table. The younger girl sat watching her mother, listening, but the older girl, Dena, sat with her head turned away. She kept touching the bandage on her face with the tips of her fingers, feeling along the edges of the tape, and she refused to look at her mother and would not say anything at all. She had formed an idea already of what was coming for herself.

37

WHEN RAYMOND AND THE BOY CAME UP TO THE HOUSE after working outside all that Saturday afternoon, Victoria said it would be a good idea if they both took a shower and cleaned up before they sat down to supper. Do we smell that bad? Raymond said.

It wouldn't hurt you to clean up a little.

You go ahead, the boy said. I'll shower after you.

If that's what it takes to get any supper around here, Raymond said. All right then.

He went back to the bathroom and showered and scraped off the bristles on his face and came out with his hair wetted down, wearing a freshly laundered pair of work jeans and a worn-out flannel shirt. Victoria said supper was ready and they should sit down and eat.

You're going to let him eat without cleaning up first? Raymond said. How come?

He's not as dirty as you were. And you've taken so long in the bathroom this food'll burn up if we don't eat it now.

Well by God, Raymond said. That don't seem fair. It sounds like you got favorites, Victoria.

Maybe I do, she said.

Huh, he said.

They sat down together at the table in the kitchen as they had for each of the meals that week, and before they had eaten much of their supper a pickup drove up in the yard and stopped in front of the house. Raymond went out onto the little screened porch to see who it was. Maggie Jones and Tom Guthrie were coming up through the wire gate.

You timed it about right, Raymond said. We just sat down to eat. Come on in.

We've already eaten, Maggie said.

Well. Is something wrong?

We came out to see you. There's something we want to talk to you about.

Come in. I'll be done eating pretty quick. Can it wait that long?

Yes, of course, Maggie said.

They came inside and Victoria brought chairs from the dining room. Raymond started to introduce Maggie and Guthrie to Del Gutierrez, but Maggie said they had met the night before at the movie theater.

Then I guess we're all acquainted here, Raymond said. He turned to Victoria. They say they don't want to eat. Maybe they'll drink some of your coffee.

Victoria poured them each a cup and Raymond sat down and began to eat again. Victoria and Maggie talked about school and about Katie's day care in Fort Collins. Then Raymond was finished and he wiped his mouth on a napkin. What did you want to talk to me about? Can you talk about it here, or is it something we better go into the other room for?

We can talk about it here, Maggie said. We just came out to take you into town to the Legion. To the firemen's ball.

Raymond stared at her. Say that again, he said.

We want to take you out dancing.

He looked at Tom Guthrie. What in hell's she talking about? he said. Has she been drinking?

Not yet, Guthrie said. But we'll probably have a few drinks pretty soon. We just thought we'd better get you out for a night.

You did.

Yes. We did.

You want to take me to the firemen's ball at the Legion.

We figured we'd come out and pry you loose. You wouldn't go otherwise.

Raymond looked at him and turned and now he looked at Victoria.

Yes, why don't you? she said. I want you to have some fun.

I thought you kids would want to go into town again yourselves. This is your last night. You have to go back to school tomorrow.

We need to get packed and you can't do anything to help with that. Why don't you go? I want you to.

He looked across at the boy and Katie as if they might be of some help. Then he looked at nobody. It just appears to me like this is a goddamn conspiracy, he said. That's what it appears like.

It is, Maggie said. Now go put on your town clothes so we can get going. The dance has already started.

I might do that, he said. But I'm going to tell you something first. I've never been so pushed around in all my life. I don't know if I care for it, either.

I'll buy you a drink, Maggie said. Will that help?

It'll take more than just one drink to wash this down.

You can have as many as you like.

All right, he said. I seem to be outvoted. But it's not right, to treat a man like this in his own house. In his own kitchen, when he's just trying to settle his supper.

He stood up from the table and went upstairs to his bedroom and put on his good dark slacks and the blue wool shirt Victoria had given him and got into his brown boots, then he came back downstairs. He told Victoria and Del and Katie good night, then followed Maggie Jones and Guthrie outside. They waited for him to get into Guthrie's old red pickup, but Raymond said he would drive his own vehicle so he could come home when he wanted to. At least you can't stop me from doing that, he said.

But we'll follow you into town, Maggie said. So you don't get lost on the way.

Well, Maggie, Raymond said. I'm beginning to think you got kind of a mean streak in you. I never noticed it before.

I'm not mean, she said. But I've been around you men for too long to harbor any illusions.

You hear that, Tom?

I hear it, Guthrie said. The best thing to do is just go along with her when she gets like this.

I guess so, Raymond said. But I'll tell you what. She's going to make me think of a barn-sour horse yet, if she keeps on this way.

THEY DROVE OUT THE LANE AND ALONG THE GRAVEL county road onto the blacktop, the headlights of the two pickups shining into the night one after the other along the barrow ditches. Then they entered town and turned west on US 34. There was a wreck across from the grocery store and the highway patrol routed them around it. They went on through town and parked in the crowded graveled lot outside the white-stuccoed American Legion and went downstairs and paid the cover charge to a woman sitting on a stool at the entrance to the barroom and dance hall. A country band was playing at the back. The music was loud, and the long smoky room was already filled with people standing two and three deep at the bar and sitting in the booths along the walls, and there were more people clustered at the foldout tables in the big side room where the sliding doors had been pushed back. Men in western suits and women in bright dresses were dancing in the thin scatter of sawdust on the floor in front of the band.

Come on, Maggie said. Follow me.

She led Raymond and Guthrie to a dark booth in the far corner that a friend from school had been saving for them. It's about time, the woman said. I couldn't have kept it much longer.

We're here now, Maggie said. Thank you. We'll take care of it.

They sat down. Raymond peered around in silent amazement and interest. There were other ranchers and farmers he knew, out for a Saturday night of dancing and partying, and a great number of people from town. He turned to look at the band and the people out on the floor dancing in wide circles. Presently a barmaid came up and they ordered drinks, then Guthrie and Maggie got up to dance to a song she said she liked. While they were gone the barmaid brought the tray of drinks and Raymond paid for them, and then the band stopped for a break and stepped down off the riser, and Maggie and Guthrie came back to the booth looking sweaty and red-faced and sat down across from him.

Did you pay for these? Guthrie said.

Yeah. It's all right.

I still owe you a drink, Maggie said.

I ain't forgetting.

Good, she said. I'm not either.

Maggie drank deeply from her glass, then she stood up and said she'd be back in a minute. Don't let him disappear, she said to Guthrie.

He's not going anywhere, Guthrie said.

The two men drank and talked about cattle, and Guthrie smoked, and Raymond asked him how his boys were doing, and all around them the big room stayed alive with movement and noise.

BEFORE THE BAND STARTED UP AGAIN MAGGIE RETURNED to the booth. With her was a woman Raymond didn't know. She was short and middle-aged with curly dark hair, and she had on a shiny green dress with a bright floral pattern and short sleeves that revealed her round fleshy arms. Raymond, Maggie said, I want you to meet someone.

Raymond stood up out of the booth.

This is my friend Rose Tyler, Maggie said. And Rose, this is Raymond McPheron. I thought it was time you two got to know each other.

How do you do, Rose said.

Ma'am, Raymond said. They shook hands and he glanced at the booth. Would you care to join us?

Thank you, she said. I would.

She slid in and Raymond sat down beside her on the outside edge of the seat. Maggie sat down beside Guthrie across from them. Raymond put his hands forward on the table. He removed his hands and set them in his lap. Would you care to have a drink? he said.

That would be a very good idea, Rose said.

What would you like?

A whiskey sour.

He turned and peered out into the crowded dance hall. I wonder what you got to do to get that barmaid to come back, he said.

The band was playing a fast song, and Maggie nudged Guthrie and they stood up.

Where you two going? Raymond said. You're not leaving, are you?

Oh, we'll be back, Maggie said, then they moved out onto the floor and Guthrie swung her out and they began to dance.

Raymond watched them. He turned toward Rose. Maybe I should move over there to the other side.

You don't have to, she said.

Well. He drank from his glass and swallowed. I'm sorry, I don't believe I've ever heard of you, he said. Do you mind if I ask you about yourself?

I've lived in Holt a long time, Rose said. I work for Holt County Social Services.

Welfare, you mean.

Yes. But we don't call it that anymore. I take care of people who need help. I have a caseload and try to help these people sort out their lives. I distribute food stamps and see that my clients get medical treatment, that kind of thing.

It must be a hard job.

It can be. But what about you? Rose said. I know you live out in the country. Maggie tells me you have a cattle ranch south of town.

Yes ma'am. We have a few cattle.

What kind?

Mostly crossbred blackbaldys.

I think I know that means they're black with white faces.

Those are the ones. That's correct.

I've heard of you, she said. About you and your brother. I suppose everybody in Holt heard about two men out in the country taking in a pregnant girl to live with them.

It was kind of hot news for a while, I guess, Raymond said. I didn't much care for it myself. The way people talked. I couldn't see how it was much of anybody else's business.

No, Rose said. She looked at him and touched his arm. And I'm so sorry about your brother. I heard about that too. It must have been very hard.

Yes ma'am, it was. It was pretty bad.

He looked out to the dance floor but couldn't see Maggie and Guthrie. Finally he said: I wonder what become of that barmaid.

Oh, she'll be here after a while, Rose said. Wouldn't you care to dance while we're waiting?

Ma'am?

I said wouldn't you care to dance.

Well, no ma'am. I don't dance any. I never have done any dancing.

I have, she said. I can show you.

I'm afraid I'd step all over your toes.

They've been stepped on before. Will you try it?

You don't think we could just sit here.

Let me show you.

Ma'am, I don't know. You'd be awful sorry.

Let me worry about that. Let's try.

Well, he said. He stood up and she slid out of the seat and took his hand and led him onto the floor. People were swirling around in what seemed to Raymond a violent and complicated commotion. The band finished the song to a small scattered applause, then began another in slow four-beat time. Raymond and Rose Tyler stood in the middle of the dance floor, and she drew his hand around the soft silky waist of her dress and set one of her hands on the shoulder of his wool shirt. Now just follow me, she said. She clasped his free hand and stepped back, pulling him toward her. He took a little step. Don't look at your feet, she said.

What am I supposed to look at?

Look over my shoulder. Or you could look at me.

She moved backward and he followed her. She backed again and he stayed with her, moving slowly. Can you hear the beat? she said.

No ma'am. I can't think about that and not step on you at the same time.

Listen to the music. Just try it. She began to count softly, looking at his face as she did, and he looked back at her, watching her lips.

His face was concentrated, almost as if in pain, and he was holding himself back from her, so as not to press too close. They moved slowly around the floor among the other dancers, Rose still counting. They made a complete circuit. Then the song ended.

All right, thank you, Raymond said. Now I guess we better sit down.

Why? You're doing fine. Didn't you enjoy it?

I don't know if you'd say enjoy exactly.

She smiled. You're a nice man, she said.

I don't know about that, either, he said.

The band began to play again. Oh, she said. A waltz. Now this is in three-four time.

The hell it is.

She laughed. Yes, it is.

I wasn't even getting used to that other kind yet. I don't know a thing about waltzes. Maybe I better take my seat.

No you don't. You just have to count it out. Like before. I'll teach you if you let me.

I suppose I can't do no worse than I already done.

Put your arm around me again, please.

Like before?

Yes. Exactly like before.

He encircled her waist with his arm and she began to count it out for him. They moved slowly, one step, two steps, sliding around the floor, part of the crowd. Rose kept them moving.

LATER THEY WERE SITTING IN THE BOOTH AGAIN WITH Maggie Jones and Guthrie and they had each taken a second drink and were talking, and then a tall heavy man in a string tie and a brown western suit came up and asked Rose if she would care to dance. Raymond looked at her. All right, she said. He stood up and she slid out of the booth and the man led her onto the floor. Raymond watched them. The man knew how to dance, and was light on his feet despite his weight, and he twirled her around and they disappeared among the crowd of dancers.

I guess I'll go on home now, Raymond said.

Why ever would you do that? Maggie said.

Because I know how this comes out.

No, you don't. She's only dancing with him. She'll be back.

I don't know that.

He turned toward the floor again as Rose and the man came swinging past.

Just wait, Maggie said. You'll see.

Then the music ended and the man brought Rose back to the booth and thanked her. Raymond stood as she slid past him onto the seat and then sat back down beside her. There were little drops of sweat at her temples and her hair was damp at the edges of her face, her cheeks bright red. Would you get me another drink, please? she said.

I believe I can do that, Raymond said. He caught the eye of the barmaid and ordered them each another drink and they all began talking where they'd left off. After a while the big man in the string tie came back again to ask if Rose cared to dance, but she said she would sit this one out, that she was happy where she was.

Then Maggie and Guthrie went over to the bar to see some people they knew. Raymond waited until he saw they were talking with the other people, then turned back to Rose. Can I ask you something?

If you want to, Rose said.

I don't even know how to ask it.

What do you want to know?

Well. I just want you to tell me right now if I got any chance of seeing you again. If you got somebody else hiding in the bushes I wish you'd tell me, so I don't make a fool of myself.

She smiled. Hiding in the bushes? What bushes?

Any bushes.

There's nobody hiding in the bushes.

There ain't.

No. So does that mean you might call me?

Yes ma'am. That's pretty much what it does mean.

When?

How about some night this coming week? Maybe you'd let me take you out for supper.

I'd look forward to it.

Would you?

Yes, I would.

Then I guess I'll call you.

Then I guess I'll be waiting.

Ma'am, I'll be waiting myself, Raymond said.

THE DANCE ENDED AT MIDNIGHT AND THE LIGHTS CAME on in the dance hall, and the people in attendance at the firemen's ball got up and moved up the stairs to the parking lot. Raymond walked Rose Tyler to her car and wished her good night, then turned toward home. Out in the country the wind had stopped and the entire vault of the moonless sky was crowded with stars. When he stepped out of the pickup, the house was dark and Victoria and Katie and Del Gutierrez were all in their beds. In the kitchen he turned the light on and got down a glass and drank some water, standing at the window looking out where the yardlight was shining across the outbuildings and over the horse barn and corrals.

Then Victoria came out to the kitchen in her nightgown and robe. She looked sleepy and dark-eyed.

Did I wake you? he said.

I heard you out here.

I thought I was being quiet.

How was it? she said. Did you have a good time?

I did.

What did you do?

Well, I spent most of the night with Tom and Maggie and a woman named Rose Tyler. Are you acquainted with her?

I don't think so.

She's a pretty nice woman.

What did she look like?

What did she look like? Well, she had dark hair. And she was about the same size as you, only not so thin.

What was she wearing?

I believe she had on a green dress. Kind of silky to the feel. She looked nice in it too.

And did you dance with her?

Yes ma'am. I was a dancing fool. She got me out there.

What kind of dancing?

Well, for one thing we did the waltz.

I don't even know how to do that.

All you got to do is count it out. It's three-four time Rose said.

Show me.

Now?

Yes.

Okay then. He took her hand and she set her other hand on his shoulder.

Go ahead. What's wrong?

I'm trying to remember. Then he began to count and they danced twice around the kitchen table in a slow swaying movement, the old man with his stiff iron-gray hair and wool shirt and dark slacks, and the black-haired girl just risen from bed, come out to the room in her blue robe.

Thank you, she said when they had stopped.

I had me a good time tonight, he said.

I'm so glad.

And I know one other thing too. There's a young girl that had her finger mixed up in this.

I might have had something to do with it, Victoria said. But not the dancing. I didn't know about you and Rose Tyler.

He kissed her forehead. But don't you do nothing else. I want to think I can manage the next step by myself.

38

ON AN EVENING IN THE MIDDLE OF THE WEEK RAYMOND drove into Holt in his pickup. He had shaved and showered and put on cologne, and again was wearing his dark trousers and blue wool shirt and the silver-belly Bailey hat. After Rose invited him inside, he looked around the front rooms of her house, at the good furniture and the lamps and the good pictures on the walls. Raymond, how are you tonight? she said.

I'm doing okay, he said.

Shall we go?

Yes ma'am. Whenever you're ready.

I'm ready now.

Where would you like to eat?

You decide, Rose said.

Well. Would the Wagon Wheel Café suit you?

That'd be fine, she said.

He walked her out to the pickup and opened the door and she slid onto the seat holding the skirt of her dress in place. In the warm spring night she was wearing a light cotton dress the color of peaches and a thin pale-green sweater.

You look awful nice, Raymond said when he came around and got into the cab. That's a real pretty dress you're wearing. It's a different one from last time.

Yes, she said. Thank you. You look nice too, Raymond.

Oh, I wouldn't say that.

Why wouldn't you?

Ma'am. Look at me.

I am looking at you, Rose said.

AT THE WAGON WHEEL CAFÉ OUT EAST ON THE HIGHWAY there were a great many cars and pickups in the parking lot, and when they got inside the front door of the café people were standing about in groups, waiting to be seated. The hostess wrote Raymond's name on her list and said it would be about twenty minutes.

Would you rather wait outside? Rose said.

Will she find us out there?

I'm sure she will.

Outside, Rose sat down on the brick ledge of the café's flower bed. More people were coming in from the parking lot.

I should of made us a reservation, Raymond said. I never thought so many people came out in the middle of the week.

It's because it's such a pleasant night, Rose said. It's finally spring-time.

Yes ma'am. But I still didn't think we'd have so much competition.

A middle-aged couple stopped to speak with Rose, and she said: Do you know Raymond McPheron?

How do you do, the man said.

I'm doing pretty good. If I could get us something to eat, I'd be doing even better.

How long have you been waiting?

We just got here. But the woman said it'd be about twenty minutes.

It better be worth the wait, hadn't it.

I have nice company to wait with anyhow, Raymond said.

HALF AN HOUR LATER THE HOSTESS STEPPED OUTSIDE THE door and called Raymond's name and they followed her to a table in the second room, and Raymond held Rose's chair out, then sat down across from her. The hostess left their menus on the table. The waiter will be with you in a minute, she said.

Raymond looked around the crowded rooms. I was in here with Victoria about a year ago, he said. With her and Katie. But not since. I just thought of this place because this is where she and Del come last week. It's no telling how soon we'll get waited on.

Is there any rush? Rose said.

He looked across the table at her and she was smiling at him. Her hair was shining under the light and she had taken her sweater off. You're right. I better quit talking about it.

Aren't you having a good time?

I wouldn't be no other place right now, Raymond said. It's just kind of late to be eating supper, that's all I mean. He looked at his watch. It's getting awful close to seven-thirty.

You wouldn't do well in New York or Paris, would you.

I wouldn't even do very good in Fort Morgan, he said.

She laughed. Let's relax and enjoy ourselves.

Yes ma'am. That's the right idea.

IN FACT, THE WAITRESS CAME RIGHT THEN, A YOUNG woman whose face was flushed from hurrying back and forth in the crowded rooms. She and Rose knew each other. You're really busy tonight, Rose said.

Isn't this crazy, for a Wednesday, she said. I'm about to lose my mind. Can I get you something to drink?

Rose ordered a glass of the house wine and Raymond ordered a bottle of beer, then the young woman rushed away.

It looks like you about know everybody here, Raymond said.

Oh no, not everyone. But quite a few.

While they waited, another couple paused to speak with Rose, then the waitress brought their drinks and they each ordered a steak and a baked potato and salad, and then Rose held up her glass and said: Cheers.

Happy days to you, Raymond said, and they clinked glasses and drank, and Rose smiled at him.

Happy days to you too, Raymond.

Later, after their steaks had been served, an old man on his way out of the café came over wearing his black hat, and Raymond was able to introduce Rose to someone she didn't know. This here's Bob Schramm, Raymond said. I want you to meet my friend Rose Tyler. Bob here has a nice place out north of town.

Schramm took his hat off. Not like the McPherons' place, he said. How you been, Raymond?

Well, I'm doing all right.

You take care then. Ma'am, it was a pleasure meeting you.

Schramm put his hat back on his head and left, and they talked and ordered another round of drinks. Rose explained to Raymond that she had a grown son who lived on the western slope. Her husband had died twenty years ago of a heart attack at the age of thirty. No one expected it, she said. There had been no warning and no one on his side of the family had had heart trouble before. Afterward she had raised their son by herself, and he'd gone on to study at the university in Boulder and now was an architect in Glenwood Springs, and married, with two little boys. I see them as often as I can, she said.

So you're a grandmother, he said.

Yes. Aren't I lucky.

Yes ma'am. I'm pretty lucky myself, he said. Having Victoria and Katie in my life.

I knew Victoria's mother, Rose said. She came in to Social Services one time, but she wasn't eligible.

Well, she come out to the house one time too, Raymond said, not long after Katie was born. Showed up at the house one afternoon kind of unexpected. I think she had in mind to get close to Victoria again, but her and Victoria didn't get along. Victoria didn't want anything to do with her. I didn't say nothing about it myself, it was up to her to decide. Anyway, I think her mother went off to Pueblo where she come from originally. I ain't saying anything against the woman. But it was kind of miserable for a while there.

THEY FINISHED THEIR DINNER AND RAYMOND GOT THE check from the waitress and paid it.

Let me leave the tip, Rose said.

You don't need to.

I know. But I want to.

They went outside to his pickup. The parking lot was half empty now and a soft breeze was blowing. Raymond opened the door for her and she got in.

Would you care to drive out in the country a little ways? she said. It's such a nice night.

If you'd care to.

Rose rolled the window down and Raymond drove them out east on the highway in the dark night, the fresh air blowing in on them through the opened windows. They drove about ten miles and then he stopped, backed up and turned around and came back. In town the lights of Main Street seemed very bright after the dark on the highway in the flat country. He pulled up to her house and stopped.

Will you come in? she said.

Ma'am, I don't know. I'm not much good in other people's houses.

Come in. Let me make you some coffee.

He shut off the engine and came around and opened her door and they walked up to her house. While she went back to the kitchen, he sat down in a large upholstered chair in the front room and looked around at her pictures, everything so clean and carefully arranged and put in order. Rose stepped into the room and said: Do you want sugar and milk with your coffee?

No thank you, ma'am. Just black.

She brought the cups in and handed him one. She took a seat on the couch across from him.

You have a beautiful place here, he said.

Thank you.

They drank their coffee and talked a little more. Finally Raymond had a last sip and stood up. I think it's time for me to get on home, he said.

You don't have to go yet.

I better, he said.

She put her cup down and walked over to him. She took his hand. I would like to kiss you, she said. Would you allow me to do that?

Now ma'am, I —

You'll have to bend down. I'm not very tall.

He bent his head and she took his face in her hands and kissed him thoroughly on the mouth. He held his arms straight at his sides. After she'd kissed him he reached up and touched at his mouth with his fingers.

Wouldn't you like to come back to the bedroom? she said.

He looked at her in surprise. Ma'am, he said. I'm a old man.

I know how old you are.

I doubt if I could do you any good.

Let's just see.

She led him back to her bedroom and turned on a low lamp beside the bed. Then she stood in front of him and unbuttoned his blue wool shirt and drew it off his shoulders. He was lean and stringy, with a growth of white hair spread over his chest.

Now will you unbutton me? she said. She turned around.

I don't know about this.

Yes, you do. I know you know how to undo buttons.

Not on a woman's dress.

Try.

Well, he said. I suppose it's kind of like counting out the steps in a waltz dance, ain't it.

She laughed. You see. It's not so bad. You've made a joke.

A awful little one, he said.

He began awkwardly to unbutton her peach dress. She waited. It took him a long time. But she didn't say anything, and when he was finished she slipped out of the dress and laid it over the back of a chair and turned to face him. Her slip was peach-colored too, and she looked very pretty in the slip. Her round shoulders were freckled and she had full breasts and wide hips. What would you think of getting out of your pants and boots now? she said.

I've come this far.

That's right. You can't turn back now.

They finished undressing and got into bed.

In bed Raymond was amazed at how it felt to be next to her. It was past all his experience, to be lying next to a woman, both of them unclothed, her body so smooth and warm and full-fleshed, and she herself so good-hearted. She lay facing him with her arms around him, and he slid his hand across the smooth point of her hip, feeling along the upper reaches of her leg. She leaned close and kissed him. Shut your eyes, she said. Try kissing me with your eyes shut.

Yes ma'am.

She kissed him again. Wasn't that better?

I like looking at your face too, though. At all of you.

Oh my, she said. Aren't you a nice man. Aren't we going to have us some fun together.

I'm having a pretty good time already, Raymond said.

Are you?

Yes ma'am. I am.

There's more, she said.

LATER SHE LAY WITH HER HEAD ON HIS ARM AND HE SAID: Rose. You're awful good for a old man like me.

You're not so old, she said. We've just had evidence of that.

You're going to embarrass me now.

There's no reason for embarrassment. You're just a healthy man. And you're good for me too. There aren't many men like you available in Holt. I know, I've looked.

HE LEFT HER HOUSE AT MIDNIGHT AND DROVE HOME IN the dark on the narrow blacktop highway. Out in the flat treeless country he counted himself more than lucky. Victoria and Katie in his life, and now to have whatever was starting with this generous woman, Rose Tyler. He drove with the windows rolled down, and the night air came in and brought with it the smell of green grass and sage.

39

THE FIRST SATURDAY NIGHT OF APRIL. AND DJ AND HIS grandfather were at the tavern on Main Street and it was not yet late, only about eight-thirty. The old man's pension check had come and he wanted his monthly night out.

They had been at the tavern for an hour sitting at the table near the wall with the other old men. DJ was seated behind his grandfather, watching the blonde barmaid as she moved around in the crowded smoky room. She had not asked him to come up to the bar and do his homework as she had before, though he had brought his school papers specially with that in mind. She seemed indifferent to him this night and had done no more than smile at him when she'd brought his cup of black coffee. He sat and watched her, while he listened to the old men's stories.

She was not wearing the low-cut blouse this time. Instead she had on a long-sleeved black blouse that came up to her neck. She was wearing the same pair of tight blue jeans though, with the deliberate hole in the thigh that revealed that much of her tanned skin. While he watched her he noticed that every time she passed along the bar a man turned on his barstool to look at her and say something. DJ had only a vague idea what a grown man like that one would be saying to her. He had seen the man before around town on the streets, but didn't know anything about him, not even his name. He seemed to be upsetting her. The blonde woman looked tired and unhappy, and appeared to be much bothered by whatever he was saying, and she gave him no response of any kind after the first two times she passed by, but just went on working in the loud crowded room.

AT THE TABLE ONE OF THE OLD MEN BEGAN TO TELL A story about a lawyer living across the state line in Gilbert Nebraska who had recently disappeared. He owed the bank two hundred and fifty thousand dollars on bad loans, and two weeks ago he went home for lunch and took a single bite out of a meatloaf sandwich his wife had set on his plate, then stood up and walked out the door with his wife in tow and disappeared, leaving the house unlocked and the rest of the sandwich uneaten. The coffeepot was still plugged in and the chair was pushed back from the table, as if they'd decided to leave all at once and couldn't wait a minute longer. The whole town was surprised. Except the bankers, perhaps. Nobody in Gilbert Nebraska had seen or heard from either one of them since.

I bet they disappeared in Denver, one of the old men said.

Maybe. But they looked for them in Denver. They looked all over. They looked in Omaha.

They probably escaped down south somewhere then. He's probably one of these front-door people-greeters at Wal-Mart someplace. Was he a old man?

Pretty old.

A old lawyer would do that. That'd be just right for a old lawyer. They should look for him down south in Wal-Mart.

THE OLD MEN WENT ON TALKING AND A HALF HOUR LATER DJ stood up and walked back through the tables to the rest room at the rear of the tavern, past the pool tables and the crowded booths. He went into one of the stalls and read the graffiti and used the toilet. Afterward he was washing his hands at the sink when the man from the bar came in. He was glassy-eyed and weaving. What you doing in here, you little shit?

Washing my hands.

Can't you read that sign on the door? This is for men, not little kids. Get the fuck out of here.

DJ looked at him and went back out and sat down behind his grandfather. His face was hot and red. He looked for the blonde woman. She was out in the room waiting on a table, standing with her back to him, her blonde hair bright against her black blouse. He opened his papers and did a page of homework. His face was burning and he kept thinking what he should have said or done in the rest room.

When he looked up fifteen minutes later he saw the man was bothering the barmaid again. Without considering what he might do, he stood up from his chair and walked to where they stood at the bar. The man had her by the wrist and was talking in a low mean voice.

Don't, DJ said. You're going to hurt her.

What? the man said. Why you little son of a bitch. He slapped DJ across the eyes and nose, knocking him into a table behind him, scattering glasses and ashtrays across the floor.

Well, what in the hell, one of the men at the table said. Hoyt, what you think you're doing?

The boy straightened himself and ran at him with his head down, but again the man slapped him away and he fell against an empty chair and crashed over with it.

Here, the bartender yelled. Raines, goddamn it, quit that.

The boy's grandfather came hurrying over and grabbed Hoyt by the shirt. I know how to deal with pups like you, he said.

I'm going to knock the shit out of you, Hoyt Raines said. Let go of me.

They commenced to fight. Hoyt slapped at the old man's white head and they whirled around and suddenly from behind them the blonde barmaid reached in and grabbed a fistful of Hoyt's hair. Hoyt's head jerked backward and his eyes rolled up in their sockets, and he swung about with the old man still hanging on to him and grabbed the woman by the throat and hurled her against the bar. Her blouse tore open, uncovering her breasts in the skimpy pink brassiere, and she let go and clutched at her blouse. Then the boy grabbed a bottle from the bar and smashed Hoyt Raines across the face with it. The bottle broke on his temple and tore his ear and he fell sideways, his knees buckling, and he righted himself and bent forward, bleeding from the side of the face onto the barroom floor. The boy waited to see what else he would do. He held the jagged bottle as if he'd stab him with it if he tried anything.

But the bartender had rushed out from behind the bar, and now he and two other men dragged Hoyt by the arms out the front door onto the sidewalk. When he turned and tried to push past them to come back inside, they shoved him violently away and he fell across the hood of one of the parked cars at the curb and lay sprawled. His face was cut and he was bleeding from the ear, the blood streamed down his neck. He rose gasping, weaving. He began to curse them.

Get the hell out of here, the bartender said. You're not coming back in here. Go on. He shoved Hoyt.

Fuck you, Hoyt said. He stood glaring at them, wobbly on his feet. Fuck every last one of you.

The bartender shoved him again and he stumbled backward off the sidewalk and sat down in the gutter. He looked all around, then rose and staggered southward down the middle of Main Street in the midst of Saturday night traffic. The cars veered around him, honking and blaring, the people inside the cars, high-school kids, shouting at him, whistling, jeering, and he cursed them too, cursed them all, gesturing at each car obscenely as it went by. He staggered on. Then he turned off into a side street and stumbled into the back alley. Halfway into the alley he stopped and leaned against the brick wall at the rear of one of the stores. A patrol car drove by out in the street. He squatted down behind a trash barrel. Blood was dripping from his ear, and the side of his face felt raw and numb. He waited, panting, squatted in the dark. He managed to light a cigarette and he cupped it in his hand. Then he stood and pissed against the brick wall of the store and stepped away in the shadows, headed out toward the street. When he saw no patrol car he turned toward Detroit.

INSIDE THE TAVERN THE BARMAID HAD HURRIED BACK TO the rest room holding her blouse together, and the men were tending to the old man, who'd bumped his head on one of the tables and was sitting awkwardly on the floor. There was a knot above his ear and he kept mumbling something. They lifted him to his feet and one of the men patted the boy on the back, congratulating him for what he'd done, but the boy ducked away from under the man's hand.

Leave us alone! he cried. All of you, leave us alone! He stood facing the ring of men. He was almost in tears. Leave us alone, goddamn you!

Why, what the hell? one of the men said. You little son of a bitch, we were trying to help you.

We don't want your help. Leave us alone.

He took his grandfather by the arm and led him back to their table. We got to go home, he said. He helped the old man into his coat and put on his own coat and gathered up his homework papers, and they went outside.

They walked down the sidewalk past the darkened storefronts. Cars drove past in the street. Across the tracks they turned in at their quiet neighborhood, and went on toward the little dark house. He put his grandfather to bed in the back room, helping him remove his overalls and workshirt and covering him with blankets. The old man lay back in his long underwear and shut his eyes.

Will you be all right now, Grandpa?

The old man opened one eye and peered at him. Yes. Go on, get to bed.

DJ turned the light off and went to his room. Once he was undressed he began to cry. He lay across the bed, hitting at the pillow in the dark. Goddamn you, he sobbed. Goddamn you.

After a while he got up and dressed once more and went into the other bedroom to check on his grandfather, then he went outside to wander the night streets. He crossed the railroad tracks and walked into the south side of Holt, out along the shadowed dark sidewalks past the silent houses.

40

It was late but not yet midnight when Raymond walked out of Rose's house to his pickup. They had gone again to the Wagon Wheel Café for dinner and the café had been even more crowded this time, but it didn't matter, they were having a good time, and afterward they had gone back to her house and drunk coffee and made love. Now he was going home. It was a fine spring night and he was feeling full of pleasure, fortunate beyond any accounting. He started the pickup and he was thinking warmly about Rose, then he got to the corner and there was a boy about to cross the street. Raymond slowed down and the boy stood under the light waiting for him to pass. He saw who it was and stopped. Son, is that you?

The boy didn't say anything.

DJ, that's you, isn't it?

Yes, it's me.

He stood at the edge of the street, his hands in his coat pockets.

What are you doing? Raymond said. Are you all right?

I'm all right.

Where you going to?

I'm just out walking.

Well. Raymond sat looking at him. Why don't you get in and let me drive you home. It's late out here.

I'm not going home yet.

I see. Raymond studied him. Then why don't you get in and we'll just drive a little.

You probably need to be somewhere.

Son, there's no place else for me to be right now. I'd be glad for the company. Why don't you come get in.

The boy stood looking at him. He looked away up the street. He stood for some time looking up the street. Raymond waited. Then the boy came around in front of the pickup and got in on the passenger side.

You're just out walking. Is that it? Taking the night air.

Yes sir.

Well, it's a nice night for it.

Raymond started the pickup and drove out of the dark neighborhood onto Main Street and turned south among the high-school kids in their cars, past the closed stores and the movie house, which had already let out for the night. When they passed the tavern the boy stared at the front of the building, and then turned sideways to look out the back window. At the highway Raymond headed west and drove out past the Legion and Shattuck's Café, where people were parked in cars at the drive-up under the long tin canopy roof, and then on out of town.

You want to just drive on a ways? Raymond said. Would that be all right with you?

Yes sir.

I wouldn't mind it myself. Crank that window down if you want some air.

The boy rolled down his window and they went on. The yard-lights of the farms were scattered out beyond the dark open fields and at every mile a graveled section road ran exactly north and south, and all along the new spring weeds were growing up at the roadside. A rabbit darted across the pavement in front of them, heading off into the weeds, its white scut flashing as it zigzagged away.

Raymond glanced at the boy. What you suppose spooked him out on the highway?

I wouldn't know.

The boy was looking straight ahead.

Son, is there something bothering you? Raymond said. You seem a little upset to me.

Maybe.

You kind of seem like it. Is it something you'd care to talk about?

I don't know.

Well, I can sure listen anyhow. If you want to try.

The boy turned to look out the side window, the headlights shining ahead on the dark road. Then all at once he began to talk. It came pouring out of him, about the fight at the tavern and about the man hurting the barmaid and his grandfather. And he was crying now. Raymond drove on and the boy kept crying and talking. After a while he stopped, he seemed to have spent himself. He wiped at his face.

Is that pretty much all of it? Raymond said. Was there anything else you wanted to tell?

No.

Did he hurt you?

He was hurting her. And Grandpa.

But they're all right now. Is that what you think?

I guess so.

What about him? Did he get hurt?

He was bleeding.

From where you hit him with the bottle?

Yes sir.

How bad was it?

I don't know. His face was pretty cut up.

Well. He'll probably be all right. Don't you think?

I don't know if he will or not.

RAYMOND DROVE ON A WAYS FARTHER, THEN THEY CAME back into town. At Shattuck's Café he pulled in under the canopy and without asking he ordered them each a hamburger and a black coffee and then turned to look at him.

Do you reckon he'd do anything else to you or your grandfather?

I don't even know who he is.

What did he look like?

He was kind of tall. With dark hair.

That could be any number of people.

They called him Hoyt something.

Oh, Raymond said. Hoyt Raines then. I know who he is. Well, you stay clear of him.

I don't want him to hurt that woman.

I doubt if he'd try again. Did they kick him out?

Yes.

Then he probably won't be allowed to go back in there. But you let me know if he bothers you again. Will you promise me to do that?

Yes sir.

All right then.

They finished their hamburgers and coffee and the girl came and took away their tray.

You think you're about ready to go home now?

Yes.

Raymond backed out onto the highway and drove up through town and stopped at the little house where he'd let the boy and his grandfather out months ago. The boy started to get out.

Son, Raymond said. I'm just wondering here, but do you think you would want to help me some? I could use a hand on the weekends.

Doing what?

Doing whatever needs doing. Working around the ranch.

I guess I could.

I'll give you a call. How about next weekend? How would next Saturday suit you?

It'd suit me fine.

You'd have to get up early.

What time?

Five-thirty. You think you could do that?

Yes sir. I always get up early.

All right. You take care now. Get yourself some sleep. I'll give you a call next week.

The boy got out and went up to the house. Raymond sat watching him until the door closed, then drove home. He drove out south and by the time he turned off the highway onto the gravel road he was thinking again about Rose Tyler.

41

LUTHER AND BETTY WALLACE WOKE TO A SUDDEN
pounding on the front door. Who's out there? he called.

It's Donna, Betty said. She come back to us.

Maybe it ain't her, Luther said.

She climbed out of bed and called: Donna, I'm coming, honey.

They went down the hallway, Luther in his underwear, Betty in
her worn yellow nightdress, and when Luther opened the door Hoyt
Raines shoved violently into the room.

No! Betty cried. You can't come in here. Get back.

Shut up, Hoyt said. He stood before them, his face ragged and
blood-smeared, his ear still bleeding a little, his eyes glassy. You two
are going to help me whether you like it or not. Those sonsabitches
over at the tavern—

You get out of here, Luther said. Just get out.

Goddamn you, Hoyt said. He hit Luther in the chest and Luther
stepped backward and sat down all at once on the couch. I got no
damn place else to go, Hoyt said.

You can't stay here, Betty said. They won't allow it.

Shut up. Hoyt took her arm and flung her onto the couch
beside her husband. Just sit there, he said. And keep your goddamn
mouth shut.

He went across to the kitchen sink and ducked his head under the faucet, soaking his head, the blood running thinly from his face over the dirty dishes, and then he stood blindly, his lank hair dripping, and grabbed a dish towel to wipe at his head and neck. Luther and Betty sat on the couch, watching him.

So, you heard what I said. I'm staying here tonight.

You can't, Betty said.

I told you to shut up. Now by God, shut your mouth. He glared at her. It won't be long. Just for tonight. Maybe two nights. I don't know yet. Now I want both of you to go back to your room and stay there and keep quiet.

What are you going to do? Luther said.

I'm staying in that back room. And you listen to me: I'll kill you if you try to call somebody. I'll hear you on the phone. He looked at them. Did you hear what I just said?

They looked back at him.

Did you?

We ain't suppose to talk, Luther said. You said for us to shut up.

Now I'm saying you can talk. Did you hear what I said would happen if you try and call somebody?

Yes.

What'd I say?

You said you'd kill us.

Remember that, Hoyt said. Now get up from there.

He herded them back to their room and shut the door, then walked down the hall to the last room. When he opened the door Joy Rae was sitting up in bed in her nightgown, one hand cupped over her mouth. He walked across the room and pulled her onto her feet, and when she began to scream he slapped her. Stop that, he said. He pulled her out in the hall and into the next room, where Richie was crouched on the floor in his pajamas, waiting in the dark, as if preparing to run off. But seeing Hoyt with his sister he lost control of himself. The front of his pajamas suddenly went damp.

You stupid little son of a bitch, Hoyt said. He shoved Joy Rae into the room and lifted the little boy by the arm. Look at you. He slapped him. The boy slipped out of his hands and fell on the wet dirty carpet.

Now take those goddamn pants off. Get out of them.

The boy whimpered and pulled off the soaked pajamas. Then Hoyt took out his belt and began to whip him. The boy screamed, squirming wildly on the floor, his thin bare legs kicking, his hands reaching out to catch the belt. His sister began to scream too, and Hoyt turned and caught her by the nightgown, lifting it up, and began to whip her legs and thin flanks. He seemed crazed, whipping at both of them in an indiscriminate fury, his face contorted with drink and rage, his arm rising and falling, flailing at them, until Luther appeared in the bedroom doorway. Stop it, Luther shouted. You can't do that no more, so just stop it. Hoyt turned and walked at him and Luther stepped back and he lashed Luther across the neck and Luther yelped and retreated hollering down the hall. Then Hoyt turned on the children again and went on whipping them until he was sweating and panting. Finally he slammed the door and walked back to Joy Rae's bedroom at the end of the hall.

When he was gone the two children crawled into the bed, crying and sobbing, scarcely able to breathe, and rubbed at their legs and buttocks. Their legs burned and throbbed. Some of the welts were bleeding. In the brief silence between their sobs they could hear their parents wailing from the room down the hall.

THE NEXT MORNING HOYT HAD LUTHER AND BETTY AND Joy Rae and Richie sit in the living room on the couch. He switched on the television and pulled the heavy window curtains shut. The light from the TV flickered in the shadowy room.

At noon he told Betty to make something to eat, and when she'd heated the frozen pizza he made them sit together at the table. Nobody said anything, and only Hoyt ate very much. After this silent meal he forced them back into the living room where he could watch them.

Once in the long afternoon a car drove up and stopped out front in Detroit Street. When he heard the door of the car shut Hoyt looked past the edge of the curtains, and a sheriff's deputy was walking up the path toward the door, then the deputy knocked and Hoyt cursed between his teeth. He motioned Betty and the two children back to the bedrooms and hissed at Luther to answer the door. Get rid of him. And you goddamn better remember what I said.

Luther went out onto the porch and talked and answered a few questions in his slow manner. Finally the deputy left and Luther came back in and shut the door. Hoyt came out of the hall and watched through the curtains as the car drove off. Then he sat them down on the couch again, to watch television. In the evening he forced them to their beds and in this way the second night passed in the trailer.

The next morning in the gray dawn he was gone. They came out of their bedrooms and discovered that he had vanished without a sound.

AT DAYBREAK HOYT HAD WALKED ACROSS TOWN TO ELTON Chatfield's house. He had waited at the curb beside Elton's old pickup until he came out, then caught a ride with him to the feedlot east of Holt. At the feedlot he entered the office and stood at the desk where the manager was talking on the phone to a cattle buyer. The manager looked up at him and frowned and went on talking. After a while he hung up. What are you doing in here? he said. You're suppose to be riding pens.

I quit, Hoyt said.

What do you mean you quit?

I come to draw my pay.

The hell you have.

You owe me for two weeks. I'll take it now.

The manager pushed his hat back on his head. You don't give much notice, do you. He took out a checkbook from a middle drawer and started to write.

I'll take it in cash, Hoyt said.

What?

I want cash. I don't need a check.

Well, I'll be goddamned. You expect me to come up with cash on a Monday morning.

That's right.

What if I don't have no cash?

I'll take what you got.

He studied Hoyt closely. Where you running off to, Hoyt?

That ain't none of your business.

Some woman chasing you? he said. He took out his wallet and removed what few bills there were and dropped them forward onto the desktop. Now get your ass out of here.

Hoyt stuffed the bills in his pocket. How about giving me a lift over to the highway? he said.

You want a ride?

I want to get over to the highway.

You better start in to walking then. I wouldn't give you a lift to a goddamn dog fight. Get the fuck out of here.

Hoyt stood for a moment, looking at him, thinking if there was something he needed to say, then he turned and stepped out of the office into the fenced yard. It was already beginning to warm up, the sun risen higher in the sky, the sky completely clear and blue. He walked out past the cattle yards, where the fat cattle were all feeding at the plank troughs at the fences, and walked out onto the gravel road, headed south toward the highway two miles in the distance. There were fields of corn stubble along the road, and small birds flew up from the ditches, chittering as he approached. A pheasant cackled from across the stubble. When he reached the highway he stood at the roadside, leaning against a signpost, waiting for a ride to come along.

Half an hour later a man in a blue Ford pickup stopped beside the road. The man leaned across and rolled down the window. Bud, where you headed to?

Denver, Hoyt said.

Well, get in here. You can ride as far as I'm going.

Hoyt climbed in and shut the door and they drove west toward town. The man glanced at him. What you gone and done to your face there?

Where?

Your nigh ear.

I wasn't looking and snatched it on a tree limb.

Well. All right then. You got to watch that.

They drove on and passed through Holt and went west on US 34. The highway stretched out before them, lined on both sides by the shallow barrow ditches. Above the ditches the four-strand barbed-wire fences ran along beside the pastures in the flat sandy country, and above the fences the line of telephone poles rose up out of the ground like truncated trees strung together with black wire. Hoyt rode with him through Norka and as far as Brush. Then he got another ride and traveled on, headed west on a Monday morning in springtime.

42

IN SCHOOL THAT MORNING THE CHILDREN WERE DISCOVERED almost at once. One of the young girls in Joy Rae's fifth-grade class, a girl who had been briefly interested in her weeks before when she had appeared at school with lipstick on her mouth, slipped up to the front of the room in the first hour of classes and addressed the teacher in a voice scarcely above a whisper. The teacher at her desk said: I can't hear you, come here. What is it you want?

The girl leaned next to the woman's head and whispered in her ear. The teacher studied her and turned to look out into the classroom at Joy Rae. Joy Rae was bent forward over her desktop. Go back to your seat, the teacher said.

The girl returned to her desk at the middle of the room and the teacher rose and walked as if on some routine inspection out among the rows of students, and stopped near Joy Rae and then caught her breath, raising her hand to her mouth, but collected herself immediately and led Joy Rae out into the hall and down to the nurse.

The little boy, her brother, was called in from his classroom.

Then, as before, against their will and despite their protestations they were examined in the nurse's room. The boy's pants were lowered, the girl's dress was raised, and seeing what she saw this time the nurse said angrily: Oh Jesus Christ, where is Thy mercy, and left to bring the principal into the room, and the principal took one look and went back to his office and called the sheriff's office at the courthouse and then phoned Rose Tyler at Holt County Social Services.

THE CHILDREN WERE QUESTIONED SEPARATELY. PHOTO-graphs were taken and a tape was made of their remarks. They each gave the same story. Nothing had happened. They'd been out playing in the alley and had scratched their legs.

Honey, Rose said, don't lie now. You don't have to lie for him. Did he threaten you?

We scratched them on the bushes, the girl said.

Her brother was waiting beyond the door in the hall, and she was standing before the cot in the nurse's room, her hands twisted in the waist of her thin dress, her eyes filled with tears. Her face looked red and desperate. Rose and the sheriff's deputy sat across from her, watching her.

What did he threaten you with? the deputy said.

He never done nothing to us. The girl wiped at her eyes and glared at them. It was bushes.

That'll do, honey, Rose said. Never mind now. We know. You don't have to say anything more. She put her arm around the girl. You don't have to lie to protect anybody.

The girl jerked away. You ain't suppose to touch me, she said.

Honey. Nobody's going to hurt you anymore.

Nobody can touch me.

The deputy looked at Rose and Rose nodded, and he went out to the principal's office and phoned the judge who was on call that day and got a verbal emergency custody order. Then he phoned Luther and Betty. He told them to stay at the trailer, that he'd want to see them in a few minutes. Then he came back to the nurse's room, where Rose had both children with her now, sitting with her arms around them, talking to them quietly. The deputy motioned for her to come out to the hall, and they went out and stood below the vivid artwork of schoolchildren taped to the tiled walls and discussed in low voices what to do next. Rose would take the children to the hospital to be examined by the doctor while he drove to the trailer and talked to Luther and Betty. Afterward they would consult again.

THE SHERIFF'S DEPUTY DROVE ACROSS TOWN TO DETROIT Street and parked the car and got out and stood for a moment looking at the trailer. The spring sun appeared to be too bright against the washed-out siding and the sagging roof, the plank porch, the unwashed windows. In the yard redroot and cheatgrass had begun to sprout up in the pale dirt. When he stepped onto the porch Luther let him in.

He sat down in the living room facing the couch where Luther and Betty sat watching him talk, studying his mouth, as if he were some preacher uttering everlasting pronouncements or the county judge himself saying out the law. He began to feel sick. He decided to make this as brief as possible. He told them they already knew about the children, what had been done to them and when and who had done it.

Betty's pocked face went all to pieces. We never wanted him in here, she said. We told him he couldn't come in.

You should of called us.

He was going to kill us, Luther said.

Did he say that?

Yes sir. That's what he said. He wasn't fooling.

But it's too late now, isn't it. He's already abused your children. You have any idea where he's run off to?

No sir.

No idea?

He was already gone when we got up this morning.

And he never said anything to you about where he might go.

He never told us nothing about what he was fixing to do.

Except for how he was going to kill us, Betty said.

The sheriff's deputy looked around the room for a moment, then turned back. Was he still here yesterday when somebody from the sheriff's office came to the door?

He was back in the hall there, Luther said. Waiting and listening.

He was?

Yes sir.

Well, we'll find him. He can't disappear forever.

But mister, Betty said, where's our kids?

The deputy looked at her. She sat slumped in the couch, her hands in the lap of her dress, her eyes red with tears. Mrs. Tyler has taken them to the doctor, he said. We have to see how bad your uncle hurt them.

When do we get to see them?

That's up to Mrs. Tyler. But they won't be allowed to come back here. You understand that, don't you? Not to live anyhow. There'll be a hearing about this, probably on Wednesday.

What do you mean?

Ma'am, the judge has issued an emergency custody order and your children are going to be placed in a foster home. There'll be a hearing about this within forty-eight hours.

Betty stared at him. Suddenly she threw her head back and wailed. You're taking my children! I knew you was going to! She began to pull at her hair and scratch at her face. Luther leaned toward her and tried to catch her hands but she shoved him away. The sheriff's deputy stepped across the room and bent over her. Here, he said. He took hold of her hands. Stop that now. That's not going to do you any good. What good is that going to do anybody?

Betty shook her head, her eyes rolling unfocused, and she continued to wail into the rank and odoriferous air.

ROSE TOOK THE CHILDREN OUT OF SCHOOL AND DROVE TO the hospital and the doctor examined them in the emergency room. The lacerations were bad but he could find no broken bones. He applied antiseptic ointment to the cuts and welts and dressed the worst ones with bandages.

Afterward Rose drove them to her house and gave them lunch, then she took them with her to Social Services at the courthouse and sat them at a table in the interview room with magazines to look at while she went next door to her office. She spoke with the deputy on the phone and then called three different foster homes and finally reached one with a vacancy in a house at the west side of Holt that belonged to a fifty-year-old woman who had two children already in her care. Then she went back to the interview room and told Joy Rae and Richie what was going to happen. We'll go by your house first to get some clothes, she said. You can see your parents for a moment. Do you want to?

The children looked at her out of their grave eyes and said nothing. They appeared to have retreated to some unassailable place.

She drove them to Detroit Street to the trailer and went with them inside. Betty was calmer now but there were the distinct red scratches on her cheeks, like the excoriations after an attack by some animal. The children went back to their rooms and gathered several changes of clothes into a grocery bag, and Betty followed behind and petted and whispered to them and cried over them, while Luther stood in the front room looking up the hall, waiting as if he had been blunted by a sudden blow.

When they went outside to the car Betty and Luther followed them into the street, and when the car started away Betty trotted beside it, her face close to the rear window, crying and moaning, calling: I'll see you soon. I'll see you tomorrow sometime.

Mama! Richie called.

Joy Rae covered her face with her hands and Luther lumbered along beside Betty until the car sped up. It disappeared around the corner. They stood out in the empty street then, watching where the car had gone, watching nothing.

ON THE WEST SIDE OF TOWN THE WOMAN LET THEM IN. She was tall and thin in a flowered apron and she had a bright way of talking. I'm going to have to learn your names, she said. I just think you'll like it here. Won't you. I hope you will. We're going to try anyway. Now I'm going to show you around first. I just always think people want to see how things are located the first thing. Then they feel better.

Rose waited in the living room while the woman showed the

children through her house, starting with the bedrooms they'd be using, then the bathroom and the other children's room. Then they came back out and Rose told them what they could expect over the next few days. She hugged them before she left and said they should call her at home if they needed anything at all, and printed out her number and the one at the office on a piece of paper and gave the paper to Joy Rae.

ON TUESDAY THERE WERE MEETINGS AND INTERVIEWS.

Luther and Betty met for an hour at the courthouse with a lawyer assigned to them by the court.

The two children were interviewed at the foster home by the guardian ad litem, a young attorney appointed to act in their behalf and represent their best interests. He listened to their story and took notes and they did not go to school that day but stayed at the woman's house.

The county attorney met with Rose Tyler and the investigating sheriff's deputy in Rose's office and drew up the Petition of Dependency and Neglect, which would be filed with the court.

But no one who met that Tuesday in these various meetings was pleased by what was decided in any instance.

ON WEDNESDAY THE SHELTER HEARING WAS CONDUCTED in the middle of the afternoon on the third floor of the courthouse in the civil court across the wide hall from the criminal court. It was a dark wood-paneled room with a high ceiling and tall mullioned windows and benches arranged in rows behind the two tables left and right that were reserved for the attorneys and other involved parties. In front of the two tables was the judge's bench raised on a dais. The two children did not attend.

Luther and Betty entered the courtroom that afternoon dressed for the formal proceedings. Betty wore a brown dress and new sheer hose, and she had rouged her cheeks to cover the scratches. Her hair was freshly washed and brushed, held back on the sides by a pair of

Joy Rae's plastic barrettes. She looked peculiarly childlike. Luther wore his blue slacks and a plaid shirt with a red tie wound under the collar that was not drawn tight under his chin since the collar could not be buttoned. The tie reached only to the middle of his stomach. They entered and sat down behind the table on the right.

Their attorney came in and sat in the bench behind them, across the aisle from the guardian ad litem. After a while Rose came in with the sheriff's deputy. He sat next to the G.A.L. and Rose slid in beside Betty and Luther, and she leaned over and took their hands and said they must speak the truth and do the best they could.

Rose, what's going to happen? Betty said.

We'll have to see what the judge decides.

I don't want to lose my kids, Rose. I couldn't bear that.

Yes. I know, dear.

Rose stood and moved to the other side of the aisle and sat at the table with the county attorney who'd entered the courtroom while she had talked to Luther and Betty. Everyone sat and waited. Outside the courthouse the wind was blowing, they could hear it in the trees. Somebody went by in the hallway, the footsteps echoing. Still, they waited. Finally the judge came in from a side door and the clerk said: All rise, and they rose. Be seated, the clerk said, and they sat down again.

There was just the one civil case this Wednesday. The courtroom was largely empty, and it was hot and stale, smelling of dust and old furniture polish.

The judge called the case from the file before him. Then the county attorney stood and spoke briefly. The judge had already seen the Petition of Dependency and Neglect and the county attorney began to review it for the record. The Petition explained why the children had been taken into emergency custody, described what had been done to them by their mother's uncle, and stated what both the county attorney's office and Social Services recommended. The Petition stipulated that the children be kept in foster care until such time as the uncle was apprehended and brought to trial. Until then the children should not be allowed to return to the home, since their parents had not shown that they were capable of protecting them from their uncle thus far. The parents should be granted regular visitations with the children under the supervision of Social Services, and the case should be reviewed at some future time and date.

Then the Wallaces' lawyer rose and said what he could in their defense, telling the court that Luther and Betty Wallace had been good parents, under the circumstances, and had done the best they could.

Are the parents in the room? the judge said.

Yes, Your Honor. They're here.

The lawyer motioned to Betty and Luther. They came forward and stood beside him at the table.

You're aware of what injury was done to your children, aren't you? the judge said.

Yes sir, Luther said. Your Honor.

Did you make any effort to prevent the injury to your children?

He wouldn't let us.

Your wife's uncle. You're referring to him.

Pardon?

You're talking about Hoyt Raines. You're referring to Mr. Raines.

Yes. That's him.

Did you witness what Mr. Raines was doing to your children?

My husband did, Betty said. I never seen it. Afterward I just seen what he done.

What did you do yourself?

You mean me?

Yes.

I told him he couldn't do it. When he first come in our house I says, You can't come in here.

Mr. Wallace. What did you do?

I went on in there, Luther said. I seen him using his belt and I says, You can't do that. You got to stop that.

Did you physically try to stop him?

Well, like I says, I was in there. Then he come and hit me cross the neck. It's still stinging me. Luther rubbed at his neck beneath the shirt collar.

What did you do after he whipped you with his belt?

I went back to take care of my wife.

What was she doing?

She was laid out bawling about all what was going on.

So in fact you didn't do anything.

Luther looked at the judge, then he glanced at Betty, then he faced forward again. I went in there to stop him. But he whipped me cross my neck. With that belt of his.

Yes. I heard you tell the court that you did that much. But just entering the room where he was whipping your children didn't stop him, did it. That wasn't enough.

He says he's going to kill us.

Sir?

He says he's going to kill us if we done anything.

Mr. Raines told you he would kill you?

Yes sir. That's exactly what he told us.

That he would kill you if you tried to prevent him from whipping your children.

Yes sir.

If we told on him too, Betty said. If we called somebody on the phone.

That's right, Luther said. If we called somebody, he says he's going to hear us, and he's going to kill us like we was dogs.

So he threatened you both.

He put a threat on us both right in our own house, Luther said.

The judge looked at the file on his desk for a moment. Then he raised his head. This is the second time this has occurred. Isn't that right?

Yes sir, Your Honor. He done it once before, Luther said.

Do you know where he is now?

No.

Where do you think he might be?

He could be about anywhere. He might be in New York City.

New York City. Do you think that's where he is?

Might be Vegas too. He's always talking bout making a killing in Las Vegas.

The judge looked at him. Well. I thank you both for your testimony. You may sit down.

The judge then called the guardian ad litem. The young attorney stood and approached the table and reported his interview with the two children. He closed by submitting his own recommendation to the court.

I'm to understand from what you've just informed the court that you concur with the recommendation of the county attorney and the Social Services? the judge said.

That's right, Your Honor.

Thank you, the judge said. He looked out into the courtroom. In a case like this one, he said, I have to make two determinations. First, on the filing of the Petition of Dependency and Neglect. Secondly, I must make a determination about the custody of the two children. The court has heard the various parties involved in this case. Is there anyone who wants to say something more?

Betty stood up from where she sat behind the table.

Yes? the judge said. Do you have something more to say, Mrs. Wallace?

You're not going to take my children, are you? Betty said. I love my children.

Yes, ma'am. I appreciate that, the judge said. I believe you and your husband do love your children. That's not in dispute here.

Don't take them. Please.

But Mrs. Wallace, it's evident to the court from the testimony we've heard today, including your own testimony, that you can't protect them. Your uncle has abused them twice. For now, they're better off in foster care.

But don't take them. Please don't.

The court has to decide what is in the best interest of the children.

They're suppose to be with their mama and daddy.

In most instances, that's right. The court makes every effort to keep the children with their parents. But in this case, it's the court's decision that they're better served by being placed in foster care. At least for the time being. Until your uncle has been found, Mrs. Wallace.

You mean you're going to take them away?

You may still see them. Under supervision. They won't be taken out of the local vicinity. They'll still be in Holt County and you can visit them on a regular basis.

Oh no! Betty cried. Oh no! No! No! Then she screamed something that was not even words. Her voice rang in the room and it echoed shrilly against the dark paneled walls. She fell back into the church bench and banged her head. Her eyes rolled wildly. Luther tried to help her and she bit his hand.

The judge stood up in surprise. Somebody help her there, he said. Somebody bring this woman a glass of water.

43

AFTER HIS SUPPER OF FRIED MEAT AND FRIED POTATOES, sitting alone at the pinewood table in the kitchen, the house so silent and still with just the sough of wind outside, he rinsed off his meager dishes at the sink and moved into the dining room. He took down the phone from the wall and carried it on its long cord to the parlor and sat in his old recliner chair and called Victoria Roubideaux in Fort Collins.

I was just picking up the phone to call you, she said.

Were you, honey? I just figured it was about my turn. I was wondering if you knew when you and Katie was coming home for the summer. I hope you're still coming.

Oh, yes. Nothing would change that.

I'll sure be glad to see you. Both of you.

I've only got another couple weeks of classes, then finals.

How's your classes going?

Okay. You know. It's school.

Well. It'll be nice to have you home for a while. How's my little Katie?

Oh, she's fine. She talks about you all the time. Here, do you want to say something to her?

The little girl came on.

That you, Katie? he said.

She began to talk immediately and her high voice was clear and excited at once, and she was telling him something about day care and some other little girl there with her, and he couldn't make out much of what she was saying, but he was satisfied just to hear her voice. Then Victoria took the phone again.

I couldn't get all of that, Raymond said. She's a talker, ain't she.

She talks all the time.

Well, that's good.

Anyway, I plan to be home by Memorial Day, she said. I've been thinking I wanted to take some flowers out to the cemetery.

He'd like that.

I think about him just about every day.

I know. I been catching myself talking to him again.

What do you talk about?

Oh, just the work around here. Like we used to do. Making up our minds about what to do concerning one thing or another. I'm just turning old and crazy, I reckon. Somebody ought to take me out back of the barn and shoot me.

I wouldn't worry about that. You're not really worried, are you?

No. I guess not, he said. Well. Now how about Del. I guess he's still in the picture.

Yes. We were out together last night. We took Katie to a movie downtown. That reminds me—do you think you could use him this summer during haying?

Does he want to do that?

He was asking about it. He wanted me to ask you if you thought that would be all right. If he came out for a while this summer.

Well sure, I could always use another hand. He'd be welcome.

Okay, I'll tell him, she said. But what about you? Have you seen Rose Tyler again?

Well. We been out several times. We been out to eat dinner.

Are you having fun?

Yes ma'am. I believe you could call it that. At least I think so.

I'm glad. I want to meet her. I haven't even met her yet.

I believe you're going to like her. She's a awful fine woman to me. I want to get us all together once you get home.

And have you been taking care of yourself?

Yes. I'd say so.

Have you been eating right?

Pretty good.

I know you haven't. I know you don't eat right. I wish you would.

It's just awful quiet around here, honey. You say you'll be home by Memorial Day?

Yes. As soon as I can.

That'll be good, he said. It'll be good to see you.

They hung up then and Raymond sat in the parlor at the back of the house with the phone in his lap, musing and remembering. Thinking about Victoria and Katie and about Rose Tyler, and about his dead brother, gone on ahead, already this half year and more.

44

In a borrowed car Mary Wells drove to Greeley, out across the high plains two hours west of Holt, and spent all that warm day going around to various places of business applying for work. She finally found a job late in the afternoon in an insurance office downtown in the old part of the city. Afterward she went to a phone booth and called home. She had begun to feel lighter, she believed things were going to be better now. When she called, the girls were home from school and she told them she would be back by nightfall and they'd all have supper together.

In Holt she returned the car to her friend and then walked along the streets to her own small house on the south side of town. The streets were all empty, with everyone inside eating supper. At home the two girls were waiting for her on the front steps when she walked up to the house. Were you worried about me? she said.

You took so long.

I came as fast as I could. But it's all right now. I'm home.

They went inside and she cooked supper for them, and they sat in the kitchen and she told them about finding a job in Greeley that afternoon. It'll be better there, she said. We can make a fresh start.

I don't want to move, Dena said.

I know, honey. But I think we should. I'm sorry. But I can't stay here and you know I have to work and support us. I can't do that here. We'll have to rent an apartment at first. That's all I can afford for right now. I'll have a truck rented for three or four days to move us out. And then we'll stay in a motel and look for an apartment. She looked at both of the girls, their faces so young and dear. Maybe we can find one with a view of the mountains. How would that be?

We won't have any friends there, Dena said.

Not yet. But you will have. We'll all make new friends.

What about DJ?

What do you mean?

He's going to be alone. After we leave.

You can write him. And it's only two hours away, so he can come visit sometime. And maybe you can come back here to visit him.

It's not the same.

Oh, honey, I can't fix everything, she said. She looked at them and both girls were ready to cry.

But I brought you something, she said. She went out to the front room and returned with two packages and set them on the table. One was a yellow dress for Emma, who tried it on and twirled around for them to see. The other package was a little container of concealer. The slogan said: Covers completely. I'll show you how to use it, their mother said.

What is it?

I'll show you.

She stood over Dena and squeezed the little tube and caught some of the beige paste onto her finger and dabbed it on the girl's scar beside her eye and smoothed it in. The scar was still red and shiny and the makeup dulled it a little. The girl went into the bathroom to look at herself in the mirror and then came back out.

What do you think? Mary Wells said. Isn't that better?

You can still see it, though.

But it's better, honey. Don't you think it is? I think it looks a lot better.

It's okay, Mama.

ON FRIDAY AFTERNOON WHEN MARY WELLS AND THE girls were loading the rental truck, DJ came to the house after school and helped them carry out the last things. Mary Wells had decided she could wait no longer. The manager at the insurance office wanted her to start work by the middle of the next week and she knew if she put off the move she might not be able to move at all. She doubted she would still have the volition and energy. She had listed the house with a realtor, and at school she had spoken to the principal and the girls' teachers, and the girls would be allowed to withdraw with passing grades since there were only two weeks of classes left and both girls had done satisfactory work throughout the year.

In those last few days, DJ and Dena went to the shed at the back alley every afternoon and sat at the table across from each other in the little dark room and lit the candles. They ate their snacks of crackers and cheese and drank cold coffee and talked.

Mama said I can write you, Dena told him. Will you write me back?

I guess so. I never wrote any letters before.

But you can write me. And Mama said you can visit sometime.

All right.

Don't you want to?

I said all right.

What do you think of my face?

Your face?

My scar.

It looks okay. I don't know.

Do you think this makeup helps it not show as much?

It looks okay to me. I didn't mind it before.

Everybody keeps looking at me. I hate it.

The hell with them, he said. Never mind those other kids. They don't know anything.

Dena stared at him and touched his hand, and he kept looking at her, then she drew her hand back and he turned away.

Do you want any more of these crackers here? he said.

Do you?

Yes.

Then I do too.

THEN IN THE AFTERNOON THE TRUCK WAS LOADED AND the big overhead door was pulled down at the back. They came out of the house and Mary Wells locked up for the last time. DJ was standing at the curb waiting and she came out to the street and suddenly took him in her arms. Oh, we're going to miss you, DJ, she said. We're going to miss you so much. You take care of yourself now. She released him and looked in his face. Will you do that?

Yes ma'am.

I mean it. You have to take care of yourself.

I will.

All right. We need to go. She went around and climbed into the cab. The two girls stood facing him and Emma was already crying. She hugged him quickly around the waist and ran and climbed up into the truck and buried her face in her mother's lap.

I'll write you, Dena said. Don't forget.

I won't.

She stepped forward and kissed him on the cheek, then stood back and looked at him, and he stood watching her, his hands in his pockets, looking forlorn and desolate already, and then she turned and got into the truck. The truck started up and she sat at the window, lifting her hand, waving slightly, whispering good-bye to him, and he stood on the curb until they had pulled away and had turned the corner and disappeared.

After they were gone he went up on the porch and looked through the front window. All empty inside, it looked strange to him now. He walked around behind into the alley past the widows' houses and the vacant lot and his grandfather's house.

THE LITTLE WOODEN SHED WAS DIM AND FILLED WITH shadows. He lit one of the candles and sat down at the table, looking

around at the dark back wall and the shelf. The candlelight was flickering and dancing on the walls. There was little to see. The framed
picture of the baby Jesus hanging on the wall. Some of their board
games. Old plates and pieces of silverware in a box. It didn't feel
good in the shed without her. Nothing there was the same. He whistled through his teeth, softly, a tune he thought of. Then he stopped.
He stood and blew out the candle and went outside and fastened the
latch. He stood looking for a long time at the old abandoned house
across the backyard grown up in weeds, the old black Desoto rusting
among the bushes. Then he entered the alley once more. Night was
falling. He'd have to go home and make supper. His grandfather
would be waiting. It was already past the hour at which his grandfather wanted his supper.

45

ON A WARM WINDLESS AFTERNOON ROSE TYLER STOPPED at the trailer on Detroit Street and honked and waited, and after a while Luther and Betty Wallace stepped out onto the porch. Luther lifted his hand to shade his eyes, then he removed a washrag from the pocket of his sweatpants and dabbed at his eyes, and afterward put the rag away and took Betty by the arm and led her down the porch steps out along the dirt path to the car at the edge of the weeds. They got in and Rose drove them across town. Everything's going to be all right, she said. Try not to worry.

The woman was wearing an apron when she let them in. Hello, Rose said. We're here.

Come in, the woman said.

This is Mr. and Mrs. Wallace.

I've been expecting you. How do you do.

How do you do, ma'am, Luther said. He shook her hand. Betty shook hands, but said nothing.

Please come in. I'll go get Joy Rae and Richie.

The Wallaces entered her house as if they were entering some formal place where circumspection was the custom. They sat together on the couch. She got a nice house here, don't she, Luther said. Real nice.

Rose sat down across from them, and presently the woman brought their children out from the back room. They stood beside her and glanced once shyly at their parents, then looked away. Their clothes appeared to have been freshly washed and ironed, and Joy Rae's bangs were trimmed in a straight line across her forehead.

You can sit there with your mother and father, the woman said. She gave them a little push.

The children sat down on the couch next to Betty. They didn't say anything. They seemed to be much embarrassed by the occasion. Betty took Joy Rae's hand and pulled her close and kissed her face and then leaned across and kissed Richie. Both children sat back and wiped at their faces and looked out into the room.

The woman excused herself to go into the kitchen, and Rose stood up. I'm going to leave you too. You'll want to catch up a little, by yourselves, won't you. Then she followed the woman into the kitchen.

You look so nice, honey, Betty told Joy Rae. Did you get your hair cut?

Yes.

It looks so nice. Did she cut it for you?

She cut it last week.

Well, it looks real nice on you. And how you been doing, Richie?

Okay.

What you been doing with yourself?

Reading.

Is it a book from school?

No, it's from church. They said I could keep it.

And I guess you been playing with other kids?

Sometimes we have.

Then the front door opened. Two young girls in bright dresses came in and stopped and stood looking at the Wallace family and then went on to the back of the house.

Who's that? Betty whispered.

Her other ones.

Her other foster kids?

We don't see them much, Joy Rae said. They don't want nothing to do with us.

ROSE CAME BACK IN AND THE WOMAN FOLLOWED HER WITH a plate of cookies and set the plate on the side table.

Joy Rae, the woman said, why don't you ask your parents if they would like a cookie. And Richie, would you pass around these napkins.

The children rose and did as they were asked.

Would you care for some tea? the woman said.

Oh, no thank you, ma'am, Luther said. We're doing pretty good just the way we are.

They all sat and ate the cookies and tried to think what there was to say.

Finally Luther leaned forward on the couch toward the woman. My eyes been burning me some, he said. I reckon I got me some kind of eye infection. Might be pinkeye. I don't know what it is. He took a bite of his cookie and set what was left of it on a napkin on the arm of the couch and pulled out the washrag from his pocket and dabbed at his weepy eyes. And my wife, he said, her stomach's been acting up again on her too. Ain't it, dear? Acting up bad.

It's been acting up real bad, Betty said. She laid her hand over her stomach and massaged at a place under her breasts.

We'll make appointments for both of you to see the doctor, Rose said. It's time again, isn't it.

When you think that'll be? Luther said.

As soon as I can get you in. I'll call yet today.

I don't want to see that same doctor I seen the last time, Betty said. I don't want to see him again ever.

He ain't never done you no good, has he, Luther said.

He give me some pills. That's bout all he ever did.

We'll see, Rose said. I'll try to get you in to see Dr. Martin. You'll like him better.

Then they fell again into an awkward silence.

Joy Rae, the woman said, why don't you see if your parents are ready for another cookie.

I could stand me another one, Luther said. How bout you, dear?

If it don't grip my stomach too much, Betty said.

Joy Rae stood in front of each of them offering the plate of cookies and then set it down and returned to the couch and sat beside her brother and put her arm around him. The little boy moved closer to her and laid his head on her shoulder, as if there were nothing else to do in such circumstances.

46

SHE CALLED RAYMOND IN THE LATE AFTERNOON AND HE was still outside. She called him again an hour later and he had come up from the horse barn by that time in the lowering afternoon sun, and he picked up the phone. I want to go out for dinner, she said.

When would you want to do that?

Now. This evening. I want you to take me out for dinner right now this evening.

It'll be my pleasure, he said. I'll have to clean up first.

I'll be waiting for you, Rose said, and hung up.

He showered and changed into his town clothes and drove into Holt in the pickup. It was still light outside and would be yet, now that daylight savings had started, for another two hours.

He went up to the door and she came out at once and he walked her to the pickup. She seemed disturbed by something. They went out to the Wagon Wheel Café on the highway as before, and over dinner she told him about taking the Wallaces to see their children at the foster home at the west side of town. He asked questions when he needed to, but mostly he only listened, and afterward he drove her back to her house.

Will you come in for a while? she said. Please.

Of course. If you want me to.

They stepped inside and she said: Why don't you have a seat and I'll make coffee.

Thank you, he said. He sat in his accustomed chair and looked around, studying a painting of hers he particularly liked, a watercolor of a stand of trees with their leaves all gone, just the bare trunks remaining, a windbreak on a hill, and brown grass on the hill against a winter sky. She had other pictures on the walls, but they seemed too bright to him and he didn't like them as well. He could hear her out in the kitchen. You want any help? he called.

No, she called back. I'm coming.

She came in and set his cup on the side table next to his chair and she sat down on the couch across the room and placed her cup on the coffee table before her. Then, without warning, she began to cry.

Raymond set his cup down and looked at her. Rose. What is it? Have I done something wrong?

No, she said. She wiped at her eyes with the back of her hands. It's not you. It's not you at all. I've just felt sad all afternoon. Ever since we went to the foster home. It was okay really, but it just seemed sad to me.

There wasn't nothing else to be done about it, was there? he said.

No. But I've felt like weeping all afternoon. I told them everything would be all right. That was a lie. I didn't tell them the truth. This isn't any kind of a priority for the police. The police aren't going to find her uncle and they won't get their children back. Those kids will be kept in foster homes till they're eighteen or till they just run away. Everything is not going to be all right.

Probably not, Raymond said.

Her eyes filled with tears again and she took out a handkerchief, and Raymond sat watching her, then he stood and crossed to the couch and sat down and put his arm around her shoulder.

She wiped at her tears and turned to face him. I've done this kind of thing so many times, she said. And today they could only mention their physical ailments. I don't blame them for that. That's all they know how to talk about. So I called the doctor and made them an appointment. But what good can any doctor do?

Not enough, Raymond said. A doctor couldn't of done nothing for my brother, either.

She looked up at him. His iron-gray hair was so stiff on his head, his face so red from all the years of fierce weather he'd worked in. Still, she could see the kindness there. She settled into his shoulder.

I'm sorry to go on so, she said. Thank you for listening. And coming over here to sit next to me without my having to ask. It means a lot to me, Raymond. You mean a lot to me.

Well, Raymond said. He drew her slightly closer to him. That goes both ways, Rose.

Then she began to weep again, against his shoulder while he held her. They sat for a long time in this way, without moving, without talking.

AND NOW, OUTSIDE THE HOUSE, BEYOND THE SILENT ROOM they sat in, the dark began to collect along the street.

And soon now the streetlamps would come on, flickering and shuddering, to illuminate all the corners of Holt.

And farther away, outside of town, out on the high plains, there would be the blue yardlights shining from the tall poles at all the isolated farms and ranches in all the flat treeless country, and presently the wind would come up, blowing across the open spaces, traveling without obstruction across the wide fields of winter wheat and across the ancient native pastures and the graveled county roads, carrying with it a pale dust as the dark approached and the nighttime gathered round.

And still in the room they sat together quietly, the old man with his arm around this kind woman, waiting for what would come.

Acknowledgments

The author wishes to acknowledge the generous support and encouragement of:

Mark Haruf, Verne Haruf, Edith Russell, Sorel Haruf Arnold, Whitney Haruf, Chaney Haruf, Mark and Gin Spragg, Rod Bina, Tony Watkins, Kit and Sandy Carpenter, Jeff Donlan, Liz Gersbacher, Stephanie Dillard, Theresa Saucke, John Niedfeldt, Rollie Deering, Dr. Tom Parks, Dr. Paul Ammatelli, Karen Greenberg, Meg Viets, Peter Brown, Carol Devine Carson, Liz Van Hoose, Kathryn Laughon, and especially JJ Laughon; and Peter Matson and Jody Hotchkiss, longtime friends and agents; and Gary Fisketjon, friend and the best of all editors; and Cathy Haruf, always.

KENT HARUF

The Tie That Binds

PICADOR

In his critically acclaimed first novel, Kent Haruf delivers the sweeping tale of eighty-year-old Edith Goodnough. Narrated by her neighbour, Edith's tragedies unfold: a tough childhood, a mother's death, a violence that leaves a father dependent on his children, forever enraged. She is a woman who sacrifices everything in the name of family – until she is forced to reclaim her freedom in one dramatic and unexpected gesture. Breathtaking and truthful, *The Tie That Binds* is a powerful tribute to the demands of rural life, and to the tenacity of the human spirit.

'A novel which dramatically and accurately explores the lives
of people who work the land in the stark American
Middle West'
New York Times Book Review

KENT HARUF

Where You Once Belonged

PICADOR

Heavy-built Jack Burdette is quite literally too big for his boots – and too big, certainly for the small-town attitudes of Holt, Colorado. But when he fails to make the grade as a college footballer, and takes a job with the local farmers' co-operative, it seems he has finally settled into the rhythm and routine of everyday life. Outward appearances can be deceptive, however, as Jack proves: returning from a weekend conference with a new wife in tow, then leaving her behind and skipping town with a bundle of other folks' money.

Nearly a decade later, no one has forgiven or forgotten, and when Jack reappears, resentment runs high. Once again though, it is Jack whose presence – even more than his eight-year absence – proves the most devastating.

'Each phrase is spare and straightforward, yet out of all of them together, an extraordinary poetry emerges'
Los Angeles Times

KENT HARUF

Plainsong

PICADOR

Combining the stories of high-school teacher Tom Guthrie, bringing up his two young sons alone, pregnant teenager Victoria Roubideaux, and Raymond and Harold McPheron, the uncommunicative cattle-farming brothers who take her in, *Plainsong* paints a convincing, compelling picture of small-town life in Holt County, Colorado.

'True to its title, *Plainsong* is a vocal book that deserves
to be read out loud'
Observer

'Kent Haruf's prose murmurs a haunting melody through the
intertwined lives of a Colorado community. It is a simple
tale of life, death, love and hatred'
The Times

OTHER PICADOR BOOKS
AVAILABLE FROM PAN MACMILLAN

KENT HARUF

THE TIE THAT BINDS	0 330 49045 1	£6.99
WHERE YOU ONCE BELONGED	0 330 49046 X	£7.99
PLAINSONG	0 330 39314 6	£7.99

TIM WINTON

THE TURNING	0 330 44135 3	£7.99
DIRT MUSIC	0 330 49026 5	£6.99
THE RIDERS	0 330 33942 7	£7.99
SCISSION	0 330 41260 4	£7.99
MINIMUM OF TWO	0 330 41262 0	£7.99

All Pan Macmillan titles can be ordered from our website,
www.panmacmillan.com, or from your local bookshop
and are also available by post from:

Bookpost, PO Box 29, Douglas, Isle of Man IM99 1BQ
Credit cards accepted. For details:
Telephone: +44 (0)1624 677237
Fax: +44 (0)1624 670923
E-mail: bookshop@enterprise.net
www.bookpost.co.uk

Free postage and packing in the United Kingdom

Prices shown above were correct at the time of going to press.
Pan Macmillan reserve the right to show new retail prices on covers
which may differ from those previously advertised in the text
or elsewhere.